## Acclaim for the authors of
### *Snow-Kissed Proposals*

#### JENNI FLETCHER

"Jenni Fletcher has such a great style, which includes being able to set the scene of the story along with creating a great base of characters... With all these great traits Fletcher doesn't disappoint."

—*Yeah Lifestyle* on *The Duke's Runaway Bride*

#### ELISABETH HOBBES

"A wonderful story, one that captured my attention with brilliant characters and an engaging story."

—*Rae Reads Book Blog* on
*The Silk Merchant's Convenient Wife*

**Jenni Fletcher** was born in the north of Scotland and now lives in Yorkshire with her husband and two children. She wanted to be a writer as a child but became distracted by reading instead, finally getting past her first paragraph thirty years later. She's had more jobs than she can remember but has finally found one she loves. She can be contacted on Twitter, @jenniauthor, or via her Facebook author page.

**Elisabeth Hobbes** grew up in York, England, where she spent most of her teenage years wandering around the city looking for a handsome Roman or Viking to sweep her off her feet. Elisabeth's hobbies include skiing, Arabic dance and fencing—none of which has made it into a story yet. When she isn't writing, she spends her time reading and is a pro at cooking while holding a book! Elisabeth lives in Cheshire, England, with her husband, two children and three cats with ridiculous names.

# SNOW-KISSED
# PROPOSALS

———

## Jenni Fletcher
## Elisabeth Hobbes

Recycling programs
for this product may
not exist in your area.

ISBN-13: 978-1-335-40751-1

Snow-Kissed Proposals

Copyright © 2021 by Harlequin Books S.A.

The Christmas Runaway
Copyright © 2021 by Jenni Fletcher

Their Snowbound Reunion
Copyright © 2021 by Claire Lackford

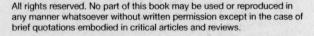

This edition published by arrangement with Harlequin Books S.A.

For questions and comments about the quality of this book,
please contact us at CustomerService@Harlequin.com.

Harlequin Enterprises ULC
22 Adelaide St. West, 41st Floor
Toronto, Ontario M5H 4E3, Canada
www.Harlequin.com

**Printed in U.S.A.**

# CONTENTS

# THE CHRISTMAS RUNAWAY

## Jenni Fletcher

Dear Reader,

Part of the reason I love reading and writing romance is because it's such a positive, happy and hopeful genre. It looks at the best in people and the world, and Christmas romances are arguably the happiest and most hopeful of all. On top of that, they're set at the coziest time of year in the northern hemisphere, when curling up in front of a roaring fire with a book, mug of tea and box of chocolates is one of the great joys in life—or it is to me anyway—and if you can get snowed in, so much the better.

I wrote this story between lockdowns at the end of 2020, and it helped me to stay positive throughout that difficult time as I channeled all of those warm vibes and biscuits! So I hope you enjoy this story, set in the northeast of Scotland where it still snows in December, and it leaves you feeling happy and hopeful, too.

Wishing you a happy and peaceful Christmas, wherever you are.

*Jenni*

# *Chapter One*

*Northern Aberdeenshire, Scotland, 1892*

Splash!

A drop of rain landed directly on the tip of Fiona's nose, soaking through the gauze veil that hung from her fashionably bead-trimmed but woefully impractical bonnet, before sliding its way over her lips and down to her chin. Curiously enough, it tasted of salt.

She stopped walking and deposited her small travelling case in the middle of the track. That was it. The final straw. The last in a long line of events that had conspired to land her here, in this desolate spot in the middle of nowhere, a hundred miles, or so it seemed, from civilisation, alone, vulnerable and inadequately dressed, with daylight fading and now, apparently, an oncoming deluge.

In a few minutes, she'd probably be drenched and by the morning, if she managed to survive that long, she'd be forced to admit defeat and go home. Her plan, which had seemed so brilliantly inspired that morning, appeared destined to end in humiliation, failure and quite likely a head cold.

And, if all that wasn't enough, her new ankle boots were killing her. She stuck one of the offending items out from beneath her skirts and then shook her head indulgently. It wasn't fair to blame the boots themselves. The green leather still looked as gorgeous as it had when she'd first purchased them a week ago, ornamented by a row of shiny brass buckles. The fault was hers for not breaking them in before venturing out on a walk in the wilderness; although, in her defence, she hadn't expected to do much wandering. She'd expected to find a hansom cab at the small village station to carry her and Emily on to their destination. Or a cart. Or even a lone horse. Not *nothing*. Perhaps they ought to have stayed the night in Aberdeen, as Emily had tentatively suggested, but as usual Fiona had been too stubborn, determined to push on that day...

She sat down on her case in order to take stock of her drizzly surroundings. The whole world looked oyster-coloured and hazy, as if she were sitting in the middle of an actual rain cloud. Scraggly hawthorn and skeletal trees bordered both sides of the track, obscuring any view of the village behind and the sea ahead. Her last glimpse of it had been from the train, a thick ribbon of grey interspersed with foaming breakers of white surf, as tumultuous as her own emotions.

She'd left the station probably half an hour before, following the directions given to her by a porter, but the man had obviously made a mistake. Or possibly she'd misunderstood his strong Broch accent which had sounded almost indecipherable to her lowlander ears. Now there was no point in denying that she had no idea where she was and no obvious way to find out. All she *did* know was that her bonnet was starting to feel soggy and her feet were developing blisters.

Still, she wasn't about to concede defeat just yet. She was making a stand, after all, one that would demonstrate to her father just what lengths she, his only child, the pride and joy of his heart—or so he'd always called her until three months ago—was prepared to go to stop him making a terrible mistake. The moral superiority of her position would be severely undermined if she went home after only one day.

If only she'd thought to bring a map!

She pressed her lips together, swallowing a sob. She was absolutely *not* going to cry. She never cried. Or rarely, anyway, and absolutely never in public, where anyone might see her. Not that anyone was likely to see her if she burst into tears here so she might as well. A passing deer or cow might take some mild interest, but the chances of an actual human coming across her seemed roughly equivalent to...

*Oh.*

The clatter of approaching hooves brought her back to her feet with an unladylike leap. Someone was coming! She crossed her fingers, hoping that it would be an older, respectable gentleman—a doctor or a minister, perhaps, preferably one who lived close by with an equally respectable wife, in a house with a warm hearth and conveniently empty bedroom. As well as having the ability to give her clear directions to Windy Heads Tower in the morning.

Unfortunately, it was not. Her hopes plummeted as an unkempt-looking man on a grey-and-white-dappled mare rounded the corner of the hedge and drew rein, apparently in surprise, at the sight of her. At first glance, his appearance struck her as somewhat alarming, since he appeared not to have washed in a week, if that opinion wasn't too generous. He was dressed in a massive grey greatcoat with an overlaying cape though, since he hadn't bothered to fasten the buttons, she was treated to an unobstructed view of the filthy shirt and shocking absence of cravat beneath.

Worse than that, there was a strange, peaty, almost medicinal smell about him. If she wasn't mistaken, he'd been drinking.

'Good afternoon.' She tossed her head, trying to make her isolated position in the middle of the road seem like the most natural thing in the world.

'Are ye lost?' The man removed his hat to reveal a tangle of dark auburn curls, pale eyes and a blunt, unshaven chin.

'Not at all.' She cleared her throat, unwilling to admit the truth to such a dishevelled-looking individual. 'I was just taking a rest.'

The man glanced pointedly up at the sky and then back again without comment.

'I'm rather hot from walking, if you must know. The drizzle feels very refreshing.'

'It may be a bit too refreshing in a few minutes. There's a lot more rain coming.' He lifted both eyebrows, holding them there for a few seconds as if he were waiting for her to ask for help, before putting his hat back on with a shrug. 'I'll leave ye to it, then.'

'Oh, all right!' she called out as he directed his horse around her. 'I suppose I *am* lost, just a little. I'm looking for Windy Heads Tower.'

He drew rein again, looking her up and down more frankly this time. 'What do ye want there?'

She stiffened at the impertinence of both the look *and* the question. 'I believe that would be my business. Now, can you tell me or not?'

'Aye, I could. It's no' far at all.'

'Thank goodness.' She heaved a sigh of relief then waved a hand impatiently when no further details seemed forthcoming. 'Well?'

'I said that I could, no' that I would. You have nae said please.'

'It was implied.' She gritted her teeth, summoning as much dignity as her increasingly soggy state would allow. 'However, if it *pleases* you, sir, would you *please* be so kind as to tell me the way to Windy Heads Tower? *Please?*'

If she wasn't mistaken, the man's lips quirked into a half-smile before he jumped down from his horse and made what she could only assume was a deliberately obsequious bow. 'I'll do better than that. I'll take ye.'

'Oh, no, that won't be necessary.' She took a hasty step backwards, alarmed by how very big he seemed, standing in front of her. She was reasonably tall for a woman, but she still found herself raising her chin to meet his eyes which, up close, were the brightest shade of blue she'd ever seen. They were like a midsummer sky, contrasting sharply with his sun-bronzed face— although how anybody could ever become sun-bronzed in such a frigid climate, she had no idea. 'Directions will do nicely.'

'Perhaps, but since I'm heading to the same place myself, it would make sense to travel together, would it no'?'

'*You're* going to Windy Heads Tower?' She regarded him with patent disbelief. Why on earth would such a disreputable-looking and possibly drunken individual be heading to her friend's house? 'Why?'

'As I believe you commented earlier, that would be my business.' He picked up her bag, hoisting it over one shoulder before reaching for his horse's bridle. 'Here, you can ride if you like.'

'No, thank you. I'm perfectly fine on foot.'

'Suit yourself. Is this all your luggage?'

'Those are my essential items. The bulk of my baggage is still at the station with my maid.'

*'Maid?'* He gave her another appraising look before shaking his head and starting off down the road. 'This way, then.'

'Wait!' She dug her heels in. 'How do I know you're really taking me there? How can I be sure you're not a criminal?'

'How do I know *you're* not? You're the one who wants to know where I live.'

'I've no interest in where you live! I'm here to visit Miss Drummond.'

He stopped for a third time, looking back over his shoulder. 'You know Mhairi?'

'Yes. Very well.'

'How?'

She blinked at the new note of suspicion in his voice. It gave the distinct impression that he wasn't going to take her anywhere until she told him the truth, the infuriating man!

'We were at school together in Edinburgh, as it happens.'

'At Mrs Kerr's Academy?'

'Ye…es.' She tilted her head. 'How do you know about that?'

'What's your name?'

'I asked *you* a question first!' She put her hands on her hips, glaring at his insolence. Apparently there was no limit to the man's bad manners. This was absolutely *not* the way introductions ought to be made, but at this particular moment it seemed she had no choice. The sooner she reached Windy Heads Tower and was out of his impudent company, the better.

'Miss Fiona MacKay.' She wrenched her shoulders back, refusing to add anything about it being a pleasure to meet him, as it most definitely was not!

'Fiona MacKay...' Blue eyes widened slightly as if in surprise. '*You're* Fiona MacKay?'

'*Miss* Fiona MacKay, yes. And you are?'

'Angus Drummond, *esquire*.' His lips twitched before curving upwards again. 'Otherwise known as Mhairi's brother—and that'll be my home you're looking for. Now, shall we go?'

On which note, the skies finally opened.

## Chapter Two

'**Y**ou might have said something sooner!'

Angus chuckled to himself as the woman—lady, he supposed he ought to call her—trotted at his heels like an extremely persistent and bedraggled terrier. 'Aye, I might have.'

'I certainly wouldn't have accused you of being a criminal if I'd known who you really were.'

He almost laughed aloud at that. To be honest, he couldn't blame her for being suspicious. He wasn't exactly looking his best. Due to a mishap involving one of the copper stills, his shirt and trousers were liberally splattered with recently fermented whisky. Personally, he hardly noticed the smell any more, but it was probably quite powerful. She'd obviously taken him for a drunkard.

Funnily enough, he already knew her, or *of* her anyway, as his sister had talked almost incessantly about her best friend during holidays from school. At thirteen, following the death of their mother, Mhairi had been sent to a ladies' establishment in Edinburgh, conveniently close to the home of their maternal aunt. It would have been hard for her otherwise, growing up on a remote farm with only a grieving father and a taciturn four-years-older brother for company, although she'd still objected strongly at first. Thankfully, all her complaining had stopped once she'd met the notorious Miss MacKay.

He was aware that the two women had kept up a correspondence since they'd finished school four years ago. Mhairi had even visited Miss MacKay in Edinburgh on several occasions since, although the woman—*lady*— in person was nothing remotely like he'd imagined. From all the stories of mice in beds, arm wrestling in classrooms and one hilarious but distinctly unladylike incident involving a chamber pot over a door—he'd advised his sister not to share *that* particular story with their father—he'd envisaged a firebrand.

Instead, he found a tall, straight-backed woman, looking as if she'd just stepped out of a fashion plate, in clothes more suited to an English picnic than a Scottish winter, with. sleek blonde hair, slate-grey eyes, and a pretty face that spoiled itself with an expression of disapproval. Those angular cheekbones struck him as being permanently sucked in. Judging by her imperious manner, she also believed herself to be some kind of empress.

Despite all of that, however, she was his sister's friend, which meant that he was honour-bound to take care of her, at least until the moment when he could hand her over to Mhairi and get back to his own business. Which, frankly speaking, couldn't come soon enough.

Thankfully, it was less than a quarter of an hour before they trudged beneath the great sandstone archway that led into the courtyard of Windy Heads and one of the farmhands came running for his horse. It was too dark now to see the full dramatic effect of the white tower, and besides, Miss MacKay was keeping her head down, using it as a kind of battering ram against the driving wind and rain, not that he could blame her. The rain was coming down in heavy sheets now, soaking them both to the skin, though she'd still refused the loan of his greatcoat, evidently preferring a chill to being indebted to him.

Well, it was her choice, however foolhardy. Hastily, he led her across to the front door, though it burst open before he could reach for the handle.

'There you are!' His sister's anxious face, framed with a mass of copper-red ringlets, peered out into the darkness. 'I was starting to worry about— *Fiona?*' Her expression lit up with a comical blend of amazement and delight as she leapt forward suddenly, throwing her arms around his companion's neck and needlessly soaking herself in the process. 'What on earth are you doing here?'

'It's a long story, but before I tell it I'm afraid I need to ask a favour.' Miss MacKay looked equally pleased to see Mhairi, hugging her back. 'My maid Emily was tired after the journey, so I left her behind at the station while I came to look for your house. I only expected to be ten minutes or so, but it must have been an hour, and she's probably desperately worried by now. All of my luggage is there, too. Do you think somebody could—?'

'I'll go.' Angus interrupted before she could finish.

'Oh, I couldn't possibly ask you to do that.' She shook her head in protest. 'You're wet enough already.'

'Which is why a little more rain won't make any difference.'

'Angus, you can't go looking like that!' Mhairi sounded mortified. 'What happened to your clothes?'

'A problem with one of the stills.'

'Well, the poor girl will take one look, not to mention sniff, of you and run for the hills.'

'Aye, I seem to be having that effect on women today.' He cast a sideways glance at Miss MacKay. 'But I cannae ask anyone else to go and get drenched. It won't take me half an hour in the cart.'

'Well, for goodness sake, at least do your coat up.'

'I'm truly sorry to put you to this bother, Mr Drummond.' To his surprise, Miss MacKay sounded genuinely apologetic. 'If I could find my own way back in the dark then I would.'

'Dinna fash.' He started to turn away and then paused. 'When you say luggage, how many bags exactly are we talking about?'

'Only five. I thought I should travel light.'

'You call five light?'

'Well, that's settled, then.' Mhairi gave him a pointed look before drawing her friend inside and into the warm. 'Away you go, Angus. There'll be a nice hot dinner waiting when you get back.'

The parlour at Windy Heads was a veritable sight for sore eyes, Fiona thought, heaving a heartfelt sigh of relief. It wasn't remotely fashionable, but it was definitely cosy, with a mismatched assortment of brightly coloured furniture vying for space with a pair of large, shaggy dogs that she might easily have mistaken for rugs if they hadn't lifted their heads briefly from their paws to examine her, before lowering them again. Best of all was a large, roaring fire that filled the room with warmth and the air with the heady aroma of smouldering peat. After the unrelenting rain and chilly greyness of the world outside, it was a very welcome scene.

'Here you go…' Mhairi picked up a foot stool and placed it directly in front of the fireplace. 'Don't mind Rory and Hamish. They wouldn't bat an eyelid if you'd come to rob the place. Now, sit here in the warm and tell me everything.'

'Thank you.' Fiona spread her skirts out in an attempt to dry them. 'Like I said, it's a long story, but the upshot is that I've run away. The situation at home was becoming unbearable and I just couldn't stand it a day longer. It's all because of my father.'

'Oh, no!' Mhairi's blue eyes—a slightly darker shade than her brother's, Fiona noticed—widened in alarm. 'Is he unwell?'

'Not in body, but he's certainly not thinking straight. He wants to marry again—at Christmas, would you believe?—and the woman in question is completely unsuitable.'

'Ah.' Mhairi's expression seemed, if anything, to relax.

'She's a widow, but twenty years younger than him.' Fiona sat up straighter, trying to emphasise the gravity of the situation. 'Unfortunately, he's completely besotted.'

'Oh dear, that does sound difficult. Thank you, Aileen.' Mhairi glanced up as a maid brought in a tea tray. 'But when you say run away, do you mean in secret?'

'Oh no, I left a note to explain I was coming here. I would never worry Father unduly, but I need him to understand that I won't be a party to his ridiculous plans. I've tried telling him how I feel, but he just assumes I'll come round eventually. So I *had* to do something dramatic. With any luck, the shock will bring him to his senses.'

'I see.' Mhairi poured out two cups of tea. 'Well,

it's wonderful to see you again no matter what the circumstances. Now, drink this and then we'll see about changing your clothes for dinner.'

'Actually…' Fiona glanced longingly at the door. 'If you don't mind, would it be all right if I went straight to bed? I don't mean to be ungrateful, but it was *such* a long journey.'

'Of course, but surely you haven't travelled all the way from Edinburgh today?'

'Yes. Emily was quite unhappy about it, but you know me. Once I make up my mind to do something…'

'You go ahead and do it.' Mhairi smiled affectionately. 'I remember.'

'Quite.' Fiona made a wry face before draining her tea in a matter of gulps. 'That was delicious.'

'Good. Come on, then.' Mhairi put her own cup aside and stood up. 'Let's get you to bed.'

'This is why you're such a good friend.' Fiona stifled a yawn as they headed back out to the hallway. 'Although I really am sorry to spring myself on you like this. I know I ought to have sent word ahead, but the idea only came to me in the early hours. I hope it's not too much of an imposition.'

'Don't be silly. I'm glad to finally repay you for all those years of looking after me. Besides, I've invited you to visit enough times.'

'That's true.' Fiona smiled, feeling better at the thought. 'Well, in that case, it's about time I came. Please do thank your brother again for helping me. I think we both made a bad first impression on each other.'

'That sounds about right. For Angus, that is.' Mhairi rolled her eyes. 'It's a good thing he's so handsome or no woman in her right mind would ever speak to him twice.'

Fiona knitted her brows thoughtfully as they made their way up first one, then a second, winding staircase. *Was* Mr Drummond handsome? It hadn't occurred to her to think of him as such before, but she supposed he was, in an unshaven, unrefined, uncouth and yet undeniably masculine sort of way. 'Rugged' was probably the best word. Or 'earthy.'

Honestly, she didn't think she'd ever met anyone quite *so* rugged or earthy before. She had the sudden, startling idea that she might enjoy tidying him up a bit. Only not too much. Now that she thought of it, ruggedness actually suited him... And what on earth made her think that? She was obviously even more exhausted than she'd realised! Either that or she'd already caught a head cold...

'Mhairi...' She tried to think of a polite way to phrase her next question. 'What *was* that smell on him?'

'*Uisge beatha.*' Her friend laughed. 'It means "the water of life" in Gaelic. Otherwise known as whisky. He's been at the distillery all day.'

'You have a distillery?'

'Sort of. It's called Meggie's, after my mother. My father built it ten years ago with what was left of her dowry, but unfortunately there was a fire not long after. The building survived, for the most part, but most of the equipment was destroyed. Angus has been trying to revive the old place ever since. It's become a bit of an obsession, to be honest, but hopefully it'll be a success this time.'

'Do you know, I have a vague memory of your telling me about it once, but I'd completely forgotten. As for your brother, I'm afraid I thought he was a drunkard.'

'I'm not surprised. It's a terrible smell.'

At last, after yet another flight of stairs, Mhairi opened the door to a bedroom and Fiona forgot all about Angus Drummond, handsome, sober or otherwise. At that moment, the cast-iron bed frame on the far side of the room, covered in elaborate lace pillows and a thick, patchwork quilt, struck her as the most attractive sight she'd ever set eyes on. She could hardly wait to crawl under the sheets.

'Mhairi, this is wonderful!'

'Then it's yours for as long as you want. Now, I'll go and fetch one of my night gowns and you can have a good night's sleep.'

'And Emily...?'

'I'll look after her when she arrives, I promise. In the meantime, I'm sure Angus is taking good care of her.'

'Thank you...' Fiona took a few steps into the room, surprised to discover that the thought of her pretty young maid in the company of her friend's arguably handsome, but definitely rugged, brother was suddenly undermining her desire to sleep.

## Chapter Three

'Are you going to explain to me what's going on, then?' Angus sat down at the table with a heaped plateful of bacon, eggs, tatties and haggis.

'Yes.' Mhairi set her spoon aside, finishing the last of her porridge. 'I would have explained last night if you hadn't gone straight off to bed when you got back. I ended up eating dinner all by myself.'

'Sorry. I thought you'd be catching up with your friend.'

'She was too exhausted. Just mind you eat properly today.'

'Already seen to.' He gestured at his plate. 'So, what's she doing here?'

'*She* has a name and she needs a place to stay for a while.'

'Why? Is she in trouble with the law?' He lifted his eyebrows, prepared to be impressed.

'No. She just wants to get away from home. Her father is planning to marry some unsuitable woman and Fiona thinks he's making a terrible mistake.'

'Who's her father?'

'A lawyer in Edinburgh. Something to do with merchant law, if I remember correctly.'

'Not a laird, then?'

'No.' Mhairi looked confused. 'What makes you ask that?'

'Just an impression I got, that's all. So she's stormed away from home in a temper?'

'I'm sure she didn't storm.'

'You didna' meet her on the road yesterday. *That's* a woman who storms.'

'She was probably at the end of her tether after the journey. She'll be a whole different person today, you'll see.'

'Mmm.'

'Angus…' Mhairi gave him a chiding look. 'You know how miserable and homesick I was when I first went to Edinburgh. It was so soon after Mother's death and all of the other girls seemed so much smarter and more accomplished than I was. If it hadn't been for Fiona, I don't know what I would have done. She didn't have a mother either, and she understood that I was grieving. She stood up for me and even took me home with her sometimes at the weekends. I owe her a great deal.'

'All right.' Angus swallowed a mouthful of bacon, conceding the point. 'So, how long is she planning to stay?'

'Well…' Mhairi smoothed her hands over the table cloth before folding them together. 'The truth is, I've told her she can stay for as long as she wants.'

He paused with his fork in mid-air, hoping that he'd just misheard. 'You've told her *what*?'

'I'm sure it won't be for long. I mean, once her father realises how upset she is then I'm sure that he'll come to his senses.'

'*As long as she wants?*' He set his cutlery down with a clatter. 'It's November!'

'I'm aware of that fact.'

'We've been lucky with the weather so far, but winter could arrive any day. Once the snow starts, it'll likely be here until February at least. We could be stuck with her for months!'

'Well, maybe I'd be happy if she *was* stuck here!' Mhairi's eyes flashed. 'It would be nice to have some company for a change. Or do you disapprove of anyone visiting me now? Are all guests *dangerous*?'

'Mhairi—'

'Don't "Mhairi" me!' His usually placid sister thrust her chair back so forcefully that it almost toppled over. 'This is still Father's house and you're not in charge yet!'

'I didnae say that I was. Where are you going?'

'To see if he needs anything. I've had enough of your company this morning!' She shot him a scathing look as she swept through the doorway. 'And it wouldn't hurt you to try and behave like a gentleman for once. You're supposed to be one, after all!'

Angus muttered an oath and turned his attention back to his plate, impaling a slice of haggis on the end of his fork. Faced with the prospect of a semi-permanent house guest, he'd lost most of his appetite, but he had a hard day's work ahead and needed a full stomach.

'Good morning.'

He jerked his head up again at the sound of another voice. Miss McKay was standing in the spot where Mhairi had just been, mouth screwed up disapprovingly and cheeks firmly sucked in, wearing a dress so bright it looked capable of causing headaches. More bizarrely, it had the largest leg-of-mutton sleeves he'd ever seen, making her upper arms look around the same circumference as her waist. No wonder she'd brought five bags with her if this was what she considered a day gown. Five *heavy* bags, too. He'd actually feared for his back when he'd lifted them into the cart. In general, he was starting to think that this woman was potentially dangerous to his health.

'Good morning.' He put his napkin aside and stood up, wondering how much of his conversation with Mhairi she'd just overheard. 'I'm afraid you've missed my sister.'

'Yes. I saw her in the hall as I was coming downstairs, although I don't think she noticed me. She seemed upset.'

'She'll get over it.' He gestured towards the sideboard. 'There's plenty to eat if you're hungry.'

'Toast will be sufficient, thank you.' She inclined her head, revealing a complicated arrangement of curls at the nape of her neck. Oddly enough, her hair looked different this morning, less of a uniform blonde and more an assortment of different shades, from white-gold to dark honey. The effect was surprisingly attractive, even if it was probably due to so much light reflecting off her dress.

'Sleep well?' He made a half-hearted attempt at conversation.

'Very well. So did Emily, or so she tells me. Thank you again for collecting her last night.'

'It was no bother. She seems a nice lass.'

'Yes.' She paused briefly as she sat down. 'She is.'

'What colour would you call that?' He couldn't resist asking.

'I'm sorry?'

'Your dress. It's not a shade I've ever seen before.'

'Oh.' She plucked at the sleeve. 'Chartreuse with a cerise trim. Don't you like it?'

'I didnae say that.' He tilted his head, taking a moment to consider. In fact, the shade complemented her very well, even if he was still feeling somewhat blinded. 'It's certainly...vivid.'

'I suppose so.' She gave him a measured look before turning her face towards the window. 'Speaking of colours, there was a beautiful sky this morning. I've never seen such a mixture of pink and gold.'

'The rain washes the sky clean. That's what my mother used to say.'

'What a lovely idea. It almost makes getting soaked last night worthwhile.' A smile softened her features. *'Almost.'*

'Aye.' He nodded and pushed his plate away. It was time to be getting on with work, but Mhairi was right. If her friend was going to be staying for the foreseeable, though hopefully not too lengthy, future then perhaps he ought to try and behave a bit more like a gentleman. It wouldn't hurt to clear the air indoors as well as out.

'Miss MacKay.' He shifted in his seat. 'I apologise if my previous behaviour might have offended you.'

'When?' She put her toast down and looked straight at him, her gaze very direct all of a sudden. 'Last night?'

'Aye.' He felt a twinge of conscience. 'Or...this morning.'

'Ah. Last night is probably better forgotten. I wasn't particularly polite myself. As for this morning, I confess that I did overhear some of your conversation and, to be honest, the possibility of being snowed in never occurred to me. Does the weather really get so bad here?'

'It can do. There's usually a month or two of the year when the roads are impassable.'

'Then I appreciate the information. As for the rest of what you said… Well, since we're barely acquainted, I suppose I can hardly blame you for not wanting to be *stuck with me.*'

'I shouldn't have said that.'

'No, it wasn't very polite, but it *was* honest and that's a quality I always appreciate. Besides, I ought to apologise to you for having arrived unannounced. I'll endeavour to stay no longer than ten days, if that's not too inconvenient?'

'Not at all.'

'Good. Then we have an understanding.' She picked up her toast again as if the subject were settled. 'As to what Mhairi said about visitors being dangerous, I admit I don't understand that at all.' Her gaze flickered pointedly towards him again. 'Not that it's any of my business, of course.'

Angus grimaced inwardly. It *wasn't* any of her business, but then he was the one who'd been indiscreet, not to mention rude. He couldn't help but be impressed by her forthrightness, too. All things considered, she'd let him off the hook for his behaviour surprisingly easily, accepting his apology and even offering one of her own. Maybe she wasn't as objectionable as he'd first thought. Maybe it would even be useful to have her as an ally. And she was actually quite pretty now that she didn't look so disapproving. He let his gaze linger on her mouth for a second longer than was polite. Her lips were thin but wide, with a rounded Cupid's bow in a slightly lighter shade of *cerise*…

He cleared his throat heavily. 'I was referring to my sister's health.'

'Is she unwell?' Her expression seemed to freeze.

'Not at the moment, but…' He rubbed a knuckle across the bridge of his nose, wondering how best to explain. 'You've been writing to my sister for several years, I understand.'

'Yes, every month. She's an excellent correspondent.'

'Aye, well…' Excellent correspondent or not, he doubted that his sister had been entirely honest. 'Has she mentioned her condition at all?'

'Her condition?' A small furrow appeared between her brows. 'No, although there was a period last winter when she didn't write. As I recall, she mentioned something afterwards about a chest cold.'

'I'm afraid it was a bit worse than that.'

'How much worse?'

He winced, leaning back in his chair. 'The truth is, she's always been prone to coughs and colds—you may remember that from school—but this time was more serious. We honestly weren't sure that she'd come through it.'

'I see.' Miss MacKay's grey gaze appeared to mist before she dropped it to the table, long lashes fanning over her cheeks. 'No, she never mentioned that.'

'She wouldn't like me mentioning it now. She prefers to think that I'm overly cautious. It can make her reckless with her health on occasion.'

'Reckless in what way?'

'She thinks that she can do things, over-exert herself.' He glanced towards the doorway, half expecting his sister to burst through it and start berating him again. 'You ought to know in case she takes it into her head to show you the district.'

'I'll bear it in mind…' Her voice faded away before she looked up abruptly, her gaze clear again. 'Although

I believe that Mhairi must be the best judge of her own condition, as you call it. I'm a firm believer in a woman's right to make her own decisions.'

'Even when those decisions might be dangerous to her health?'

'Dangerous in *your* opinion. Does her doctor share these concerns?'

Angus laid his hands on the table, pushing himself to his feet. The last person he wanted to discuss was Mhairi's doctor. So much for getting their house guest on his side. Forthright was one thing, but she seemed determined to argue.

'I thought that you ought to be aware, that's all. Now, if you'll excuse me, I have a busy day ahead. I'll see you at dinner, Miss MacKay.'

'Good morning.' Mhairi smiled brightly when Fiona entered the parlour after breakfast, brimful of tea and toast. If the argument with her brother was still bothering her then she showed no sign of it. 'Now, what would you like to do today?'

'What would you suggest?' Fiona took her cue and smiled back. 'I have to say, it looks a little cold outside.'

'If we wait for a warm day then we could be trapped inside until May—and that's optimistic.' Mhairi laughed. 'Why don't you let me show you around the farm? Then maybe I'll take you up to see Papa.'

'That would be lovely. To be honest, I thought I might see your father at breakfast. I remember him from that spring he came to visit you at school and we had a picnic together on Arthur's Seat.'

'I'm afraid he's a different man these days.' Mhairi's expression became strained. 'He prefers to stay in his room most of the time and he forgets things easily.

Sometimes, he's not even sure where he is, then at other times, he's just like his old self. The truth is, he's never been the same since we lost my mother. He seemed well enough this morning, but I'll check again later.'

'Oh, Mhairi...' Fiona reached out and clasped hold of her hands. 'I'm so sorry. And there I was yesterday, talking about my father losing his mind over a woman...'

'You weren't to know.'

'I'm still sorry and I'll leave it up to you to decide when or whether your father's well enough to see me. Your parents were a love match, weren't they?'

'Very much so. My mother married my father despite her family's objections. She was much wealthier than he was. Just like with your parents.'

'At least your grandparents came round.' Fiona made a face. 'Mine never thought my father was good enough. That's why they put their whole fortune in a trust for me.'

'Sometimes I wish mine had done the same. Then Father would never have taken it into his head to build the distillery and maybe things would have been different.' She lowered her voice even though they were alone. 'Sometimes, I wonder if it was the stress of what happened that caused my mother's heart to fail. It was such a terrible time. And now Angus is determined to restart the business all over again. I can't help but worry about the effect it might have on him.'

'I'm sure he knows what he's doing.'

'I hope so.' Mhairi smiled weakly as Fiona reached across and squeezed her hand. '*And* I hope that you've brought a warmer coat than the one you were wearing yesterday. You're going to need it.'

\* \* \*

Ten minutes later and Fiona was wearing one of Mhairi's three-quarter-length tweed capes over her own giant sleeves. The winter sun was shining, but the wind whipping in from the sea and across the bare fields was bitter, numbing her nose and cheeks despite her borrowed wool-lined bonnet.

In daylight, however, she was able to see Windy Heads in its full splendour. And it *was* splendid—a whitewashed, five-storeyed, seventeenth-century fortified tower, with turrets at each corner and crenellations around the top of the roof, all surrounded by a panorama of gently rolling hills. It was hard to believe that it was the same barren, waterlogged landscape she'd traipsed through the day before. Oh, there was still a wildness about it—it *was* winter, after all—but there was a stark kind of beauty, too. Now that the sun had finally risen, the very light seemed unique, shining with a pale, silvery lustre that sparkled off the sea in the distance and made her heart glow in response. Simply put, it was stunning.

She cast occasional sideways glances at Mhairi as they walked arm in arm through the gardens, wondering if what the objectionable Mr Drummond had said at breakfast was true. There was surely no reason for him to lie, but perhaps he'd exaggerated? Admittedly, her friend had never been very robust, but she'd also always recovered, and she certainly seemed well enough now.

She was aware, too, of feeling slightly subdued, unable to forget the other comments she'd overheard. *Stuck with her* were hardly words to make a woman feel very good about herself. And that was before his pointed remarks about her dress and their subsequent disagreement. Obviously he was just like every other man she'd ever met and thought that women ought to blend into the background and keep their mouths closed. She'd expected—*hoped* for—better from her friend's brother, especially when his blue eyes had looked even bluer that morning...

On the other hand, Mhairi herself appeared genuinely pleased to see her so what did Angus Drummond's opinion matter, really? She hadn't come to visit *him*. He might not be quite as uncouth as he'd first appeared, but he was still a long, very long, way from being a gentleman. Nonetheless, she would be careful not to outstay her welcome. There was no sign of snow at that moment and hopefully ten days would be enough to bring her father to his senses...

'Angus spoke to you about me, didn't he?' Mhairi came to an abrupt halt halfway down the garden path. 'He told you that I was ill. That's why you're being so quiet this morning.'

'Am I?' Fiona fiddled with the buttons of her cape evasively before spreading out her hands. 'Yes. I'm sorry. He mentioned something about a bad illness last year.'

'Did he tell you that I shouldn't exert myself?'

She nodded, holding onto Mhairi's gaze. 'Was it so very serious?'

'I suppose so, at the time, but I'm much better now, no matter what Angus thinks. And I want to live my life, not spend it wrapped up in shawls by the fireplace.'

'Well, I can understand that...if you're certain you're completely recovered?'

'I am. I admit it was all quite frightening at the time, but some good came from it, too.'

'What do you mean?'

A wash of colour suffused Mhairi's cheeks, her eyes

positively glowing with happiness. 'I met someone. The doctor who took care of me. He only moved to the area from Perth a year ago and he was so kind and thoughtful. Then, after I recovered, he kept on coming to visit, though at first I thought it was just to check on Father. I never mentioned him in my letters to you because I didn't dare even dream he might feel the same way about me as I felt about him. I would have felt so foolish if I'd been imagining it all, but then three months ago he asked me to marry him.'

'But that's wonderful! So you're engaged?'

Mhairi's face fell again. 'Yes and no. That's the other reason I didn't tell you. My father gave us his blessing, but Angus doesn't approve. He thinks that marriage would be too much of a risk for my health.'

'Surely he can think what he likes? If your father's given permission, then your brother can't forbid you to marry.'

'No, but how could I be happy going against his wishes?' Mhairi sighed heavily. 'He just walks away every time I mention the subject. He won't even stay in the same room as Graham. That's his name, by the way—Dr Graham Tomlinson.'

'But surely if a *doctor* thinks you're healthy enough for marriage…?'

'That's what I keep saying, but Angus claims he's letting his heart rule his head.' She threw a quick look around the gardens as if somebody else might be listening. 'Actually, he used a much more vulgar phrase, but it's not fair. Graham has never treated me with anything but respect. And he says he'll wait for as long as it takes for Angus to come round, but I don't want to wait. I'm already twenty-two.' Her flush deepened.

'Not that there's anything wrong with being unmarried at twenty-two.'

'Oh, don't apologise. I'm perfectly happy with my spinster state, I assure you—or I was until Margery Gibson came along.'

'What will you do if your father does marry her?'

'I refuse to accept that possibility.' Fiona shuddered. 'I'm sure that Papa will see sense before long and then things can go back to the way they were. I'd like to see *her* manage his household as efficiently as I do. Or his social life. You know, my musical soirees were becoming quite famous in Edinburgh. *And* I was thinking of starting a literary salon.'

'Don't you ever want to marry?'

'I doubt it. I've no objection to the institution in principle, but men don't like me.'

'Oh, I can't believe that. You're pretty and intelligent...'

'And much too independent and forthright in my opinions. Which I also have too many of, or so I've been told. No, it's no use. I won't claim that such comments don't hurt sometimes, but if it's a choice between having opinions and having a husband, then I'll keep my opinions, thank you very much.'

'But surely you must have some suitors?'

'Oh yes, the ones with their eyes on my grandparents' fortune. Unfortunately, they're all such terrible actors. I can actually see the horror in their eyes whenever I open my mouth and yet they pretend to be *so* charmed.'

'I'm sure there's somebody out there who *would* be charmed.'

'Write to me immediately when you meet such a

paragon. In the meantime, I'll settle for meeting your Dr Tomlinson.'

'I wish that you could.'

'Then why can't I? Invite him for tea. Your brother said that he was going to be busy all day.'

'Really?' Mhairi's expression wavered for a moment before breaking into a mischievous grin. 'Oh, I *knew* you'd be on my side. That would be wonderful. And I know you're going to love Graham just as much as I do.'

'Probably not quite as much.' Fiona laughed. 'But I'm sure he'll be perfectly charming.'

'Come on!' Mhairi hooked a hand through her arm, dragging her back towards the house with a surprising show of strength. 'I'll send a note at once.'

# Chapter Four

Angus whistled a few bars of 'Bonnie Doon' to himself as he opened the front door to the tower and peeled off his greatcoat in the hallway. He was back home several hours earlier than anticipated, but there wasn't much more he could have done that day. There was, however, always plenty to do on the farm, a whole backlog of tasks to catch up on just as soon as he changed his clothes and had something to eat.

He was in a good mood. After years of hard work, planning and saving, the distillery was finally ready. Soon he could open one of his father's ten-year-old casks and, provided the contents tasted as good as he hoped, he could start his own brewing in earnest. And the best part was that he'd done it all on his own, rebuilding Meggie's brick by laborious brick. Nobody could ever accuse him of using somebody else's fortune. Before long, he would prove to the world that the Aberdeenshire Drummonds were still a family to be reckoned with, not one to be pitied.

He put one foot on the staircase and then stopped at the sound of voices and laughter coming from the direction of the parlour. The door had been left slightly ajar, giving him a narrow view of Miss MacKay sitting in an arm chair, looking markedly happier and more relaxed than she had at breakfast, her complexion flushed with laughter and her grey eyes sparkling with warmth.

She looked, he had to admit, quite surprisingly attractive. Even more surprisingly, she struck him as desirable, too, so much so that for a moment he found himself imagining what it would be like to peel away those ridiculous sleeves and press his lips to the bare skin beneath, to find the pulse in her wrist and then work his way up her elbows and shoulders, all the way to the hollow at the base of her throat.

Of course, he'd have to unbutton her high collar in order to reach it, which would be just a step towards removing the rest of her dress. Given the amount of material, the whole process would probably take some considerable time, but he suspected the results would be worth it…

He came back to reality with a jolt as he heard a man's voice, the fantasy evaporating into thin air when he pushed the door open to find his sister sitting on a sofa beside the fireplace, several inches too close to her so-called fiancé.

'Mhairi?' He burst into the room. 'What's going on? Is Father unwell?'

'Mr Drummond.' The smile dropped from Dr Tomlinson's face as he stood up and bowed.

'Nothing's the matter with Father.' All Mhairi's facial muscles tensed at the sight of him. 'He wants to stay in his room today, but he's perfectly well.'

'Then why is *he* here?'

'*Angus!* I invited Dr Tomlinson for tea as my guest.'

'*Tea?*' He lowered his brows. Ever since Angus had made his displeasure about her engagement known, Mhairi had been discreet in her dealings with the man.

Dr Tomlinson had only ever visited the tower for medical reasons—as far as he knew, anyway. The fact that she'd seen fit to invite him for tea today was obviously due to somebody else's influence and it wasn't hard to guess whose. His gaze slid accusingly towards her friend.

'Yes, tea.' Miss MacKay's eyes narrowed in reply. 'Would you care for a cup? There's plenty left in the pot.'

Angus gritted his teeth. The woman had some nerve, offering him tea in his own house, although she was obviously daring him to say so. The look of challenge on her face was unmistakeable. And *this* was the woman he'd been fantasising about undressing! He felt as if he'd just been tricked.

'No, thank you. Some of us have work to do!' He let his scowl rest on each of them in turn before pivoting away and slamming the parlour door hard behind him.


'Oh, dear.' The defiant look on Mhairi's face turned to one of distress the moment Angus had gone. 'I'm sorry about that.'

'There's no need to be on my account.' Fiona tore her gaze away from the door, realising that she was scowling even more fiercely than the man who'd just stormed through it. She, Mhairi and Dr Tomlinson had been having such a delightful time before *he'd* arrived, looking even more dishevelled than he had the day before—a feat she hadn't thought possible—with his waistcoat hanging open and the top few buttons of his shirt undone to reveal the strong muscles of his neck, as well as a patch of dark hair at the top of his chest. Was the man incapable of remaining decently clothed for a full day?

'It wasn't your fault.'

'But it *was* mine.' Dr Tomlinson sounded sombre as he sat down again. 'Perhaps I shouldn't have come.'

'Don't say that.' Mhairi's eyes widened with an expression of hurt. 'I invited you.'

'Yes, but—'

'If it's anyone's fault, then it's mine,' Fiona interrupted briskly, picking up the teapot and refilling their cups. There weren't many problems that couldn't be fixed with tea, or so Mrs Kerr had always taught her pupils, and it was one of the few lessons she hadn't taken issue with. '*I* was the one who insisted on inviting you. I was just so thrilled when Mhairi told me about your engagement.'

'Thank you. That means a great deal, Miss MacKay. I hope that you'll be able to attend the wedding?'

'There's no way you'd be able to stop me.' Fiona smiled warmly. As fiancés went, Dr Tomlinson had exceeded her expectations. In his mid-thirties, with dark hair and coffee-coloured eyes, he had a pleasant face, a deliberate, thoughtful way of speaking and what she imagined would be an excellent bedside manner. Best of all, his affection for Mhairi radiated from his eyes in a way that made her feel almost wistful.

'If there ever *is* a wedding…' Mhairi's face crumpled suddenly before she stood up and rushed out of the room. 'Excuse me…'

'Mhairi…' Dr Tomlinson made a move as if to go after her and then changed his mind, lifting a hand to his brow instead. 'I'm sorry about that, Miss MacKay. Whatever must you think of us?'

'I think that Mhairi is my dear friend and that she's found a good and decent man to marry.' Fiona regarded him sympathetically. 'And that her brother needs to mind his own business.'

He gave a short laugh. 'I admit, something similar has crossed my mind. As a doctor, I understand his objections, but I would never put Mhairi in danger deliberately.'

'Then you disagree with his views?'

An expression of anguish crossed his face. 'Marriage…childbirth especially…is a risk for all women. Mhairi has a certain weakness of the chest, but I don't believe that it puts her at any substantially greater risk.'

'I see.'

'But perhaps…' He glanced at the door and then shook his head. 'Perhaps it's selfish of me to come between her and her brother. I thought that, with time, he'd come to realise how much we care for each other, but if anything he's only become more intractable. I fear I'm causing them both unhappiness.'

'You'd cause Mhairi even more if you changed your mind about the engagement. Somebody just needs to talk some sense into Mr Drummond, that's all.' Fiona lifted her teacup to her lips, a new idea rooting itself in her mind. 'And that someone is me.'

Dr Tomlinson's eyebrows almost disappeared into his hairline. 'Please don't feel that you have to. Mr Drummond can be somewhat terse.'

'I've noticed, but it's exactly why he needs to be challenged! And I've absolutely no trouble in speaking my mind, I assure you. I want Mhairi to be happy.'

'I can see that.' Dr Tomlinson's anxious expression turned into a smile. 'In that case, if you could help us, I'd be eternally grateful.'

'You can thank me in your wedding speech. In the meantime, let's finish our tea and give Mhairi a chance to recover, shall we? I believe that there's another slice of gingerbread for each of us, too. I do so hate to see good cake wasted.'

# *Chapter Five*

'Pass the butter, please.' Mhairi addressed her brother across the breakfast table the following morning. It was the first sentence anyone had uttered since they'd sat down and sounded unnaturally loud and jarring amidst the light clatter of cups and cutlery. 'Thank you.' She gave him a second look as he slid it towards her. 'Aren't you going to the distillery? It's almost nine o'clock.'

'Not today, no.' Mr Drummond was being uncharacteristically polite, Fiona noticed. Not only had he stood up and bowed when she'd entered, but he'd actually managed to shave and put on a waistcoat *and* cravat. No doubt he was feeling guilty about his behaviour towards Dr Tomlinson the previous afternoon *or* about the dour silence he'd inflicted upon them all afterwards. Dinner had been a downright depressing affair.

'I thought we might go down to the beach.' Mhairi turned her attention back to Fiona. 'Aberdour has a beautiful cove and the tide should be out at the moment.'

'That sounds delightful. I love the seaside.'

'I'd be happy to escort you, if you wish?'

'You'll…what?' Mhairi gaped at her brother in surprise.

'That would be very kind of you, Mr Drummond.' Fiona inclined her head graciously before Mhairi could refuse. Unpleasant as the thought of spending any more time with him was, it would give her the perfect opportunity to discuss his sister's situation.

'Good. I'll need to pay a quick visit to Pennan on the way back, but otherwise I'm at your service.'

'Oh, that means I can visit Annie!' Mhairi clasped her hands together excitedly. 'She was a maid here until she got married last winter and she just had a baby.'

'Aye, well...' Angus pushed his chair back and stood up. 'I'll get the cart ready and see you outside in ten minutes.'

'How stunning...' Fiona stood on the shore, gazing out at a seemingly endless expanse of rippling green water. She was used to the wide, sandy beaches at Dunbar and Tantallon that she and her father often visited in the summer, but Aberdour was a whole different landscape, with tall, red sandstone cliffs dropping away into a narrow beach of sand, shingle and pebbles.

She closed her eyes, listening to the low rumble of approaching waves, followed by the screeching of stones being sucked backwards and then tossed forward again in the surf. The combination of sounds was incessant, a constant churning and whirring like the wind in some never-ending tempest, and yet it was also soothing somehow. In truth, there was no point in being anything but soothed. There was no holding back the sea. She felt as though she'd be happy to stand there all day, just listening.

'True enough, it's a bonny sight.' Angus came to stand beside her. He was wearing his usual greatcoat, the ends billowing around his legs in the morning breeze. 'This is one of my favourite places.'

'No wonder. I'm just surprised Mhairi doesn't want to come down to the shore.' Fiona waved over her shoulder at her friend who was sitting on a bench at the edge of the grass.

'She wants to stay where it's sheltered. That's St. Drostan's Spring beside her.'

'St Drostan?'

'He landed here with St Columba in the sixth century and founded Deer Abbey. He was known for his miracle cures and used to baptise local people with the spring water.' He gestured along the beach. 'Would you care to walk? The tide's only just on the turn.'

'I'd be delighted.' She fell into step alongside him, bending occasionally to pick up a few pieces of green sea glass. 'You're being very obliging today, Mr Drummond.'

'Am I?' He gave her a sharp sideways look.

'Yes. Anyone might think you were suffering from a guilty conscience after yesterday.'

'Anyone might keep their opinions to themselves.'

She gave a distinctly unladylike snort. 'If I did that then I'd hardly speak at all.'

'I don't doubt it.'

'I find it interesting that it's mostly men who suggest it, though. And yet *they're* usually eager to share their opinions with all and sundry. It's almost as if they don't *like* a woman thinking for herself.'

'Not necessarily. Maybe it's just the way she expresses those thoughts.'

'Ah, so you think that I ought to be discreet and subtle? Those are supposedly feminine attributes, are they not?'

'I can't say I've ever given the matter much thought.'

'Maybe that's the problem.'

'And what problem would that be?' He stopped walking abruptly. 'Why do I get the impression that all these comments are building up to something, Miss MacKay?'

'Because they are.' She slid the sea glass into her pocket and brushed her hands together to get rid of the sand. 'Honestly, I'd like to know why you're so against Mhairi marrying Dr Tomlinson.'

'What does it matter to you?'

'*She* matters to me.'

'And you think that she doesn't to me?' His gaze darkened. 'Anyway, it doesn't matter what I think. Father already gave his permission for the marriage.'

'But you're the one stopping her from going ahead.'

'I haven't said anything.'

'You don't have to. You make your feelings perfectly obvious in the way you behave.'

'And you've been here for how long? Not even two days.'

'I saw your behaviour towards Dr Tomlinson yesterday and I know what Mhairi's told me. It's not fair. She has a right to be happy.'

'Then she can go ahead and marry him.'

'No, she *can't*. She doesn't want to hurt you and he doesn't want to cause a rift with her family.'

'Or maybe deep down he knows that I'm right and she's *not* strong enough.'

'Or maybe as a doctor he's better placed to judge her strength than you.'

'Or maybe he's selfish.'

'Oh, yes, Mhairi's told me all about his selfishness.

How he gives free treatment to those who can't afford it. He sounds utterly monstrous.'

Mr Drummond's jaw tightened visibly. 'Maybe it's time we went back. It's getting cold.'

'Then you should fasten your coat. Personally, I think the temperature quite pleasant, but by all means go back to the cart if you're feeling delicate.' She climbed up onto a plateau of rusty-coloured rock, moulded into smooth, swirling shapes by the water. 'But at least be honest and admit that you just don't like a woman challenging you. Most men can't cope with it.'

'I've no problem with a woman speaking her mind.'

'Except when she contradicts *your* opinions.'

'You ought to be careful up there.' He sounded as if he were speaking from between clenched teeth. 'The rocks can get slippery.'

'Duly noted.'

'And look where you're going. There are rock pools.' He muttered something that sounded distinctly unflattering before jumping up beside her. 'I don't want you falling in one and breaking a leg.'

'How thoughtful.'

'Miss MacKay...' He appeared to take a deep breath. 'It's not that I don't like the man. From what I've seen and heard, he's an excellent doctor. I just don't want Mhairi taking any foolish risks.'

'Then what about calculated ones? You can't keep her in a silk-lined cage all her life. She won't thank you for it— Oh!' Fiona stopped mid-sentence, noticing a gap in the cliff face. 'Is that a cave?'

'Aye.' He glanced over his shoulder. 'It cuts through to the next beach at low tide.'

'It's still low tide now.'

'It's even more slippery in there.'

'Then you'd better come along and keep an eye on me!'

She didn't wait for his response, clambering over several large boulders until she reached the gap. It was bigger than it had looked from a distance, leading into a dank tunnel that gradually opened out into a large, high-roofed cavern.

'How picturesque.' She stopped to admire the view framed between the cavern walls.

'What's lovely about it?' Mr Drummond's voice behind her sounded distinctly grumpy. 'It's dark, damp and smells of seaweed.'

'It's sublime.' She ignored him. 'Like a pre-Raphaelite painting. You can just imagine a maiden standing silhouetted in the foreground, gazing out to sea, awaiting the return of her lover.'

'Can ye?' He grunted. 'Well, she'd better not stay there too long or she'd be washed out to sea herself.'

'You're not much of a romantic are you, Mr Drummond?'

'I've never been accused of it, no.'

'Well...' She crouched down beside a rock pool brimming with hermit crabs, limpets and seaweed. 'I suppose that explains a lot.'

'So you think I should just let Mhairi do as she pleases?'

'Yes.' She removed her gloves and dipped her hand into the pool, swirling the water gently with her fingertips, vaguely aware of his black leather boots coming to stand beside her. 'I think that everyone should be allowed to make their own choices in life.'

'Are you a radical, then? I've heard of women like you.'

'I'm the woman my mother taught me to be. She contracted tuberculosis when I was nine years old, but I remember her very clearly. Before she died, she called me to her bedside and told me that I was going to be the lady of the house from now on and that I should always be sure to know my own mind and make my own choices in life. In essence, she told me to think for myself and treasure my independence. She was a member of the Edinburgh chapter of the National Society for Women's Suffrage, and generally considered a bluestocking, but I was very proud of her. So was my father.'

'And you've been managing his house for him ever since?'

'Yes, although I boarded at Mrs Kerr's establishment during the week for a few years. He was often away on business and thought that the company of other girls would be good for me. Which it was, since I met Mhairi.' She stood up and drew her gloves back on. 'Now I manage his household, and do an excellent job of it, too.'

'But now he wants to marry again?' He lifted a shoulder. 'Mhairi told me.'

'I'm afraid so. To a woman only eight years older than me, if you can believe it?'

'Aye, if he cares for her.'

'It's indecent! We could be sisters.' She tossed her head. 'I don't see why he needs her anyway. We were perfectly content until she came along.'

'Perfectly content with a daughter is one thing. Perfectly content with a wife is a whole different matter.'

'I don't see why.'

He made a strange-sounding snort. 'Well, if you don't, then I'm not going to explain it to you.'

'Don't be absurd.' She felt a rush of colour flood up

her throat and over her cheeks. 'My father is almost fifty years old!'

'Speaking as a man, I don't think age makes much of a difference.'

'Of course it does! How could you even think such a thing?' She turned her face to one side, horribly aware that her cheeks were turning a similar shade to the rocks. 'I just want things to go back to the way they were.'

'Aye.' To her relief, he sounded thoughtful rather than gloating. 'I can understand that, but maybe there is no *way things were*. The world's always changing. You cannae stop it any more than you can stop the waves, but knowing that doesn't always make it easier to accept.'

'Are you a philosopher now?'

'No, I'm just saying I can understand why you're anxious. After my mother died, so soon after my father's business failed, I felt hopeless for a while. Lost. Everything in my life seemed to unravel so quickly. And my father's mind... Mhairi must have told you, it's not what it once was.'

'Yes. I'm sorry.' She looked up at him curiously. 'Mhairi said there was a fire at the distillery. Do you know what happened?'

'Not really. A stray candle perhaps... They're dangerous places.' He shook his head. 'Although he wasn't so upset about that as at the things people said.'

'Such as?'

'That my mother must have regretted her choice of husband, that he wasted her fortune and that she could have done better than a Drummond. We've never been the richest nor the most respectable family. And then, when she died not long afterwards of a heart seizure, it was hard not to see the two as connected.'

'How tragic. But then… Forgive me, but I don't understand why you *want* to restore the distillery.'

He gave her a look, as if the answer ought to be obvious. 'For my father. Meggie's was his dream. I want him to see it become a success and prove everyone wrong. I want to restore our family name and fortunes.'

'Ah.' She wrinkled her brow. 'But doesn't that mean you're not really accepting the situation either?'

'What?' His brows snapped together.

'Well, you just said that we ought to accept that life changes, but *you're* not. You're trying to rebuild the distillery even though it failed the first time. Whisky's a competitive industry, isn't it?'

'That doesn't mean I'll fail.'

'No, but I don't see how we're so very different. We're both trying to fix something we think is wrong. You want to make your father feel better and I'm trying to stop mine from making a terrible mistake.'

'Why are you so certain his marrying again would be?'

'It's obvious.'

'Apparently not to your father.' He folded his arms. 'You know, Mhairi told me you were the kind of person who stood up for other people.'

'Meaning what, exactly?'

'I'm just wondering whether you've given this poor woman much of a chance. Are you sure you're not just feeling threatened as lady of the house?'

'That's a horrible accusation!'

'And do you know what else? Here you are saying that women ought to be allowed to make their own decisions, and yet you object to another woman marrying your father just because you think she's too young. That's a bit of a contradiction, don't you think?

'So now you're calling me a hypocrite?'

He lifted an eyebrow. 'You were the one who said you valued honesty.'

'Well, you're an overbearing, controlling brute! You're only saying all this in revenge for me challenging you about Mhairi!'

'Aye, there might be a bit of that, but it doesn't make what I'm saying any less true.'

'I think you've made your feelings perfectly clear!' She folded her arms, mirroring his stance. 'Now, is that everything? While you're making it blindingly obvious what you think of me?'

'Just one more thing. It strikes me that, for all your talk of being an independent woman, running away from home without directions for where you were going wasn't exactly the behaviour of a rational adult, more like that of a wilful child. You were just lucky I found you when I did.'

'I *thought* I knew where I was going. How was I to know a tower would be so hard to find?'

'You could have planned ahead. Instead, you put yourself and your maid in danger, acting like you know best, wearing your ridiculous clothes and—'

'How dare you!' She inhaled sharply. 'My clothes are *not* ridiculous!'

'Then what's that thing on your head?'

'It's called a toque!'

'I've seen bigger saucers. It's certainly no' keeping your head warm.'

'I'm wearing a cape!'

'Which you had to borrow from my sister because you didn't bring anything suitable yourself. In how many bags was it? Five?'

'At least *I* dress properly. You can hardly keep your shirt buttoned!'

'Well, Miss MacKay.' His lips curved in a slow, taunting smile. 'I'm flattered that you've noticed.'

'You beast! I ought to—' She started to retort and then clamped her teeth together, torn between fury and sudden, horrible self-doubt.

Despite all his goading, she was aware that several of his comments contained grains of truth. Her behaviour *had* been somewhat impulsive. And, if he was right about that, then maybe there was a faint chance that he was right about other things, too. Was it possible that she'd misjudged Mrs Gibson simply because she'd felt threatened? Had she acted like a child? Not that she was going to acknowledge either possibility to *him*. She needed to get away, to get back to her room and consider... After which, she could spend the next nine days avoiding him!

'Miss MacKay?' He was looking at her strangely, she realised, as if he were waiting for her to finish the sentence.

'You're right, it *is* getting cold.' She walked around him, heading back into the darkness of the tunnel. 'I'll meet you at the cart.'

## Chapter Six

'Angus?' Mhairi murmured as he took hold of her elbow, helping her onto the bench at the front of the cart. 'Is everything all right?'

'Perfectly,' Miss MacKay answered for him, climbing up on the other side without waiting for his assistance. 'Mr Drummond just felt a little cold, that's all.'

'*You* felt cold?' Mhairi's eyebrows lifted.

'Humph.' He made a sound that was meant to be a grunt of acknowledgement but came out sounding more like a growl, then counted to ten under his breath before jumping up and taking hold of the reins.

He'd only come out that morning to make amends for his temper the day before, but instead he'd lost it all over again. He was almost as angry about that as he was about Miss MacKay's comments about the distillery. She'd sounded just like everyone else, talking as if it were nothing more than a fool's errand that he ought to let crumble away into oblivion. It was only fortunate that Mhairi was sitting between the two of them as a buffer, although she could probably feel the waves of resentment emanating from both sides.

'Well…' His sister's head turned uncertainly between them. 'I'm looking forward to seeing Annie and the baby.'

'Aye, we should get on.' He flicked the reins determinedly. 'Are *you* fond of babies, Miss MacKay?' He wasn't sure what made him ask, only that he had a feeling the question would annoy her.

'To be honest, I don't think of them very often.' As he'd expected, there was a definite coolness to her tone. 'My experience is somewhat limited.'

'You never know…you might have a new brother or sister to play with before long. Oof!' He grunted as Mhairi elbowed him violently in the ribs.

'Quite.' Miss MacKay's voice suggested that, given the opportunity, she would have applied her elbow to a more tender area. 'You know, if there's one thing I'm coming to rely on Mr Drummond, it's your ability to make an already bad situation suddenly appear ten times worse.'

'Do you see that croft?' Mhairi interjected, her breathless tone indicating her eagerness to change the topic. 'That's where Jane Whyte lives. She's our local heroine.'

'Jane Whyte…' Miss MacKay sounded thoughtful. 'The name sounds familiar.'

'She was in all the papers a few years ago. There was a shipwreck in the bay, the *William Hope*, during a bad storm. Jane waded out into the water, caught onto a rope they threw to her, tied it around her waist, made it secure and then helped the whole crew ashore. She saved fifteen lives that night.'

'Incredible.'

'She got a silver medal for bravery from the RNLI, as well as ten pounds.'

'I should think so, too. And what's that over there?'

'Oh, that's old Aberdour Castle. It's mostly a ruin now.'

'Can we go and take a look?'

'Another day.' Angus grunted as Mhairi turned enquiringly towards him. 'I want to get some fish from Murdo before it's taken to market.'

They lapsed into silence, driving along the winding road over the cliff top and then down the steep descent into the tiny fishing village of Pennan.

'Annie's house is over there.' Mhairi jumped off the cart at the bottom of the hill, pointing towards the last in a row of white cottages. 'Will you come and visit with me, Fiona?'

'No, thank you.' Miss MacKay answered stiffly, obviously still rattled by the thought of young siblings. 'I'll wait with the cart, if you don't mind?'

'Of course not. I won't be long.'

'Neither will I,' Angus commented as he moved the cart forward a few paces, drawing it to a halt beside the harbour wall.

'Take as long as you like.' She acknowledged the words without turning her head. 'I'll endeavour to manage without your company in the meantime.'

He nodded, not that there was any point in doing so when she wasn't looking, then walked away in the opposite direction from Mhairi, towards a lone cottage with a pile of lobster pots piled high at the front.

'Morning!' He waved a hand to one of the local fishermen, Murdo, who was sitting on a bench outside with one of his sons, mending nets. 'How was the haul today?'

'We did well.' Murdo glanced past him towards the cart. 'Although it looks like you've caught something yerself!'

'Not by choice. She's a friend of my sister's.'

'But nay one of yours, judging by the way she's glaring at you. Pretty lass, though.'

'With a tongue like an adder. She'd argue with herself in the mirror if there was no one else around.'

'My Sadie's the same way, but there's nothing wrong with a lass having a bit o' spirit in my book. Unless you're afraid of a challenge, o' course!'

'I have enough challenges in my life.'

'Aye, true enough.' Murdo nodded his head sagely. 'But ye should probably tell her to mind where she's walking.'

'Eh?' Angus glanced over his shoulder and frowned. Miss MacKay appeared to have changed her mind about staying put and was climbing the steps up onto the harbour wall, looking at the boats within and not paying sufficient attention to the increasingly tall waves without. Thankfully, they weren't yet big enough to be dangerous but, with the tide coming in, she'd find herself caught in the spray if she wasn't careful.

'Aye.' He turned his back on the scene, reaching into his coat pocket for a few coins. 'I'll fetch her down in a moment. Right now, Mrs Donald is after something for dinner.'

'Just a moment.' Murdo went into the cottage, coming back with a string of freshly caught silvery mackerel. 'How about these?'

'They'll do nicely. I'm obliged.'

'Ye'd best get back to your adder, then.'

'She's not *my* anything.'

Murdo chuckled. 'That's what I used to say about Sadie until she told me otherwise.'

Angus shot him a dark look before turning back to the cart. Miss MacKay was standing at the far end of the harbour wall now, her tall figure silhouetted against the sea like the heroine in the painting she'd talked about earlier. She was certainly a striking-looking woman when it came down to it, the hair beneath her ridiculously small hat glowing like gold in the midday sunshine. Murdo was right, though. She shouldn't be standing where she was. *He* shouldn't have let her walk out so far...

Quickly, Angus tossed the fish into the back of the cart and accelerated his pace. 'Miss MacKay!' He took the steps two at a time, calling out as he went, but it was too late. No sooner had the warning left his mouth than a particularly large wave smacked into the harbour wall, enveloping her in a heavy torrent of salt water.

'Damnation.' He sprinted towards her. 'Are ye all right?'

'Just a little drowned.' She spluttered between words, looking so thoroughly drenched that a reasonable person might have assumed she'd just been for a swim.

'Come on.' He wrenched his coat off and draped it around her shoulders, dragging her away before the same thing happened again, leading her dripping and shivering all the way back to Murdo's cottage.

'Fiona!' Mhairi came running along the street to join them, shooting an accusing glare in his direction. 'I saw what happened from Annie's window. You poor thing!'

'Come inside, miss.' Murdo held open the door of his cottage. 'You can warm yersel' at the hearth.'

'Thank you.' Miss MacKay's teeth were chattering as she ducked under the lintel and stumbled into the kitchen.

'Oh!' Sadie, Murdo's wife, almost dropped a pan at the sight of her. 'What on earth happened?'

'I wasn't paying enough attention to my surroundings.' To Angus's amazement, Miss MacKay managed a self-deprecating laugh. 'I think the waves took exception to it.'

'Well, come on over to the fireplace and get dry.' Sadie handed her a length of material to dry her face and then made shooing motions at her three small daughters who were all staring open-mouthed at the spectacle.

'Thank you.' Miss MacKay held her hands out in front of the fireplace. 'I admit, the water felt as if it had just come straight from the north pole. I'm so sorry to drip all over your kitchen.'

'If there's one thing we're used to, it's water. I'll just run and fetch you a dress to borrow.' Sadie paused at the bottom of a small staircase. 'If you don't mind wearing one of mine, that is?'

'On the contrary, I'd be incredibly grateful.' Miss MacKay removed her sodden toque and set it down on the floor. 'I must look quite a sight.'

'It wasn't your fault. I ought to have warned you about the harbour wall.' Mhairi's elbow poked hard into her brother's ribs.

'So should I.' Angus gave a start, aware that he was gaping at Miss MacKay almost as much as the little girls. After the initial shock had worn off, he'd expected tears or stamping of feet. Some complaining about her ruined clothes, at least. Not humour. Maybe she wasn't such a spoilt child after all. In fact, her behaviour was consummately that of a lady. Whereas his, as a gentleman, left a great, *great* deal to be desired. 'I didna' think I'd be gone long.'

'Yes, well…' Miss MacKay gave him a cursory look. 'No real harm done.'

'Here you are, miss.' Sadie came back downstairs with a dress draped over one arm. 'Now, if Mr Drummond will just step outside, you can get out of those wet things.'

Angus turned quickly towards the door, the thought of her undressing taking his thoughts in an entirely inappropriate direction. 'Just call for me if you need anything.'

'I think you've done more than enough for today, *thank you*.' Mhairi gave him a pointed shove before slamming the door in his face.

'Well, now...' Murdo was sitting on his bench again, smoking a pipe. 'I'd ask how your whisky venture was going, but something tells me you'd be better spending your time thinking up a decent apology.'

'Aye.' Angus rubbed a hand over his chin, feeling as if he'd just been doused in frigid cold sea water himself. 'I've a feeling you're right.'

## Chapter Seven

Angus slumped in his armchair, lowering his brows at his sister as they sat in front of the parlour fireplace that evening. Miss MacKay had been keen to put the whole harbour wall episode behind them, chattering away light-heartedly at dinner before retiring early to bed, but his sister was still giving him the cold shoulder. Quite literally, sitting sideways in her chair so that she wouldn't have to look at him.

'Are you going to ignore me for the rest of her stay?' he burst out finally, unable to bear the silent treatment any longer.

'Maybe I will.' Mhairi drew a thread through her embroidery, a handkerchief bearing the initials 'GT', as if she were deliberately trying to infuriate him. 'And if Fiona catches a chill then I might ignore you for years.'

'How was I to know?'

'You knew fine well what might happen with the tide coming in and you *didn't warn her*!'

'I was trying to when it happened! Besides, I said I was sorry on the way home.'

'Really? That sounded more like mumbling to me.'

'Well, *she* said it was all forgotten.'

'Because she doesn't want to upset *me*. Honestly, don't you know anything about women?'

'Apparently not.' He heaved himself up from his arm chair and walked towards the window, drawing the curtains aside to look up at the waxing half moon. 'Fine. I'll apologise again at breakfast. Will that satisfy you?'

'Not if it's said as graciously as that, no.' Mhairi threw him one last, scornful look before tossing her sewing aside. 'Now, if you'll excuse me, I'm going to bed, too.'

Angus waited until the door had closed before giving vent to his feelings, most of the words directed solely against himself. No matter which way he looked at it, he'd been utterly in the wrong, and it didn't help that Miss MacKay was being so conciliatory. The situation would have been much easier to handle if she'd simply ranted at him.

His gaze fell suddenly on a bottle of amber-coloured liquid standing on a table beside the book shelf. He'd transferred the contents from one of his father's old whisky casks the day before but still hadn't tasted a drop. After ten years, the flavours ought to have matured sufficiently for drinking, but he hadn't yet summoned the nerve to find out. He'd intended to try it this evening, but now it occurred to him that the bottle might serve another purpose. Miss MacKay wasn't exactly the person he would have chosen to share a dram with, but Mhairi was right. He owed her a decent apology and, as peace offerings went, this was the best he could do.

He filled a third of a tumbler and headed upstairs, pausing to take a deep breath on the third landing before rapping his knuckles gently on the door to her chamber. Of course, it was possible that she'd already gone to sleep. In fact, she probably had, but at least then he could go to his own bed knowing that he'd tried...

'Yes?' The door creaked open. 'Oh.' Miss MacKay's friendly expression faltered at the sight of him. 'It's you.'

'Aye.' He nodded, forcing his gaze back to her face after one swift glance downwards. She was dressed for bed in an ankle-length cotton nightgown and long red shawl, with her golden hair hanging loose around her shoulders. In the glow of the oil lamp behind her, it looked like a shimmering waterfall, so smooth, silky and radiant that it took several moments for him to find his voice again. 'I wanted to apologise again. Properly.'

'Meaning that Mhairi told you to?' She folded her arms and his eyes followed the movement, coming to rest on her fingers where they grasped the edge of her tasselled shawl. They were long and delicate, her nails clean and neatly trimmed, utterly unlike his own rough, calloused hands.

'I still mean it. I ought to have warned you about the waves.'

'Yes, you should have.' Miss MacKay pursed and then un-pursed her lips. 'But, on reflection, I can understand why you might have been somewhat irritated with me. I was insensitive about your distillery earlier and, as for Mhairi's situation, you're right. I've only been here for two days and I don't know everything.

'In my defence, however, it's possible that I was feeling a little defensive about what you said in regard to my father. Coupled with which, it's not easy being a woman, Mr Drummond. We have to speak so much louder to have our opinions heard that it makes me over-assertive on occasion. I shouldn't have called you a controlling brute.'

'I shouldn't have called you a wilful child.'

'Oh, yes.' Her brows puckered again. 'I'd forgotten about that. Still, I've been thinking about what you said about feeling lost after your mother died, and I *do* understand what it's like to lose someone you care about. It can make you afraid of losing anyone else. Maybe it can make a person controlling, too. Or even wilful.'

Something shifted in the depths of her grey eyes. 'I know that you only object to Dr Tomlinson because you're trying to protect Mhairi. And your father, too, I expect?'

He blinked, surprised by her acuity. 'Aye, he's given his consent to the wedding, but I'm afraid that if anything happens to Mhairi then he won't be able to bear it. Not after everything else.'

'I see.' She nodded slowly although, thankfully, for once she didn't try and argue.

'In any case…' He held out the tumbler. 'I've brought a peace offering.'

'Whisky?' She looked shocked. 'For me?'

'Not just any whisky. *Meggie's.*'

'Oh… Thank you.' She took the glass from his fingers, regarding the contents suspiciously for almost half a minute before taking a tentative sip. 'Eurgh!' She started spluttering almost at once. 'It's… I can't… I'm sorry, Mr Drummond, but it's *foul*!'

'What?' He reached for the tumbler, frankly alarmed by the disgusted expression on her face, and took a large mouthful himself, letting it rest on his tongue for a few seconds before swallowing. The amber-coloured liquid trickled its way slowly down his throat, rich, smooth and fiery. Perfect.

'I really am sorry.' Miss MacKay had finally stopped coughing enough to look sympathetic. 'I'm not just being mean in retaliation. I *wish* that it tasted better. Truly.' She frowned. 'Why are you laughing?'

'Because it's *meant* to taste like that!' He gave a whoop of triumph, dropping the tumbler onto a bureau on the landing before catching her up in his arms and swinging her enthusiastically around in a circle, feeling relieved and vindicated and as if his heart were soaring. 'It's everything that I hoped it would be. Peaty, smoky and deep... There are so many layers. You can *taste* the land!'

'And that's a good thing?' She started to laugh, too. 'Well, thank goodness!'

He whirled them to a halt, belatedly realising that picking up house guests and twirling them around in their nightclothes, even in celebration, was yet another example of ungentlemanly behaviour. Quickly, he lowered her back to her feet, though there was no disguising the fact that his hands were still wrapped around her un-corseted waist, and that they were standing substantially closer than decency allowed—so close that their cheeks were actually pressed together, his bristly stubble scraping against her smooth skin. He could feel her heartbeat through her nightgown, he realised, beating erratically against his chest, while her hair smelled of violets...

He inhaled subtly before dropping his hands and taking a reluctant step backwards. 'Forgive me.' His voice sounded uncharacteristically husky. 'I got a little carried away.'

'Quite understandable.' She swayed as if she were dizzy and he caught hold of her again, by her elbows this time. 'You were pleased, that's all.'

'With my foul liquid?' He gave a ragged laugh, tying to dispel the new sense of tension that was making the landing seem much smaller suddenly. 'I suppose the taste can take a bit of getting used to. Have you never tried whisky before?'

'No. I *definitely* would have remembered, although perhaps…' She swallowed and licked her lips. 'Perhaps I judged too hastily. Could I have another try?'

'Of course.' He reached for the tumbler again, holding it up to her face. 'Take in the aroma first. What can you smell?'

She buried her nose in the glass. 'Peat?'

'Good. What else?'

'Sherry?'

'*Very* good. It's been stored in old sherry casks. Now, take a small sip and make sure to roll it around your mouth for a few seconds before you drink. You want to get all the flavours.'

'All right.' She let him tip the glass back against her lips and then immediately started coughing again. 'Eurgh! I'm sorry, Mr Drummond. It really must be an acquired taste.'

He grinned and finished the rest of the tumbler in one satisfying gulp. 'In that case, why don't you come with me to the distillery tomorrow? I'll show you around.'

'Me?' Her eyes widened. 'Oh, there's really no need. I've already accepted your apology.'

'Yes, but I'd like a chance to convince you that what you just drank was delicious.' He quirked an eyebrow, surprised as much by his own offer as by how much he wanted her to say yes. Despite their disastrous outing to Pennan that day, he found that he actually wanted to spend more time with her.

'I don't know.' She caught her bottom lip between her teeth. 'Will I have to drink more of it?'

'Not if you don't want to. You can be appreciative from a distance.'

'You know, you really don't have to trouble yourself.'

'But I'd like to.'

'Well…' She rearranged her shawl, clasping the ends tightly at her throat. 'Do you promise I won't end up getting drenched again?'

'Not by the sea. Unfortunately, I cannae vouch for the weather, but I'll bring an umbrella. I'll even throw in some lunch. How does that sound?'

'Oh, well, in that case…' Her grey eyes sparked silver with amusement, her whole face lighting up in a smile that left him suddenly and utterly dazzled. 'How can I refuse?'

## Chapter Eight

How could she have refused?

Fiona asked herself the question several times as she made her way downstairs to breakfast. There were, in fact, several ways she might have done so. She might have said, quite honestly, that she detested both the smell and flavour of whisky, that she was there to visit Mhairi, not him, and that, considering the way her inner organs had reacted when he'd swept her up in his arms, it was in their best interests not to spend any more time together.

Instead, she'd agreed, with the result that she was going to spend one of her eight remaining days learning more about that noxious liquid in the company of a man she'd found mostly objectionable ever since she'd arrived.

Given the circumstances, she was much too excited.

'Good morning.' Mr Drummond stood up from the table when she entered the dining room, raking his fingers through already messy hair in a way that she found unexpectedly, inconveniently, endearing. 'How are you feeling? Did the whisky help you sleep?'

'I don't know about that.' She helped herself to

some toast and eggs from the sideboard, surreptitiously smoothing a hand over her bodice to quell the tingling sensation that appeared to have taken up residence in her stomach. 'I'm more inclined to think it was the sea air, but I slept very well, thank you.'

'It's going to be another bonny day.' He pulled out her chair, his fingers skimming lightly across the top of her back as she sat down.

'Yes, I saw the sunrise,' she answered breathlessly, something about the contact making her breath catch and her insides tighten. If she wasn't mistaken, his fingers lingered for a moment against her shoulder blades, as if he didn't want to pull them away. Which meant that she surely *was* mistaken.

'Good morning.' Mhairi entered the room at that moment.

'Oh.' Fiona gave a small start, hoping she didn't look quite as guilty as she felt. 'Good morning. We were just talking about the sunrise.'

'It *was* beautiful this morning.' Mhairi tilted her head to one side, her gaze moving speculatively between them. 'I'm glad to see the two of you getting along.'

'Aye.' Angus took his own seat again, looking perfectly at ease, as if touching her hadn't affected him at all. 'Miss MacKay's coming to the distillery with me today.'

'Really?'

'Yes. I have a lot to learn about whisky, apparently.' Fiona strove to sound brisk and business-like. 'But you'll be coming along, too, won't you?'

'Oh, no, I've heard enough about whisky to last me a lifetime.' Mhairi shook her head quickly. 'Besides, I'm feeling a bit tired this morning.'

'Then I'll stay and keep you company.'

'Don't be silly. I'll probably just curl up by the fire and read.'

'Are you feeling unwell?' Angus's voice sharpened.

'Oh, for goodness' sake.' Mhairi rolled her eyes. 'I'm tired, not ailing. Don't start fussing!'

'Fair enough.' He threw Fiona an enquiring look. 'It'll be just the two of us, then, if you don't mind?'

'Well...' She hesitated. For the sake of her reputation, she really ought to take some kind of chaperone with her. Emily, at least. Then again, Mhairi didn't seem to think the idea of them going alone particularly scandalous, and who else would know about it? And, even if someone *did* find out, it would hardly damage her marital prospects. She was already a renowned bluestocking. Nobody would ever believe that a man like Angus Drummond would have designs on a woman like her...

'No, of course I don't mind,' she answered at last. 'In fact, I...' She faltered mid-sentence, distracted by the sight of a gentleman standing in the dining room doorway. His hair was greyer, and his face slightly more wrinkled than it had been the last time she'd seen him, but his features were instantly recognisable, an older, male version of his daughter's. 'Why, good morning, Mr Drummond.'

'Father?' Both his son and daughter sounded shocked.

'I thought I'd come and join you all downstairs for breakfast today.' The old man hobbled forward. 'Mhairi told me you were visiting, Miss MacKay. I apologise for not greeting you sooner.'

'Not at all.' Fiona stood up and held out her hand. 'I'm sorry that you were indisposed yesterday, but it's a pleasure to see you again now.'

'Have you two met before?' Mr Drummond the younger looked even more surprised.

'Aye, that spring I went to visit your sister at school and you said you had too much work tae join me.' Mr Drummond Senior inclined his head towards Fiona. 'He's never liked cities, this one. But how's your own father these days?'

'Oh, he's very well, thank you.' She decided against mentioning Mrs Gibson.

'Is he not here with you?'

'No, I travelled alone—except for my maid, of course.'

'And Mhairi and Angus have been taking good care of you, I hope?'

'Excellent care. I'm having a lovely time.'

'I'm glad to hear it. I keep telling my son that he ought to spend more time with young ladies and less time working or he'll never find a bride. You'll be a good influence on him, I hope.'

'Well, I don't know about that...' She made a show of pouring some tea, horribly aware of her cheeks darkening treacherously.

'Aye, well...' For a moment, she thought she caught a mischievous glint in the older man's eyes before he turned his attention towards the breakfast. 'I'm very glad to see ye again, Miss MacKay. Almost as glad as I am to see those kippers.'


'Here we are.' Angus drew the cart to a halt outside the front door of Meggie's distillery and set down the reins, trying to imagine seeing the place through new eyes. Fortunately, the weather was working in his and its favour today, with halcyon rays of sunshine making the windowless whitewashed walls gleam even brighter than usual.

Now they'd arrived he was starting to feel decidedly nervous about letting somebody else see inside, especially somebody who didn't know the first thing about whisky, and yet for some reason her opinion seemed important to him. After his impulsive invitation the night before, he'd surprised himself by just how eager he'd been to see her at breakfast. He wouldn't have thought it possible to change his mind about a person so completely, but he had. Even the violently purple tone of her gown hadn't put him off. On the contrary, he'd felt a surge of pleasure at the sight of it—of *her*.

'It's smaller than I expected,' Miss MacKay commented before biting her lip, looking embarrassed. 'Not that I'm criticising. I just wasn't sure what to expect.'

'It's all right. My father never produced more than a few barrels.'

'It was lovely to see him again this morning,' she commented, jumping down from the cart before he could walk around to help her.

'Aye, he was on good form. He likes you.'

'You say that like it's a surprise.' She lifted her eyebrows and then craned her neck backwards before he could respond. 'What are those pagoda-like things on the roof?'

'They're a new invention. Doig's ventilators. They help clear the smoke away after malting.'

'Doig's ventilators,' she repeated, as if she were committing the words to memory. 'Now, I want you to tell me everything. When I learn about a subject, I like to do it properly.'

'Then I'll do my best.' He unlocked the padlock on the front door and moved aside to let her precede him. 'After you.'

'Thank you.' She stepped over the threshold and peered into the gloom. 'Don't you have any employees?'

'No. If I need help, I bring one of the men from the

farm and pay them a bit extra, but at the moment I do most of the work by myself.' He opened some window shutters, letting light into the long barn-like room. 'Here we are. This is where it all happens—or will, hopefully. I've managed to save enough to replace the old, damaged equipment, and tested it a few times, so it's all ready to go.'

'How does it work?'

'Are you sure you want to know?'

'Oh, yes. I hardly ever ask things just to be polite.'

'Well, there are several stages to the process. The first is malting, which happens in the next room. You steep your barley in water, then spread it all out on the floor to germinate, turning it occasionally to stop heat building up. After that comes the mashing. That's where you grind the barley into a flour, then mix it with hot water and leave it to ferment. The liquid that comes off that is called the wort. Then you add the yeast and it goes into the stills. You need to distil at least twice.

'Finally, it comes through this.' He patted a wooden and glass box. 'The spirit safe. Only the local excise officer has the key.'

'It sounds like a complicated process.'

'You get used to it.' He cleared his throat as she came to stand beside him, very aware of the subtle scent of violets emanating from her skin, reminding him of how lovely she'd looked in a night gown and how much he'd like to see her in one again... 'Then it goes into casks.'

'For how long?'

'It depends on the type of whisky, but at least ten years.'

'*Ten years?* You mean, you have to wait a whole decade just to find out if your product is any good?'

'Aye. In the meantime, you keep on brewing with your fingers crossed.'

'How extraordinary.' She walked slowly around the room, pausing to examine each piece of equipment before twirling about to face him again. 'Wait... If you've only just started brewing again, and it takes ten years to mature, what was it I drank last night?'

'Ah, that was original Meggie's. Most of my father's barrels were destroyed in the fire before they could be taken away to a warehouse for storage, but fortunately he'd already taken a couple back to the farm. What you drank came from one of those. I finally summoned the courage to open it.'

Her eyes widened. 'Then I'm honoured that you shared it with me. And also sorry for the way I reacted.'

'As if I'd just given you poison, you mean?'

'Yes. If I'd known it was so special...'

He laughed, trying not to notice the delicate sway of her hips as she walked towards him. 'I'll be honest, you made me panic for a moment there, but I probably should have mixed it with water to soften the taste.'

'Maybe next time.'

'Maybe.'

She gave him a quizzical look as she came to a halt. 'So what would you have done if it hadn't tasted as good as you hoped? All of this preparation would have been for nothing.'

'I would probably have kept going anyway.' He tapped his head. 'Stubborn.'

'*Determined.* It means a great deal to you, doesn't it?'

'Restoring my family name and honour? Aye, it does.'

'Then I truly hope it succeeds.' Her smile seemed

to ignite a warm glow in his chest. 'Now, I believe that you mentioned something about lunch?'

'Remind me again why we're not just eating at a table on the ground like normal people?' Miss MacKay sounded uncharacteristically nervous.

'It's for the view. Trust me, it'll be worth it. There's a flat section on the roof that's perfect for picnics.'

'Are you sure it's safe?'

'Aye. I replaced the slates myself.'

'I meant this ladder.' There was a sound of creaking wood. 'And do you promise you're not looking up?'

'I gave you my word!' He stifled a laugh. 'Although, I should tell ye, I've seen a woman's ankles before.'

'Not mine! And it's more than my ankles at this point. It's not easy climbing a ladder in a dress.'

'I'll take your word for it.' He focussed all of his attention on the bottom rungs of the ladder, wondering just how *much* more she was talking about. As if the temptation to steal a glance upwards wasn't strong enough already...

'I really ought to have worn bloomers. I've often thought they were a good idea.' There was a bit more creaking, followed by the clatter of boots. 'All right, I'm up.'

'Good.' He sprang up after her, the picnic basket over one arm. 'It'll be getting dark soon.'

'I choose to ignore that sarcasm, but only because you were right about the view. It *is* spectacular, especially today. I can hardly believe it's November.'

'It is,' he agreed, suddenly unable to think of a single other thing to say as their gazes met and locked together. Her grey eyes looked more blue today, he noticed, as if the sky were reflected in their depths, while the fresh air had added a fetching pink bloom to her cheeks.

'So, what do we have?'

'Mmm?'

'In the basket.'

'Ah.' He crouched down and started to unwrap several muslin-wrapped parcels. 'It looks like a week's supply of cheese sandwiches, a few pieces of shortbread and some ale.'

'Excellent.' She reached for one of the sandwiches and sat down beside him. 'Now perhaps you can tell me what the matter is?'

'What do you mean?'

'Whatever it is that's causing you to give me such funny looks.' She sighed. 'It's called heliotrope, if that's what you're wondering.'

'What is?'

'The colour of my dress.'

'Ah. It wasn't.' He turned his face towards the horizon before his expression could give anything else away. 'I was just thinking that you look different, that's all.'

'Different from when?'

'From when we first met.'

'I should hope so. I looked like a drowned rat that evening.'

'Not a rat. I remember thinking you were more like a terrier.'

She stiffened as if he'd just poked her hard between the shoulder blades. 'You thought I looked like a *dog*?'

'Not looked, just behaved. And don't get me wrong... they're a grand type of dog, just a bit unruly.'

'How so?'

'Always trying to escape and get into trouble. They like to do things their own way.'

'Mmm.' She reached for another sandwich, seemingly placated. 'In that case, they sound like a very intelligent animal.'

'They are. Loyal, too.'

'Well, I'm still not sure I like the comparison, but then I thought you were a drunken wastrel that evening. And *you*, by the way, look just as unkempt now as you did then. Do you actually own a hairbrush?'

'Aye.' He made a face. 'I just don't use it very often.'

*'Try.'* She reached into her reticule and pulled out a comb. 'Here.'

'You want me to tidy myself up now?'

'No time like the present. And you *did* say you were sorry about yesterday, didn't you?'

'That's blackmail.'

'I know.' She smiled sweetly before wrenching the comb back out of his hand. 'Not like that! Honestly, there's no need to tear all of your hair out. Here.' She moved to sit behind him. 'Now, stay still and no complaining.'

'What are you...?' He stopped talking as she drew the comb gently through his curls. It was a strange, pleasantly numbing sensation, completely different from the way it felt when he occasionally did it.

'So...' She put one hand on the top of his head, turning it slowly from one side to the other. 'Have you given any more thought to Mhairi's situation?'

He almost moaned aloud. He didn't want to talk about that now. He didn't want to talk about anything. He only wanted to close his eyes and enjoy the warm glow of contentment spreading outwards through his body, from the very roots of his hair to the tips of his toes. At that moment, he felt as if he were completely in her power. She could ask him to say or do almost anything and he would agree, like some kind of sleep-deprived kitten.

'Mr Drummond?' The comb paused briefly.

'Oh…' He cleared his throat, aware that his breathing sounded heavier than usual. 'Maybe you have a point about it being her decision. As much as I want to protect her and my father, it's her life.' He opened his eyes again when she didn't make any comment. 'So?'

'So what?'

'So don't you have anything to say to that?'

'No. You already know what I think.'

'You could at least say you told me so.'

'Not when you could say the same thing to me.' She exhaled softly, the warmth of her breath skimming the back of his neck and sending a shiver down his spine. 'I've been thinking about what you said about my father and his…fiancée. Maybe you're right and I haven't been very fair either. Maybe I *have* been feeling threatened. I suppose that, ever since my mother died, I assumed that it was *my* job to look after him. It never occurred to me that somebody else might come along. Somebody he might prefer.' Another sigh. 'It's not a very edifying thought, though. I'd much rather be morally righteous.'

'In all fairness, I've never met either of them. You could be right about it being a mistake.'

'Well, I still think she's too young, but perhaps that part's none of my business. There.' She put the comb aside and placed her hands on his shoulders. 'All done.'

'How do I look?' He twisted his head, reluctant to move any more of his body in case she took her hands away. He liked the feeling of them pressed against him.

'I'm not certain.' Her eyes held a strange, hazy expression. 'I think I might prefer you messy, after all.'

He paused for a moment to let the words sink in and then let out a shout of laughter. 'Have you ever tried *not* saying exactly what you think, woman? Honesty's all very well, but—'

'I know!' She gave a shame-faced shake of her head before dropping her hands. 'I just can't seem to help it. When I was eight years old I broke a porcelain ornament, a figure of a shepherdess that used to stand on my mother's writing desk. I was running about when I shouldn't have been, but I told my mother that I didn't know what had happened.'

'But she knew ye were lying?'

'Oh, yes. She gave me a lecture about integrity and trust and then said she was giving me a second chance to tell the truth. That was the day I realised I was no good at deceit and it was much better to just be completely honest.'

'Did your mother never mention tact?'

'Sadly, not. I've sometimes wondered if she was saving that talk for when I was older.' She shrugged apologetically. 'I do *try* to be tactful, only it never seems to come out quite right.'

'Aye, well, you shouldn't try to be something you're not.'

'Thank you. That's what I believe, too. We should all be ourselves, no matter what other people might say or think about it.'

'It suits you.' He moved to sit alongside her again. 'Being yourself, I mean. And my hair will be messy again soon enough, don't worry.'

'Well, that's certainly a relief.' She picked up a piece of shortbread and took a large bite. 'Although I should probably try a little harder to be tactful. I know a lot of people find it off-putting. Men especially.' A faint wave of pink washed across her cheek bones. 'In general, I mean.'

'Maybe you're just a new kind of woman and they're not ready for you yet.'

'*You* didn't like me at first either.'

'You caught me off-guard, that's all.'

'So now you're *on* guard?'

'I prefer to think that I've caught up.'

'Why, Mr Drummond, I think that's one of the nicest things anyone's ever said to me.'

He leaned sideways, nudging her shoulder gently. 'For what it's worth, you suit heliotrope, too.'

This time, she laughed outright. 'Not too *vivid* for you?'

'Not at all, now my eyes have adjusted.'

Their gazes snared, her lips curving as she looked at him. 'Thank you for bringing me here, Mr Drummond. It's been a lovely outing.'

'It has.' He lifted a hand before he realised what he was doing, smoothing away a lock of hair that had blown across her forehead. It didn't particularly need moving, but he couldn't seem to help himself.

'Oh… Thank you.' Her eyes widened, her voice quavering slightly as he tucked the offending hair behind her ear, as if she weren't quite sure what to make of the gesture.

'I hope I haven't bored you too much.' If he hadn't known better, he might have thought his throat had gravel in it.

'Not in the slightest. I feel much better equipped to hold a conversation about whisky now.'

'Just so long as you don't have to drink any?'

'Exactly.' Her gaze slid sideways before she shivered abruptly and stood up. 'Now, we'd better be going. Mhairi will be wondering where we've got to.'

## Chapter Nine

'You'll never guess what's happened!' Mhairi threw open the door of Fiona's bed chamber while she was still slumbering. 'Oh! I'm sorry. You're usually awake so early. I just assumed...'

'It's all right.' Fiona drew an arm across her face, opening and closing her eyes a few times as she stifled a yawn. 'I must have overslept after all that fresh air yesterday.'

'I expect so.' Mhairi gave her a strange smile. 'But you'll never guess what Angus just told me!'

*That she'd combed his hair?*

Fiona pushed herself up on her elbows, the memory of *that* particular episode from their expedition bringing her back to full consciousness with a heart-stopping jolt. In retrospect, she could hardly believe that she'd done something so intimate, yet at the time it had felt completely right. Natural, even. It still did, in a confusing kind of a way, but surely he hadn't told his *sister*?

She cleared her throat, affecting a look of innocence. 'You're right, I can't. I need a cup of tea before I even begin to think straight in the morning.'

'Well...' Mhairi perched on the edge of the bed for

almost a full second before bouncing up again. 'He apologised for his behaviour over the past few months and said that I should marry Graham as soon as I wish!'

'Oh, Mhairi!' Fiona flung the quilt aside to embrace her. 'That's wonderful! I'm so pleased for you.'

'Something tells me it's partly due to your influence. What did you say to him yesterday?'

'Nothing in particular.'

*That she preferred him messy...*

'I wore him down for you, that's all. He probably just wants me to stop pestering.'

'I don't think so. He's in an uncommonly good mood this morning. He even said he wants to throw a party to celebrate our engagement.'

'How lovely.'

'Ye-es. There's just one problem. He thinks we ought to have it as soon as possible because of the weather, so it has to be next week.'

'Well, in that case, it's about time that I got up and dressed so we can start planning.' Fiona swung her legs over the side of the bed and then hesitated. 'If you want me to help with the planning, that is? I don't want to interfere if you'd rather do it all by yourself.'

'Don't be silly. I wouldn't know where to start! I'm relying on you to help me.'

'Then you're in luck.' Fiona sprang to her feet. 'Because I absolutely adore planning. More than I enjoy parties themselves, to be honest. And there's your wedding dress to think about too...'

'We'll discuss it all over breakfast. In the meantime, I'll leave you to get dressed.'

'Do you know...?' Fiona stretched her arms above her head. 'I'm feeling in a very good mood this morning myself.'

'Yes, I had a feeling you might be.' Mhairi gave her a sly smile as she made her way to the door. 'What an *amazing* coincidence.'

'Are you certain that's everyone?' Fiona peered over Mhairi's shoulder at the guest list, counting the number of names, before pacing to the far side of the parlour and then back again. She was feeling curiously restless that morning. There had been no sign of Mr Drummond at breakfast or afterwards, while she and Mhairi had been discussing party arrangements, and the result was that she'd been unable to sit still for a single moment. It was both vexing and extremely frustrating.

'I think so.' Mhairi tapped her fountain pen thoughtfully against her teeth. 'It's pretty much all the same people that will be coming to the wedding, although Graham will probably want to add a few names. I must send him a note. I'm sure he won't have any objections to a party, but I ought to consult him first.'

'All right. We'll put off sending the invitations for now, but we need to start thinking about decorations and food as soon as possible. And dancing. We'll need music. Maybe a small orchestra?'

'Or maybe just a couple of fiddlers alongside the piano!' Mhairi laughed. 'Otherwise we'll never fit everyone into the house.'

'Oh, don't worry about that. It's amazing what you can do with a little organisation. I'm always rearranging the furniture at home.'

'It doesn't need to be grand.'

'On the contrary.' Angus's voice came from the open doorway. 'I want only the best for my wee sister.'

'Angus!' Mhairi shot out of her seat to embrace him. 'Thank you again for this.'

'Dinna fash.' He looked faintly embarrassed, meeting Fiona's gaze over his sister's shoulder. 'Good morning, Miss MacKay.'

'Good morning, Mr Drummond.' She felt her pulse quicken at the sight of him. He was looking scruffier than ever and yet, paradoxically, even more handsome. If she hadn't known better she might have thought that her stomach had just flipped over. 'And you're absolutely right. We'll make this a party to remember.'

'Aye, although I've brought someone who might have a few opinions of his own.'

'Graham!' Mhairi practically flew from her brother into her fiancé's arms. 'What are you doing here?'

'It occurred to me that you weren't the only one I owed an apology to,' Angus explained for him. 'So I rode over to do it in person. Then we thought we'd come back and tell you the good news together.'

'So the two of you...?'

'Have come to an understanding.' Angus nodded firmly. 'We're going to be brothers, after all.'

'Oh.' Mhairi wiped a tear from her eye. 'I don't know what to say. Thank you.'

'Well...' Fiona cleared her throat, starting to feel somewhat sentimental herself. 'I'm sure that the two of you would like a little time in private. Perhaps I'll take a brief stroll in the garden.'

'And I'll come with you, if you don't mind?' Angus gestured towards the patio doors. 'These two have a wedding date to decide on.'

'That was a very kind thing you just did.' Fiona threw Angus a sideways look as they stepped out into the garden and onto a gravelled path.

'Better late than never.'

'That, too, but still kind. I don't think I've ever seen Mhairi so happy.'

'Good.'

'However…' She lifted her chin, acutely aware that they were alone together again. 'I believe there's a little matter we need to discuss, as well.'

'I've been thinking the same thing, but ladies first.'

'Thank you. It's about the party. I know I said that I'd only be staying here for ten days, but I offered to help, and it looks like there might not be time—'

'You can stay for as long as you want,' he interrupted her. 'That's what Mhairi told you and I agree.'

'Really?' She lifted her eyebrows doubtfully. 'Because I'd hate to impose where I'm not wanted.'

'Ah, but that's where you're mistaken. You *are* wanted. Mhairi certainly wants you here, and as for me…' He flashed her a smile. 'Who else is going to tell me when I'm being a pig-headed fool?'

She couldn't repress a small burble of laughter. 'Perhaps in the future I could add a postscript to my letters to Mhairi? *PS Tell your brother not to be such a pig-headed fool.*'

'Aye.' He came to a halt between two fir trees, clasping his hands behind his back as he turned to face her. 'Or perhaps you might consider writing to me directly.'

'Oh…' She was aware of that strange stomach-flipping sensation again. 'I suppose I *could*, but if I did, I'd expect a reply.'

'I could probably manage a few lines. Although, I should warn you, my writing's as untidy as the rest of me.'

'I'm sure I'd be able to decipher it eventually.' She swallowed and then nodded. 'I'd be happy to correspond with you. Now, what was it you wished to discuss with me?'

'It was about what you called me before.'

'I don't recall...'

'Mr Drummond. My name's Angus.' He glanced at the horizon and then back again, his gaze intensifying. 'I wondered if we might move past the formalities? Especially if we're going to be correspondents.'

'Oh.' For the first time in as long as she could remember, she was genuinely speechless for a few seconds. 'Yes, of course... I think that sounds like an excellent idea, Angus.' She extended an arm. 'I'm Fiona.'

'I know.' He took hold of her hand, although instead of shaking it he simply folded his fingers around hers, raising them gently to his chest. 'Fiona...'

'Yes?' She found herself swaying forward as he moved his head closer towards hers. Or perhaps he was tugging her... She wasn't entirely sure. All she knew was that she was moving willingly, drawing closer and closer, her heart beating so fast she had the vague impression it was trying to pound its way out of her chest...

*'Fiona! Angus!'*

'Oh!' She started and jumped backwards, tearing her hand away as Mhairi came running down the path towards them. 'You gave me a scare. Where's Graham?'

'He had patients to visit. He said to tell you goodbye. But look!' Mhairi thrust out her hand, revealing a gold band topped with a single square-cut emerald. 'I had to come and show you straight away. He gave me this!'

'It's beautiful.' Fiona bent her head, glad of the excuse to hide her flushed cheeks as she examined the ring in more detail.

'Angus?' Thankfully, Mhairi seemed completely

oblivious to the nature of the scene she'd just inter-rupted. 'What do you think?'

'It's bonny, but if you're going to start talking about jewellery then I ought to be getting to work.' He cleared his throat and stepped backwards, his gaze lingering on Fiona's face in a way that made her heart start to ham-mer all over again. 'I'll see you both tonight.'

Two hours of invitation-writing later, Mhairi went for a lie down, leaving Fiona free to wander back through the garden, retracing the steps she'd taken with Angus earlier. She was glad to be alone, to have time to think about what had happened between them. For a moment—no, several moments—she'd had the impres-sion that he'd wanted to kiss her. Which was a pre-posterous notion. Delusional, probably. Though no less preposterous than the idea that she'd wanted to kiss him, too. Just like the day before on the distillery roof when he'd tucked her hair back inside her bonnet, his gaze profound yet unfathomable...

She shook her head as a flicker of excitement coiled in her stomach. She was being ridiculous, letting her imagination run away with her. Men didn't think of her in that way. She'd had ample evidence of that fact over the years. Oh, they might admire her looks from a dis-tance, but once they got to know her—once she opened her mouth, in other words—admiration turned swiftly to disapproval, occasionally even horror.

She'd overheard the comments. She was too indepen-dent, too opinionated, too overbearing. Mr Drummond himself—Angus—had made all of those points abun-dantly clear. Recently, his attitude towards her seemed to have changed, but he was probably just making amends for what had happened in Pennan. *She* certainly hadn't changed. She might have admitted to possibly misjudging her father's fiancée, but in all the essentials she was exactly the same as she'd ever been. And she was perfectly happy with those essentials. Only something about Angus Drummond made her wish that he was the kind of man who might like them, too.

*I prefer to think that I've caught up.*

The words floated back into her mind as she reached the gate at the bottom of the garden. *Could* he have meant them? *Could* he really like her? And…if he did… how much did she like him?

She glanced back at the tower and then turned away again quickly, reproaching herself for her silliness. For goodness' sake, she'd only met him four days ago, and she'd absolutely no wish to make any more of a fool of herself than she probably had done already. As for her own feelings, it was a waste of time and energy even to consider them! What she needed right now was a walk to clear her head and bring her back to her senses.

And fortunately she knew exactly where she wanted to go. The ruin that they'd glimpsed from the cart on their way to Pennan wasn't so far, a mile at the most, and the terrain wasn't unduly challenging, especially as she was wearing sensible boots for once. And the weather looked reasonable at that moment. The day wasn't bright, but it was dry, and the bank of grey clouds in the distance was a long way off. If she followed the main track that led to the beach and then cut across the cliff tops, she could probably be there and back before Mhairi had even woken from her nap.

She opened the gate and stepped out onto the drive, full of newly found resolve. A brisk walk was just what she needed and exactly what she was going to get.

## Chapter Ten

'Angus!'

The sound of Mhairi's panicked voice echoed across the courtyard.

'What's the matter?' He dismounted quickly, catching hold of her shoulders before she barrelled into him.

'It's Fiona!' His sister's expression was nearly wild. 'She went out for a walk an hour ago and she hasn't come back.'

'What?' He felt a sudden constricting sensation in his chest, looking out over the fields as if she might still be visible. 'Why didn't you stop her?'

'I was taking a nap. One of the maids saw her leave, and thought it was odd so she came to wake me, but by the time I rushed out there was no sign of her.' Mhairi lifted her eyes nervously. 'You know what's coming?'

'Aye.' He followed her gaze to the sky. It was going to snow, and not just a little bit. He'd noticed the gathering clouds on the horizon at midday and had hurried home as speedily as possible. Ironically, he'd actually been pleased, the idea of a cosy afternoon and evening in the company of his sister and Miss MacKay striking him as quite appealing at the time.

'Was anything wrong? Did she seem upset?' He tried to focus on the present again.

'No. She seemed perfectly happy when we were writing invitations. A little distracted, but that's all. I thought that maybe she went down to the beach for a walk, so I sent Daniel and a few of the other men to look, but they came back ten minutes ago.' Mhairi put her hands to her cheeks. 'What if she's had an accident? She could be lying in a hole injured somewhere!'

'I'm sure it's nothing so serious. There's probably a perfectly good explanation for why she's not back yet.' Angus squeezed her shoulders reassuringly, although for the life of him he couldn't think what that explanation might be. All he knew was that he couldn't sit around waiting to find out.

'I'm going to look for her. I'll need a couple of thick blankets and some food.'

'No, Angus, you can't. It's too dangerous. Once the snow starts...'

'I know, but at least I'm used to the conditions. Whereas if Fiona's out there, alone, maybe lost...' His heart clenched at the thought. 'She doesn't stand a chance. I have to go.'

'All right.' Mhairi gripped hold of his sleeves and then nodded. 'I'll get everything ready.'

'Hurry.' He looked back at the horizon and clenched his jaw. He didn't know where she was, but he wasn't going to come home without her.

The ruin, Fiona quickly discovered, was actually less of a ruin than it had appeared from a distance. It wasn't exactly habitable, but the stairs were still sturdy enough for her to climb up—even if the ledge at the top struck her as a little dubious—and there were more rooms to explore than she'd anticipated. The very stone-work seemed to grow out of the cliff-face, with open windows overlooking a sheer drop down to the sea. It was all so fascinating that she lost track of time, ducking under archways, peering into crevices and imagining the former inhabitants, including one particularly handsome knight bearing a striking resemblance to a certain Mr Angus Drummond.

It was some time before she remembered that she was only supposed to be taking a short stroll and that Mhairi was probably awake and wondering where she was. It was past time to be getting back, but at least she was in a better frame of mind now. She still wasn't entirely certain whether or not she'd imagined the scene with Angus, but she wasn't going to dwell on it any longer either. If he really wanted to kiss her then presumably he would find another opportunity to do so before she left. And if he didn't then she obviously *had* been imagining things.

As for whether or not she wanted to kiss him… Well, that was something she'd think about if and when the situation arose. Which it wouldn't. Probably.

She'd just emerged back into the open when she became aware of snowflakes swirling in the air around her. Only a few at first, but turning rapidly into an impenetrable, shifting veil that obscured her vision and left her feeling alarmingly disorientated. Quickly, she turned in the direction of the farm, but the fields in between were already invisible, covered in a thick, fluffy white blanket. The sight might have been beautiful if it hadn't also been so frightening.

A gust of icy cold air hit her full in the face, stinging her cheeks and nose and chilling her all the way to her core. It was impossible to deny the harsh reality of her situation. She was in trouble. Yes, she'd come out on her own with no food or supplies, and without telling anyone where she was going, but from this point on she needed to be sensible and think practically. Walking back across the fields wasn't an option, which meant that the next best thing she could do was take shelter in the warmest spot she could find and wait until the storm had passed.

In the meantime, she ought to leave some kind of marker to show people where she was. Unlikely as it seemed that anyone would be out searching for her in such weather, it was still worth a try...

She reached down and tore a strip off the hem of her dress—fortunately one of her brightest, a brilliant aquamarine that would hopefully be visible from the road—then pushed her way through the snow to the nearest tree and tied the material around one of the branches as a makeshift flag. Having done that, she hurried back into the centre of the ruin and crouched down in a corner, acutely aware now of the wind howling around the rafters. Crumbling stone walls weren't exactly the safest place to shelter behind, but they were still a hundred times better than staying outside.

Teeth chattering, she curled her legs up to her chest and rubbed her hands vigorously over them, trying to build up some heat, relieved that she'd put on Mhairi's warm cape instead of her own light jacket. At least she'd done one thing right, even if the snow falling through the large gap in the ceiling was becoming thicker and faster every second...

She felt her head start to nod and jerked herself upright. It was important to stay awake, she knew, although she was starting to feel unusually dizzy and light-headed, as if she'd drunk too much of the whisky

Angus had given her two nights ago… And her eyelids felt *so* heavy, as if there were weights attached to her lashes, dragging them down…

Maybe if she closed them just for a little while…?

'Fiona?'

A voice called her name, but it seemed to come from a long way away.

'Fiona?'

It sounded familiar, too…

'Can you hear me?'

'Oh!' She yelped as a pair of strong hands grasped hold of her shoulders, shaking her back to wakefulness. 'What…?' She blinked rapidly as a pair of piercing blue eyes gradually came into focus, looking down at her with a concerned expression. 'Angus?'

'Aye.' Concern turned to relief. 'Are ye all right?'

'How did you…?' she started to ask and then decided it didn't matter, launching herself forward instead. 'You found me!'

'So I did.' He rocked backwards as she clamped her arms around his neck. 'You gave me quite a scare, mind.'

'Are you sure you're real and not a figment of my imagination?' She clung tighter. '*Please* tell me you're not a dream!'

'I'm definitely not that. It's why I still need to breathe.' He coughed as he gently disentangled her arms from around his neck, although he squeezed her hands before letting them go. 'Now I need to know if you're feeling numb anywhere.'

'I don't think so.' She flexed her fingers and toes cautiously. 'No, everything seems in working order.'

'Are you certain?' He gave her a hard look. 'This isn't the time to start withholding the truth.'

'As if I could.' She looked around. 'Are you here on your own?'

'I'm afraid so. There were a few other groups out looking for ye earlier, but they'll be back at the farm by now.'

'Oh, dear, I didn't mean to cause any trouble. I just came out for a walk and lost track of time.' She shook her head apologetically. 'Thank you for coming to find me. I was afraid that I'd lose my way if I tried to make my way back on my own.'

'You were right not to move. We cannae go anywhere now until the snow stops. I'll need to build a fire.' He glanced up at the hole in the ceiling. 'Fortunately, we seem to have a reasonable-sized chimney.'

'But the snow's coming in there, too.'

'Not too badly. The wind's blowing from the north, so the walls are giving us some protection.' He laid the sack he'd brought down on the ground and reached inside, pulling out a small collection of dried logs and twigs as well as a tinder box. 'We'll be sheltered enough for a while.'

'Can I do anything to help?'

He gave her a quick, appraising look before nodding. 'You can fetch some stones to make a fire ring. It'll be good for your muscles to move around a bit.'

'Of course.' She pushed herself up and started searching the ruins, gathering several large stones in her arms and positioning them in a circle around the logs. 'How's that?'

'Perfect.' He struck a light over the pile, feeding twigs in slowly as the flame burst into life. 'There we go.'

'That was very efficient.' Fiona watched in admiration.

'It's an important skill in this part of the world. Some men can waltz, others can light fires.' He gave her a quick grin. 'Although, if we get desperate, we can always dance to keep warm, I suppose.'

'Right now, I'll take the fire.'

'Me, too.' He gave a nod of satisfaction and then spread a blanket out on the ground. 'Here, take a seat.'

'Thank you.'

'Feeling better?'

'Much.' She tucked her legs up beneath her. 'Although I was honestly doing my best to stay awake before.'

'I know. It's not easy when the cold grips you. We should be all right now with the fire, but...'

'What?' She knitted her brows as he hesitated.

'We ought to share our body heat, too. If you have no objections, that is?'

'Oh.' She swallowed against a suddenly desert-dry throat. 'I think we can put etiquette aside when it's a question of survival.'

'Aye.' He sat down beside her, leaning back against the wall and draping one arm loosely around her shoulders. 'Is this all right?'

'Mmm-hmm.' She made a sound that hopefully passed for assent, feeling a tremor run through her at the contact. Unruly reactions aside, however, his arm felt reassuringly solid.

'We'll just need this.' He pulled another blanket up over their legs. 'There. Nice and cosy.'

This time, she didn't even try and answer. Being tucked up under a blanket together was a little—*a lot*—like being in bed. Not to mention confusing. Somehow their situation struck her as both necessary and inappropriate in equal measure, although she felt completely safe, too. She was aware now of just how badly she'd misjudged him when they'd first met. He wasn't a brute. He might be stubborn and scruffy, but he was also brave, honourable and, at that moment, wonderfully warm, so much so that she couldn't resist the temptation to lay her head on his shoulder.

'I can't believe you came to find me on your own.' She snuggled closer, rubbing her cheek against his collar.

'I couldn't leave you out in the cold.'

'It was still a big risk.'

'No more than walking off on your own without telling anyone where you were heading.'

'I know. I really thought I'd just come and take a quick peek and be back before anyone noticed I'd gone.' She felt a pang of guilt. 'I should have paid more attention to the clouds.'

'I should have warned you that the weather can come in quickly.'

'So you're not angry?'

'No.' His voice sounded strangely tender. 'I'm just relieved that I found you.'

'So am I, but how *did* you guess I was here?'

'I remembered how interested you were in the ruins when we drove over the cliff top. Then I caught sight of your flag.' He gestured at the torn hem of her gown. 'Maybe your clothes aren't quite so impractical after all.'

'Angus...' She tilted her face up to look at him. There were tiny lines at the corners of his eyes, she noticed, ones she wanted to touch... 'You've probably saved my life. I don't know how I'll ever repay you.'

'You don't have to.'

'Is Mhairi very worried?'

'As much as you'd expect, but we'll deal with that to-morrow.' His arm tightened around her. 'Which is also when I'll be finding myself some new dogs.'

'Why? What's wrong with Rory and Hamish?'

'You mean aside from the fact they'd rather doze by the fire than do anything useful like tracking?'

'I don't suppose they could have tracked me through the snow anyway.'

'They could have tried. No doubt they're saving their energy to give you a good licking when you get back.'

She laughed and yawned at the same time. 'In that case, maybe you ought to get yourself a terrier. I recently learned they're an excellent breed.'

'You might be right.' He chuckled and stretched his legs out. 'Now, are ye hungry? I've brought some supplies.'

'No. Mhairi and I had luncheon just before I left.' She put a hand to her mouth, attempting to stifle another yawn. 'Although that seems a very long time ago now.'

'Aye.' He tugged her closer, his hand smoothing gently over her arm as she settled back against him, tucking her head into the curve of his neck, aware of a deep sense of gratitude and, curiously enough, contentment. Not perfect contentment, obviously, given the danger they were still in, but a kind of calm that warmed her insides despite the weather. Whatever it was, she doubted she would feel the same resting against just *any* shoulder. It was *his* particular shoulder that caused the feeling, as if she would rather be stuck in the snow with him than with anyone else in the world. Which, given the fact that she'd only known him for four days, seemed either a symptom of madness or incipient frostbite.

'Try and stay awake until the fire gets going,' Angus murmured. 'Tell me more about my faults if you like.

What was it you called me the other day, overbearing and controlling? You must have more adjectives than that.'

'I'm *not* such a harridan!'

'I know, but you're so easy to goad.'

'Oh.' She pursed her lips and then smiled. 'Yes, I suppose I am. Although, if you must know, I can't think of any more faults.'

'None at all?' He sounded surprised.

'No.'

'Well, I'll drink to that.' He reached into his pocket and drew out a small flask. 'Care for a wee dram?'

'All right, since these are strange circumstances.' She reached for the bottle and took a sip, managing not to cough this time. 'Actually, that tastes better than before. Maybe it's the cold speaking, but I may have to revise my opinion about whisky.'

'I'm glad to hear it. Now, since I lit the fire...' He took a mouthful himself before screwing the lid back on. '*You* can tell me a story to keep us awake...'

The important thing, Angus reminded himself, was not to take advantage of the situation. Their position was fraught with enough tension and peril as it was. The sky above the ruined castle was darkening, and the temperature felt as if it were plummeting with every passing second, but so long as the fire didn't go out they should make it to the next morning unscathed. Fortunately, he'd brought enough logs to get them through the night, so it was just a matter of staying awake and tending to the flames.

A bigger concern was that the depth of the snow might make it impossible for them to climb out in the morning, but even then he could probably scale the rock-

face below and make his way along the beach and cliffs
to Pennan. It wouldn't be easy, but if he left at low tide
then he should be able to escape and fetch help.

He sighed and tipped his head back against the wall.
He was thinking ten steps ahead when he ought to be
concentrating on getting through the night—and thinking about that led him back to his original point. It
was important—*vital*—not to take advantage of the
situation, even if the feeling of the woman lying in his
arms at that moment was driving his entire being to
distraction.

Fiona had fallen asleep halfway through telling him
about her latest musical soiree in Edinburgh, her head
tucked against his shoulder with one arm wrapped
around his chest. One of her legs had draped itself
across one of his, too. He doubted that she was aware
of having put it there, but its presence was doing strange
things to his body temperature despite the Baltic conditions. At least staying awake under such feverish circumstances wasn't a problem, but it was also becoming
downright uncomfortable, making his blood race and
his whole body ache with longing.

He wasn't sure when exactly she'd become so desirable. Oh, he'd noticed her attractiveness that first day
in the parlour, but only in an objective physical sense.
Now he was aware of the whole woman—every inch
of the whole woman, in fact, and she was the most gorgeous, desirable creature he'd ever set eyes on, let alone
held in his arms, all soft, warm and curled up like some
sleek and golden cat. So long as she stayed asleep, he
wouldn't do anything foolish, but if she were to wake
up, look at him with those big, grey eyes and tell him
again how grateful she was...

No! He dragged his gaze away from the soft curve

of her cheek, horribly aware of the unsteadiness of his own breathing. He'd set out to find her and, now that he had, he was duty-bound to protect her, even from himself, no matter how desirable she might be. Afterwards, when they were safely back at Windy Heads Tower… Well, maybe then he might see if she wished to be more than a correspondent.

His pulse accelerated at the thought. Would she? Marriage wasn't something he'd ever seriously considered before, but then he'd never met or even imagined any woman like Fiona. And why shouldn't he consider it? They were of a similar age and the farm was doing well enough. He was a gentleman and she was a gentleman's daughter. She might not want to live so far away from Edinburgh, but he wouldn't find out unless he tried wooing her…

He bent his head, letting the scent of violets fill his nostrils. First he'd get her to safety, and then… Well, then they could talk.

## Chapter Eleven

The first rosy glimmers of dawn were just peeking over the horizon when Angus lightly touched his fingertips against Fiona's cheek, watching as she opened her eyelids, her gaze sleepy and unfocused for a few seconds before it met his and widened abruptly. If he'd let off a firework, she could hardly have sat up any faster.

'Don't worry.' He put a hand on her shoulder to steady her. 'Nothing's wrong.'

'Nothing's wrong?' Her face wore a look of horror. 'It's getting light! Mr Drummond—*Angus*—we were supposed to help each other stay awake!'

'You seemed like you needed your rest.'

'That's not the point! If we were going to sleep then we should have taken turns. Have *you* had any rest?'

'There'll be time for that later. Right now, we need to get moving. The snow's stopped, but I don't know for how long. If we're going to get back to the house, then we need to leave now.'

'Very well, but this isn't the end of it. I'll scold you again later.' She scrambled to her feet and looked around. 'Have you packed everything already?'

'Aye, all except for this.' He handed her some oatcakes. 'It's going to be hard work trekking through the snow, and you need something in your stomach.'

'Just so long as you've eaten, too.' She took a bite and narrowed her gaze. 'I don't want you exhausted *and* hungry all because of me.'

'I've had a couple, I promise.' He stuffed the blankets into the sack and started towards one of the archways, laughing under his breath. Obviously the night hadn't done her much harm if she was still able to argue.

'It didn't take me too long to get here, I think.' She came to stand beside him, looking out over the white fields. 'Maybe fifteen minutes?'

'It'll take at least three times as long to get back.' He grimaced. By his estimation, the snow was at least two feet deep. 'Believe it or not, this isn't so bad, but it still won't be easy, and once we start we can't stop.'

'Is there any alternative?'

'Short of waiting for someone to come and find us? They're probably getting ready to come out searching again.'

'Putting their lives at risk because of my foolishness, you mean?' She straightened her shoulders. 'No, you're right, we have to go now.'

'Are you certain?'

'No, but I got myself into this mess so it's my responsibility to get myself out of it. With a little help, obviously.'

'We'll help each other.' He held a hand out and she took it. 'All right, then. Let's go.'

Fiona rubbed the back of her glove across her brow. It seemed incongruous to feel so hot in such freezing conditions, but as it turned out Angus was right. Trudging through thigh-deep snow was *extremely* hard work. So much so that she found herself dripping with sweat and panting by the time they'd made their way back to the main road. If it hadn't been for the scrap of her dress still hanging from the tree, she wouldn't have recognised the spot, but fortunately her companion seemed to know exactly which direction to walk in, carrying a long stick in one hand to prod at the earth while clasping hers in the other.

They didn't talk, conserving their energy and never stopping for more than a few seconds to catch their breaths. Most of the time she kept her eyes on the ground, unwilling to see how far they still had to go, concentrating instead on putting one foot in front of the other. Even if it hadn't been a question of survival, she was determined not to let Angus down after he'd spent a sleepless night looking after her.

'Almost there!'

Neither of them had spoken for so long that the sound of his voice made her start. Quickly, she looked up, her heart jumping with relief at the sight of Windy Heads Tower rising up ahead of them, its pale stone almost camouflaged in the snow.

'Just another ten minutes and we can set Mhairi's mind at rest.' Angus squeezed her hand as if he were trying to transfer some of his strength into her.

'Thank goodness. How do you make this look so easy?'

'I'm used to it. There's a knack to walking in snow, but you're doing well. I'm impressed.'

'Now I *know* you're just trying to cajole me.'

'I wouldn't dare.' He grinned. 'I really am impressed. You're a lot tougher than you look.'

'I'm perfectly aware of *that*.' She gave him a pointed look and then surged forward again. 'Come on, let's get this over with.'

'Angus! Fiona!' Mhairi came hurtling out of the front door as they approached the house. 'I've never been so pleased to see two people in my whole life! Where have you been?'

'In the old castle ruins.' Angus tightened his grip on Fiona's fingers as she attempted to pull hers away. 'We were able to shelter from the worst of the weather.'

'And you've walked all the way back through the snow this morning?' Mhairi gave them both an amazed look. 'Well, hurry on in and I'll send for Graham.'

'There's no need for a doctor.' Fiona stepped over the threshold with relief. 'Thanks to your brother, we're both perfectly fine.'

'I'd still like Graham to make sure, if he can get through. I'll send someone to see how bad the road from the village is, but first things first—a hot bath. After that, you need to go straight to bed and rest.'

'There's no point in trying to argue.' Angus tipped his head towards hers as Mhairi hustled them into the parlour and then hurried away to make the arrangements. 'Not when she gets bossy like this.'

'Actually, a bath sounds wonderful.' Fiona caught her breath at his close proximity. What had been mere stubble the evening before was now a short growth of beard. It was a slightly redder shade from the rest of his hair, giving him the look of a Viking—a Viking whose fingers were still tightly entwined in hers.

'Anyway...' She felt the hairs on her arm rise with tension. 'I don't know how to thank you.'

'I already told you, you don't have to.' There was a

guttural note to his voice, making her knees feel un-steady all of a sudden. Considering how far they'd just walked and in what conditions, the sensation was un-derstandable, although something told her it had noth-ing to do with the snow. 'Just don't scare me like that again, do ye promise?'

'I promise.' She drew her hands away, still wonder-ing what was going on with her legs. 'I suppose I can finally take this cape off now. If I can unfasten it, that is...'

'Here, let me.' He pulled his gloves off and took over, gently unfastening the clasp at her throat and peeling the fabric away. 'Your fingers are probably still too cold.'

'Yours should be, too.'

'Aye, but mine are as tough as cow's hide these days.'

'Thank you.' She removed her bonnet by herself. 'That's much better.'

'Now it's probably time for that bath.'

'Yes, and then...' She stopped mid-sentence, realis-ing where the sentence was leading her. She was aware that she ought to move away, but her legs were still be-having oddly, refusing to budge. She had a sense of being trapped in the depths of his penetrating blue gaze. A blue that looked darker than usual, almost black... What had she just been saying?

'Bed?' He quirked an eyebrow.

'Yes.' She cleared her throat, attempting to exert some control over her wayward thoughts. 'Which in your case is absolutely right. You've had no sleep at all.'

'I can manage without.'

'You will not. You're going straight to bed even if I have to carry you there myself.'

'I'm all yours.'

'I didn't mean... You know what I meant.'

'Aye, I do, but your way sounds much more interesting.' A slow smile spread across his face as he lifted a hand and trailed his fingers slowly across her cheek. It was the softest of caresses, barely a touch really, and yet the gesture struck her as far more intimate than anything she'd ever experienced before. It made her aware of something, too, a feeling that seemed to have been hovering at the back of her consciousness for a while and now burst forth, filling her whole being with a warm, fuzzy glow.

But it was absurd. It was simply a reaction to their dramatic ordeal, surely? She couldn't possibly be in love with him. Even if, at that moment, she was quite certain that she was.

'Your baths are ready!' Mhairi bustled into the room at that moment, carrying a tray bearing two steaming mugs. 'Now, drink this and let's get you both warmed up and to bed.'

## Chapter Twelve

Fiona sat in front of her dressing table, gazing thought-fully at her reflection as she added a few finishing touches to her evening wear. A cameo brooch at the throat, a pair of diamond teardrop earrings, two small butterfly pins in her hair and, there, she was ready.

The pale pink and cream chiffon gown she'd packed as an afterthought was somewhat muted for her tastes, but for once she wanted to blend into the background. Tonight was all about Mhairi. *She* was only there as a guest, future bridesmaid and organiser *par excellence*.

And she'd made quite a good job of the arrange-ments, too, though she said so herself. Perhaps her fa-ther would allow her to help organise his wedding when she returned to Edinburgh in a few days. That was if his marriage was still on and she hadn't caused too much of a shock with her dramatic departure. Now that she thought of it, it was strange that she hadn't received any correspondence from him since she'd arrived. Even if he was angry at her, which was a distinct possibil-ity, she would at least have expected a letter enquiring after her health. Hypocritical as it was, she felt hurt by its absence.

There was a light tap on the door and she opened it straightaway, expecting some last-minute question about the furniture arrangements, only to find a man she'd never seen before with smooth auburn hair, a clean-shaven jaw and dancing blue eyes dressed in a single-breasted black suit over a pristine white shirt and bow-tie.

'Angus?' She felt so stunned that it was an effort to get his name out. 'You look…'

'If you say "like a gentleman" then I'll take this thing off right now.' He hooked a finger beneath the tie and gave it a tug. 'I feel ridiculous.'

'Well, you shouldn't. I was going to say very dashing. I'm sure Mhairi will appreciate the effort, too.'

He put one hand on the door frame and leaned closer, his lips curving in a way that made her heart stutter and then start racing. 'I'm not wearing it for Mhairi.'

'Oh.' She opened her mouth, trying to think of something witty to say, but her thoughts seemed to have scattered. Thankfully, Angus appeared not to notice, his gaze dipping to her bodice instead.

'This is a surprise. I thought you'd be wearing scarlet tonight at least.'

'I thought I'd be subtle for once.'

'You look dazzling, but then you always do.'

'Oh…' Fiona coughed, wondering if she was falling ill. She'd never been so lost for words in her life. 'Thank you. How's the weather? Can the guests get through?'

'Dinna fash about that. It's still mild. Most of the snow has melted and there's no sign of any more yet.' He extended an arm. 'Now, are you ready to make an appearance?'

'I think so.' She turned her lamp down and then

wrapped her fingers around his bicep, forcing herself not to squeeze as she felt the muscles flex beneath.

It felt completely different, she realised, walking beside him now, from the way it had when she'd first arrived. Their night in the snow the previous week had changed something between them. With all the party organising, there hadn't been many opportunities to speak together in private afterwards, especially since Mhairi seemed determined to keep an eye on her, presumably to stop her from wandering off again. But she felt acutely conscious of him every time they were in a room together. She had the sneaking impression that he felt the same way, too, their eyes meeting almost every time one or other of them looked up.

'Fiona, I can hear hooves!' Mhairi came rushing out of the parlour as they came down the staircase, looking both very pretty and very panicked. 'Some guests are arriving!'

'Good. That's what they're supposed to do.' Fiona smiled, looking around at the decorations. As it was almost December, they'd decided to be festive. All of the doorways were framed with boughs of holly and the banister was draped with a long garland of ivy and mistletoe. There were bowls filled with pine cones and dried fruits, red ribbons and bows in as many places as she'd been able to tie them, as well as sparkling baubles hanging from the parlour mantelpiece. The only thing they *didn't* have was a Christmas tree, but there had only been so much space to surrender. Nonetheless, the combination of colours and scents was lovely. The whole tower looked like a winter wonderland. 'Has Dr Tomlinson arrived yet?'

'Not yet. Oh, dear, I feel as if I'm going to be sick.'

'It's just excitement. In an hour's time you'll wonder what you were worried about.'

'I hope you're right. I'm not used to people looking at me. I don't know how to behave.'

'Then I'll tell you.' Angus put a hand under his sister's elbow. 'You're going to lift your chin up, stand by the door like the beautiful lass you are and remember that this is supposed to be fun. Because if it's not then I'll happily tell everyone to go home again.'

'Don't you dare.' Mhairi giggled. 'But will you come and stand beside me until Graham arrives? Father's sitting by the fire and I don't want to tire him.'

'I'd be honoured.'

'In that case, *I'll* go and sit with your father,' Fiona commented, feeling strangely breathless again. 'I think it's about time we opened some champagne.'

Unlike the majority of hostesses, Fiona did *not* consider a squeeze to be the defining sign of a party's success. Personally, she found little to enjoy in being crushed amid a throng of overheated bodies, but she had to admit this particular crush was a resounding triumph. Maybe it was the recent thaw that had made everyone determined to get out and enjoy themselves before winter truly set in, because enjoying themselves was definitely what they were doing. All of the downstairs reception rooms, as well as the recently emptied dining room and hallway, were filled with happy chatter, laughter and background music of piano and violins.

'This is more people than the place has seen in years.' Angus appeared at her shoulder as she stood watching the dancing in the former dining room. 'You've done a grand job.'

'Thank you. So have you.'

'I didn't do much.'

'You helped. You moved all that furniture for me.' She felt a flush spread up her throat at the words, remembering how muscular he'd looked lifting tables and chairs with his shirt sleeves rolled up. She'd supervised a little bit more than was strictly necessary. 'And you looked after Mhairi until Graham arrived. No big brother could have done better.' She lowered her voice to a whisper. 'Not to mention the fact that you're wearing a bow-tie.'

'Not for much longer if I can help it.' He rubbed a hand around the back of his neck. 'But, before I burn the thing, I came to ask if you'd care to dance with me.'

'I'd be delighted, but it's ceilidh music. I don't know any of the steps.'

'They're not hard. I'll teach you.'

'Are you sure you won't mind your toes being crushed?'

'They're big toes. They can take it.' He lifted an eyebrow. 'Will you?'

'I will.' She smiled nervously. 'What do I do?'

'First of all, we stand side by side and you put your hands like this.' He put one of his own behind her back and reached the other across her body. 'Then we walk forward four steps, then twist about and go back four steps, then you turn under my arm and we spin into a polka. Easy at that.'

'I understood the word polka…'

She looked at him dubiously as he led her out on to the floor, although it wasn't long before she started to relax, twisting and twirling around the room so quickly that she couldn't hold back a whoop of delight.

This was *much* more fun than the staid, regimented dancing at the parties she attended in Edinburgh. As

the music sped up and the dance descended into apparently intentional chaos, the whole world seemed to spin around her. Only Angus remained as the one constant, appearing in and out of her vision every few seconds, wearing a smile so broad it looked in danger of splitting his face in half.

The sight was so unexpected and endearing that she started to laugh. Just a giggle at first, though it wasn't long before she was breathless and panting, half afraid that, if the music didn't stop soon, she was going to collapse into a giddy heap on the floor. And then it *did* stop, yet she was still swaying in Angus's arms, his hands holding her steady while his face remained just a few inches from her own, causing a shiver of excitement that dried up her giggles abruptly.

'You're a quick learner.'

'That was fun.' She took a deep breath, trying to restore some sense of equilibrium, though it was almost impossible when her pulse was racing so fast. 'I think Edinburgh balls will feel a little underwhelming from now on.'

'Maybe you shouldn't go back, then.' His voice sounded rough. Combined with the words themselves, they made her heart give a little jump, making it even harder to breathe.

'It's home.'

'Aye, but have you never thought of living somewhere else? If you had a reason, I mean?'

'I don't know. I've never thought about it. Maybe... if it was a good reason.'

'What if I—?'

Unfortunately, she didn't hear the rest of his words as they were drowned out by raised voices coming from the direction of the parlour. By the sound of it, some-

body was making a toast, calling everyone to find a glass and join in.

'Shouldn't we join them?' She looked around uncertainly as the rest of the dancers traipsed past, leaving them alone in the dining room.

'Probably.' He shrugged and moved a step closer towards her, the look in his eyes intensifying as his legs brushed against her skirts. 'Unless…?'

'Unless?'

'Unless…this.' Slowly, he lifted a hand, sliding it round the back of her neck and lowering his face towards hers.

'Oh…' She closed her eyes as his lips caught hers, softly at first, then with a building pressure as he coaxed her mouth apart and dipped his tongue inside. For a moment, she stood immobile, uncertain about what to do with the rest of her body, before deciding to follow her instincts by running her hands up his back to his shoulder blades, pressing her breasts against the solid expanse of his chest until she could feel the strong, erratic thud of his heartbeat against hers. Meanwhile she could feel his hands sliding into her hair, dislodging her butterfly pins, if the clatter of metal on the floor was anything to judge by.

She gasped at the realisation. If she wasn't careful then she was going to end up looking even more dishevelled than *he* usually did, though it was hard to care when his kisses felt so wonderful. Her nostrils were filled with the scent of his shaving soap, her fingers alive with the touch of his body, her nerve-endings all tingling and thrumming with an awareness of the body heat building between them. There was a strange throbbing sensation in her abdomen, as if she wanted him closer still… And then his lips were on her cheeks, her

chin, her throat, then back to hers again, until all of her senses felt as though they were filled to breaking point.

'Angus…' She panted as they finally came apart for air, her hands clinging to his shoulders. 'We should go into the parlour. Mhairi might need you.'

He made a sound like a growl, his lips already skimming against hers again. 'Do you *want* to go in there?'

'No.'

'Neither do I.' He grinned. 'But we cannae stay here or somebody's bound to find us. Come on.' He took hold of her hand, leading her away from the door to the parlour towards the one to the hall.

'What about Mhairi?'

'She has Graham.'

'But where are we…?'

'Shh.' He put a finger to her lips, looking up and down the hallway quickly before darting across it, wrenching another door open and pulling her through.

'Where are we?' She tried to look around, but the room was too small and dark either to move or see.

'It's a cupboard.' Angus pressed his mouth against her ear, his voice a low murmur. 'Nobody's likely to look for us here. We're safe.'

'Oh.' Fiona licked her lips nervously. *Safe* wasn't exactly the word she would have chosen. On the contrary, she felt dangerously excited, her body aching with need while her blood was pumping so fast, she was starting to feel dizzy all over again. Angus's hands were looped around her waist, one of them pressing into the small of her back, and she wanted to kiss him again so badly that apparently she was willing to risk destroying her reputation to do it.

She tilted her face up to his and then gasped as she heard more voices outside the door—two of them, both male, discussing politics, if she wasn't mistaken. She froze, just able to make out Angus's eyes in the darkness, lit up with a gleam that was part amusement, part desire. And then his mouth descended on hers and every single person on the guest list could have assembled outside and not even a tiny part of her would have noticed.

Angus tightened his hands around Fiona's waist, hauling her fast against him. Their bodies were already pressed together in the confined space, but he wanted to be closer still, until not even a sliver of air came between them. Fiona was gripping his shoulders in a way that made him want to tear off both of their clothes and debauch her right then and there. Not that there was a great deal of room for debauching, but where there was a will there was a way, and there was definitely a will. She tasted sweet, like champagne, and her response was more passionate than he'd ever dared to imagine. She didn't feign either shyness or indecision, matching his kisses with an ardour that told him she wanted him as much as he wanted her. Which was both hard to believe and incredibly stirring.

She let out a soft sigh as he slid his hands upwards and he groaned in response. Just one breast, he told himself, tugging at the edge of her bodice, that was all he needed. Just one breast, to touch and cup and graze his lips along, and that would be enough. Then he'd be able to pull away and start behaving like a gentleman—for an hour or two anyway, just until the party was over and everyone else was in bed…

He clenched his brows at a commotion outside. There were even more voices in the corridor now, as well as footsteps, then the sound of the front door banging open and closed. It was probably nothing to worry about, just some guests arriving late, except that there was one man's voice that was louder than all the rest...

He sounded indignant. Angry, even. With a low-lander accent...

'What is it?' Fiona sounded dazed.

'I'm not sure. Something's happening.'

'Oh, no!' She inhaled sharply at the sound of her own name being called. 'That's my father!'

'Your...' He felt a moment of horror. He didn't know a great deal about etiquette, but he was pretty sure that being discovered in a small, dark cupboard with a gentleman's daughter was beyond the limits of propriety. It could have only one result, too, although oddly enough that thought actually made him feel calmer. Happy, even. Which was a curious blend of emotions, not that he had any time to analyse it. He was only aware of happiness dominating. If only they had a bit more room, he thought, he would be perfectly willing to drop down on one knee right there, only he didn't want her to feel forced into anything.

'What do we do?' Fiona's voice sounded panicked.

'We should probably get out of here for a start.' He pulled her bodice back up reluctantly. 'Don't worry. It sounds like they've gone into one of the rooms.'

'Yes. I think you're right...' She pressed her ear against the door before turning the handle slowly and stepping outside. 'All clear. How do I look?'

He couldn't stop himself from smiling at the question. She looked adorable. Rumpled and crumpled and like a woman who'd just been thoroughly kissed. If her guilty expression didn't give her away, then her mussed-up attire and wild-looking hair definitely would.

'There's a mirror just around the corner.' He gestured in the direction of the kitchen. 'You tidy yourself up and I'll go and introduce myself.'

'Wait! You're all dusty.' She brushed her hands over his suit jacket before looking up into his face, her expression uncertain all of a sudden. 'Angus, I—'

'Do I have your permission to speak to your father?' he interrupted. 'If you'd like me to, that is?'

'Oh.' A pink flush stole over her cheeks. 'You don't have to. That is, you needn't feel obligated because of what just happened. I mean, we've both had champagne, and it's a special, sentimental kind of evening...'

'Is it so hard to believe that I *want* to speak with him?' He cleared his throat, trying to do things properly. 'Fiona, I'm not rich. I have the farm and Meggie's, but it'll be years before I make any money from whisky, if I do at all. On top of which, we're a long way from Edinburgh, and it would be a very different life from the one you're used to. There won't be many musical soirees, but—'

'Yes.' She interrupted *him* this time. 'Yes, you can speak to him.'

'Thank you.' He slid a finger beneath her chin, tipping it upwards that so he could kiss her one last time. 'In that case, I'll see you in a few moments.'

'I might need a little longer than that.' She made a comical face as she lifted her hands to her messy hair, laughing before darting off in the opposite direction. 'Stall for me!'

'Consider it done.' He watched until she disappeared around the corner and then tugged at the hem of his suit jacket. With any luck, they would be celebrating two engagements tonight.

## *Chapter Thirteen*

Despite the recent commotion at the front door, the party was still in full swing when Angus entered the parlour.

'There you are!' Mhairi came hurrying across the room when she saw him. 'Do you have any idea where Fiona is? Her father's here and he's very upset.'

'Is he? Why?'

His sister drew him to one side, lowering her voice. 'The thing is, I'm not sure how it's happened exactly, but it seems that he didn't know she was here after all. He's had detectives out looking for her for all this time! I've shown him into the office away from the guests.'

'Fiona's on her way.' He shrugged at her inquisitive expression. 'She's just fixing her hair.'

'I *knew* it!' Mhairi's eyes lit up with a gleam of triumph. 'I *knew* there was something going on between the two of you! You've hardly been able to keep your eyes off each other all week. Have you—?'

'I'm *not* discussing it with my sister.' He gave her a pointed look. 'I probably ought to discuss it with her father, however.'

'Are you going to propose?' She gave a small bounce of excitement. 'How wonderful!'

'Don't get ahead of yourself. He might refuse.'

'I should think he knows better than to refuse Fiona anything she's set her heart on and I've seen the way she looks at you. Besides, she's of age, and it's not as if she needs him to provide a dowry.'

'What do you mean?'

'She's been financially independent since she turned twenty-one. Now you'll be able to restore the distillery properly.'

'Mhairi, what are you talking about?'

'Oh!' His sister's eyes widened before she clapped a hand over her mouth. 'Nothing.'

'You can't just say "nothing" when it's clearly something. How is she financially independent?'

'Well…' Mhairi sounded hesitant. 'The truth is, Fiona's grandparents—her mother's parents, that is—left her their ship-building fortune. Only she doesn't like to talk about it. There are a lot of fortune hunters in Edinburgh, apparently.'

'You still could have told *me*!' He frowned, starting to feel a sick feeling in the pit of his stomach. 'You said that her father was a lawyer.'

'He is, but Fiona herself is worth at least five times as much.'

'You mean, she's an heiress?' The sick feeling became a horrible lurch. 'Just like Mother?'

'I suppose so, but what does that matter? Angus?' Mhairi drew her brows together. 'What is it? You've gone pale.'

'I thought…' He ran a finger beneath his shirt collar as it started to feel uncomfortably tight. *An heiress?* If he'd made a list of the qualities he desired in a wife, 'heiress' would have come at the very bottom. He didn't *want* to marry money. He wanted to make his own. He wanted to make the distillery a success on his own terms, and for people to know it, but if he married Fiona then everyone would assume the opposite.

And what if the business failed all over again? They'd say that he'd made the same mistake as his father, throwing away his wife's fortune on a misguided dream. He glanced at the office door and fought the temptation to turn and run in the opposite direction.

'She's by the kitchens.' His voice sounded leaden. 'You'd better go and help her tidy up while I introduce myself to her father.'

Fiona pressed a hand to her stomach, trying to control a hundred excitedly dancing butterflies as she reached for the office door handle. Mhairi had said that her father wasn't in a very good mood, but her nerves weren't about that. Angus was going to ask her to marry him. And she…unbelievably…was going to accept.

After so many hurtful comments and insincere compliments over the years, she'd never expected to answer that particular question with anything but a polite, firm refusal. But then she'd never expected to meet a man who seemed to genuinely like her for who she was. A man who didn't even know about her fortune and yet still wanted to kiss and fondle her in an under-stairs cupboard. It hadn't been her first kiss, but it had certainly been the most convincing. Just thinking about it made her breasts feel heavy and her nerves start thrumming again. She had to suck in her cheeks to stop herself from smiling.

'Papa?' She pushed the door open and sailed in. 'How lovely to see you, but what on earth are you doing here?'

'What am *I* doing here?' Her father whirled around from where he was standing facing Angus across the fireplace. 'Do you have any idea how much trouble you've caused?'

'No.' She lifted her eyebrows innocently. 'Why?'

'*Why?* Because I've had no idea where you've been for the past two weeks!'

'But I left a note.'

'Which fell down the back of your dresser! I had half the police in Scotland out looking for you before we found it!' His eyes bulged as if he were on the verge of apoplexy. 'My driver said that he'd taken you to the railway station, but you didn't tell him where you were going. I thought that you'd run away!'

'Ah.' She put a hand to her throat. 'That *is* unfortunate.'

'I've been beside myself with worry and now I find you here at a…a…*party*!'

'It's for Mhairi's engagement.'

'I don't care what kind of party it is!' Her father stormed across the room and pulled her roughly into his arms. 'I've never been so worried in my whole life.'

'Oh, dear. I really am sorry, Papa. It never occurred to me that the note might get lost. It must have been caught in a draught.'

'I know you don't approve of my wedding plans, but—'

'No!' She pulled her head back quickly. 'That is, I didn't, but I've had time to think since I've been here and…well…we have a lot to talk about.'

'Do we?'

'Yes, but we'll discuss all that later.' She gave a wide smile. 'Now, I see you've met Mr Drummond.'

Her father looked as if he was struggling to keep up with the conversation. 'Yes, a few moments ago.'

'Excellent.' She paused, waiting for him to go on, but both men were silent. There was something odd about Angus's expression, too, she noticed, a new look of tension, as if he wanted to be anywhere else in the world but there.

For a moment their eyes met and she thought she saw a flash of regret before it vanished quickly. Her smile faltered as panic replaced anticipation. Had he asked her father's permission to marry her and been refused? No, surely her father would have mentioned that? But what *had* happened? Five minutes ago, he'd seemed eager to propose, even after she'd told him he didn't have to.

'Well, then, if there's nothing else to say…?' She let the words hang unanswered in the air for a few seconds. 'Why don't we go back and join in with the celebrations? Mr Drummond's family own a distillery, Papa, did he tell you? You absolutely must try some of their whisky.'

'After the fortnight I've had, I need it.' Her father let out a long sigh. 'But I'd rather we were leaving.'

'Now? Papa, it's dark.'

'All right. First thing in the morning, then. I want to get back to Edinburgh as soon as possible. I would have been here days ago if it hadn't been for all the snow. Who knows how long this thaw will last?' He glowered in the direction of the curtained window, as if suspicious about the weather conditions behind it. 'We could wake up tomorrow and find ourselves completely snowed in.'

'So I've learned, but I'm sure everything will be perfectly fine.' She feigned another smile. 'Now, you go on through to the parlour and Mhairi will take care of you. I just need to speak with Mr Drummond for a moment.'

Her father opened his mouth as if he were about to

object and then shook his head. 'Aye, well, it seems as though you know what you're doing. You usually do.'

'Thank you, Papa.' She waited until the door had closed again before letting her cheerful demeanour drop. 'Angus?'

'You'll be leaving in the morning, then?'

She felt her expression freeze at the words, lifting her chin as if to bat them away and stop them from reaching her brain, but it was too late. Their meaning was obvious. Anything he might have said earlier had just been in the heat of the moment. On reflection, he'd changed his mind about proposing. About *her.*

'It would seem so, yes.'

'I hope you've enjoyed your stay. It's been—'

'What?' She narrowed her eyes, horribly aware of tears welling behind them. 'Fun? Interesting? An amusing way to pass the time?'

'No.' He flinched. 'I didn't mean… I'm sorry, Fiona.'

'Yes.' She turned around before he could see the hurt on her face. 'So am I. Now, if you'll excuse me, I have a party to get back to.'

Angus helped to load Fiona's bags into the carriage her father had hired from his hotel, trying not to wince with every movement. Every shaft of early-morning sunshine was like a dagger stabbing into his skull, the result of too much whisky after the guests had all left. From what he could gather, the MacKays were travelling straight back to Aberdeen and then on by rail to Edinburgh. In twenty-four hours, he and Fiona would be almost two hundred miles apart.

'Thank you for everything.' Mhairi embraced her friend one last time. 'Especially my party.'

'You're more than welcome. Thank you for taking me in.'

'You'll still come back and be my bridesmaid, won't you?'

'Of course. Have I ever broken a promise?' Fiona pressed a kiss to her cheek before looking over her shoulder, meeting his gaze with a wary expression. 'Goodbye, Mr Drummond.'

'Miss MacKay.' He inclined his head, hating the way his voice sounded, as if she were still just a woman he'd found in the middle of the road and wanted to get away from. 'Have a safe journey.'

'Good luck with your whisky venture. I hope it brings you success.'

'Thank you.'

'Come along, my dear.' Her father gave her a nudge before Angus could think of anything else to say. 'I don't like the look of those clouds.'

'Yes. Goodbye, then, both of you. Please give your father my regards.' She reserved her last glance for Mhairi, Angus noticed, before climbing into the carriage. 'Have a happy Christmas!'

'Are you proud of yourself?' Mhairi's voice rose above the sound of wheels crunching on stones, her tone accusing even as she smiled and waved a hand in farewell.

'No, if you must know.'

'Why didn't you propose?'

'I couldn't.'

'But—'

'I *don't* want to talk about it.' He spun on his heel, storming back into the house.

'Oh no, you don't, Angus Malcolm Drummond!' Mhairi followed close behind. 'You're not getting away with this kind of behaviour any longer. You spent five months refusing to discuss *my* getting married and you're not going to do the same thing for yourself. What's wrong this time?'

'We're not suited, that's all.'

'You seemed suited last night.'

He stopped halfway up the staircase and grasped hold of the banister, the memory of Fiona in his arms making his body feel tight all over again. 'That was a mistake.'

'You're lying.'

'All right, I'm lying, but she's an heiress!'

*'And?'*

'And I *can't* marry a wealthy woman. I have to restore the distillery on my own, without any help.'

'Why?'

'Because I just do!'

'But w*hy*?'

'Because that's how I started it! After Mother died and you went to Edinburgh, when Father's mind started wandering, I was all on my own. *That's* when I started making plans to rebuild the distillery, to restore our family name and put things right for us again. I started to do it on my own and I'm going to finish it on my own. And I'm not going to be called a fortune hunter! Our family name has suffered enough. I won't have people saying…'

He stopped, tightening his fist around the banister.

'Saying what?' Mhairi came to stand just below him.

'All those things they said about Father.' He turned around. 'About how he took Mother's dowry and squandered it. About how she must have wished she'd married someone else, someone better than a Drummond.'

'But you know Mother never thought that herself.

She loved Father deeply, despite everything that happened.'

'Aye, but if I marry Fiona, and the distillery's a success, everyone will think it's because of her money. And if it fails, it will be just like history repeating itself. I can't risk that.'

'So you wanted to marry her until you found out about her money? I thought you were a better man than that.'

'What?'

'I never thought you'd let pride and fear get in the way of what really matters. As for our family name, it seems to me that the only person who thinks badly of it is you!'

'I don't think badly of it!'

'No? Then why are you letting a few ugly comments made by vindictive people control your actions?'

'Because—'

'No, *you* listen to *me*! I know that our family name matters to you. I know that honour and pride, and looking after Father and keeping me safe and making the distillery a success, all matter to you. But you don't have to take responsibility for everything. I've been worried about history repeating itself with the distillery, too. Not about it failing, but because of its effect on you! You're giving it too much power over your life. It's just a building, that's all. If you really cared about Fiona—'

'Of course I care about her!'

'No, you don't. Not if you're so easily swayed.'

'You don't understand.'

'I understand love. And if you truly loved her then all of those other things wouldn't matter.'

'I *do* love her!'

'Good. I thought so.' Mhairi moved up another step.

'Angus, I'm sorry you felt so alone after Mother died. I'm sorry that I wasn't here then, but I am now. I always will be, even when I marry Graham. You're not on your own any more. You can accept help. And love, too. That's the way to finally put things right for our family.' She sighed. 'I don't suppose you told Fiona any of this?'

'No.' His insides twisted. 'I didn't say anything. I didn't know how to explain. I just…let her go.'

'In other words, you let her think you don't care?'

He met his sister's accusatory gaze, feeling his heart wrench at the words. He hadn't thought of it like that, but she was right. He'd let the woman he loved leave, believing that he didn't care.

'Do you think that maybe…?'

'Aye.' He didn't wait for her to finish as he vaulted down the staircase and charged back outside, but it was already too late. The carriage was nowhere in sight. Even worse, it was snowing.

## Chapter Fourteen

Edinburgh in winter was surely one of the most beautiful cities in the world, Fiona thought, gazing out of her sitting room window at the snow falling outside like icing sugar being sprinkled over a giant cake. It was just a light smattering, really, mere dust compared to the amounts she'd seen in Aberdeenshire, but it brought the pale grey stone of the New Town to life, as if there were actual diamonds sparkling amidst the brickwork.

Unfortunately, as with anything remotely connected to Angus, it also made her stomach churn with now familiar feelings of betrayal, regret and confusion.

*Angus...* She pushed the mental image of him out of her mind and picked up her pen determinedly. She was supposed to be writing a letter, not thinking about a man who'd led her to feel and want things she'd never expected to want or feel, and then jilted her without so much as a word of explanation. She still had no idea what had happened on the night of Mhairi's party. Nothing *had* happened in the five minutes between their parting in the hallway and her joining him in the office with her father. She'd gone over the evening so many times in her mind and yet nothing became any clearer.

All she knew was that one moment he'd wanted her and the next he'd changed his mind. Which meant that the only reason, as far as she could see, was her.

'Good afternoon, Miss MacKay.'

She turned away from the window as she became aware of a woman standing behind her. She didn't remember a visitor being announced, but then she was so distracted these days that a herd of elephants might have passed through her sitting room and she might not have noticed. In this case, however, there were no elephants, just a small woman with dark hair and serious, hazel-hued eyes.

'Mrs Gibson?' Fiona stood up to greet her guest, struck with a sudden pang of guilt. She'd been so preoccupied with her own misery since leaving Windy Heads Tower that she hadn't yet talked to her father about his wedding plans. As far as he knew, she still objected. 'I'm afraid that my father is out on business.'

'I know. It was actually you I came to see.' The other woman lifted her chin. 'I'm afraid that I resorted to subterfuge and crept past your maid. I thought you might not agree to see me otherwise.'

'Of course I would have. Please, take a seat.' Fiona gestured towards a sofa, positioning herself at one end while Mrs Gibson took the other. 'Would you care for some tea?'

'No, thank you. This shouldn't take long.'

'That sounds ominous.'

Mrs Gibson bowed her dark head, smoothing her hands over her lap as if she was nervous. 'Your father was very worried when you left so unexpectedly.'

'Yes, but it was all a big misunderstanding. I left a note.'

'I know. I was the one who found it.' She smiled tightly. 'All that money spent on detectives and the answer was down the back of your dresser, wedged in the floorboards the whole time.'

'Oh, dear.'

'The point is, I saw your father's face when he read it and I've never seen such relief. He loves you a great deal.'

'As I love him. I would never have made him suffer unnecessarily.'

'I understand, and I understand that the two of you have a special kind of bond. It was never my intention to damage it or to come between you. It was my hope that you'd get used to the idea of your father and I marrying eventually, but now...' She paused and sat up straighter. 'Now I see that I was mistaken. That's why I'm calling off our wedding.'

'What?' Fiona felt her body jolt in surprise.

'I've just been into your father's office and left my engagement ring on his desk. I'm sure he'll wish to discuss the matter in person, too, but I've made up my mind. I'll be out of both of your lives very soon.'

'I see.' Fiona sucked in a breath, waiting for some sense of triumph to kick in, but all she could feel was a combination of sadness and shame knotted together in the pit of her stomach. 'So you're calling the wedding off because of me?'

'Because I want him to be happy and I don't believe he ever will be if he's estranged from his daughter.'

'So because of me,' Fiona repeated. 'He'll be heart-broken.'

'I'm sure that with time—'

'Do you love him?'

Mrs Gibson's eyes looked suspiciously bright all of a sudden. 'Yes, I do.'

'Despite the fact that he's twenty years older than you?'

'Eighteen but, despite that, yes.'

'Enough to give him up?'

'Yes.'

'Well, then.' Fiona tossed her head. 'You must go and put your ring back on immediately. And let me be a bridesmaid, if you can find it in your heart to forgive me, just so long as the dress isn't white. Pale colours wash my cheeks out dreadfully.'

'Miss MacKay—'

'*Fiona.* I should have let you call me that before, but I've been ill-mannered and horrible. The truth is, I felt threatened. Scared, even. It's just been my father and I for so long…but that's no excuse. I've done you a terrible disservice.'

'Oh…' Mrs Gibson dashed a hand across her cheek. 'So have I. I wanted to come and speak to you weeks ago, but…forgive me…you can be a little intimidating.'

'Yes, I've been told. I'm afraid it's something of a character flaw.'

'It's not a flaw at all. You're an intelligent woman with a mind of your own and you're not afraid to say what you think. Your father's always telling me how proud he is of you. He tells everyone! You should see how fiercely he reacts if anyone dares to suggest he might have wanted a son.'

'Really?' Fiona smiled weakly. 'That's so…so…'

'Did I say something wrong?' Mrs Gibson slid across the sofa as a sob escaped her. 'Is something the matter?'

Fiona pressed her lips together and then opened them again. She didn't want to talk about Angus, but she couldn't seem to stop herself, the words pushing their way out of their own accord. 'There was a man in Aberdeenshire... I thought he was different from all the other men I've ever met. I know he found me annoying at first, but I thought that he came to respect me—to like me, even—opinions and all. I thought...'

She shook her head at her own folly. 'Stupidly, I thought he was going to propose to me. I know that sounds foolish when I'd only known him for two weeks, but I was so sure. When Father arrived he asked if he could speak to him and I said that he could. I wanted him to and I *never* thought I'd say that about any man. But then...well, he didn't. He didn't say a word. He just changed his mind about me.'

'Then he wasn't good enough for you.'

'But the problem is, I think that he was. I don't understand what happened.'

'Ah.' Mrs Gibson sounded sympathetic. 'I'm sorry. You know, my first husband was never very good at expressing how he felt. Some people aren't. It doesn't necessarily mean they don't care.'

'In Mr Drummond's case, I can't see what else it means. Whatever he might have felt for me, it wasn't enough.' Another sob burst out. 'I've always been so sure about who I was and what I wanted, and yet now I feel completely adrift. I hardly know what to do with myself any more.'

'You know you'll always have a home with us.'

'Thank you, but I think it's time I set up a household on my own. I'm always telling everyone how independent I am. I really ought to prove it.' She gave a small sniff. 'I was perfectly content *not* being married before I met Mr Drummond and I will be again. I just need a bit of time to recover, that's all.'

'Of course. It's not easy, getting over heartbreak.'

'However, as much as misery loves company, I have no intention of spoiling things for you and my father.' She reached for the other woman's hands. 'I haven't spoiled them, have I? You will go through with the wedding?'

'Are you certain that it's what you want?'

'Certain enough to do this.' Fiona slid off the sofa and onto one knee. 'Mrs Margery Gibson, would you do me the very great honour of accepting my father's hand in marriage, for better or worse, for richer or poorer, in sickness and in health, forsaking all—?'

'Enough!' Her prospective stepmother burst into peals of laughter. 'Thank you, Miss Fiona MacKay, I will.'

# Chapter Fifteen

Angus stood on the opposite side of the road to the kirk. The bride and groom had just emerged, the former looking resplendent in a trailing, violet-coloured gown, but he couldn't drag his eyes away from the bridesmaid. She looked even more beautiful, dressed in vibrant pink with a white shawl draped artlessly around her shoulders and an assortment of colourful feathers in her hair that made him smile despite his nerves.

There surely weren't many women in Scotland who could look so beautiful and original at the same time, but somehow Fiona managed it. More than that, she looked utterly breath-taking.

He glanced down at his own workaday clothes and grimaced. He'd only reached Edinburgh that morning and, having gone straight to the address that Mhairi had given him and discovered where Fiona was, hadn't paused to change. He hadn't even found a hotel, with the result that he was still carrying his travelling bag. All he'd wanted was to find her as quickly as possible.

He took a deep breath and crossed the street to where the wedding party was preparing to climb into a row of carriages, presumably waiting to carry them off to some post-nuptial celebrations.

'Mr MacKay?' He made a beeline for the groom. 'May I offer my congratulations, sir?'

'Mr Drummond.' Fiona's father hesitated before accepting his handshake, as if he were taken aback to see him. 'What brings you to Edinburgh?'

'I came to speak to your daughter, sir.'

'Indeed?' A pair of grey eyebrows rose upwards. 'Well, I'm afraid it's not a good time. As you can see, we're a little busy.'

'On the contrary, I think it's the perfect time.' The bride, a pretty, dark-haired woman who'd been regarding Angus curiously up until that point, interjected. 'I've heard so much about you, Mr Drummond. Why don't you come and celebrate with us? Fiona's organised everything so I expect great things.'

'Thank you, but I'd—'

*'Angus?'* The woman in question burst out of the crowd suddenly, the feathers on her head bobbing up and down as she gaped at him in surprise. 'What are *you* doing here?'

'He came to speak with you.' The bride put a hand on her new stepdaughter's arm, though whether it was a gesture of support or restraint he couldn't tell. 'I've just invited him to join us back at the house.'

'I don't want to impose.' Angus inclined his head, acutely aware of Fiona's back stiffening, not to mention several of the guests watching. 'Perhaps we might take a walk instead?'

'What a charming idea!' Once again, it was the bride who answered. 'Fiona, you should take Mr Drummond to see the Christmas tree in Princes Street Gardens.

I'll send one of the carriages back here to collect you in an hour.'

'But...' Fiona looked from her stepmother to her father and then back again. 'What about the wedding breakfast?'

'Oh, there's plenty of time for both. We probably won't even be seated by then. We certainly won't have reached the speeches. And then perhaps your friend will change his mind and join us, after all.' The bride beamed as she climbed into one of the carriages. 'I do hope so, Mr Drummond. It's been such a pleasure to meet you. I hope you have a charming and productive walk.'

'Now, that's a turn-up...' Mr MacKay patted his daughter on the shoulder as he followed his new wife into the carriage. 'I believe that's the first time I've ever seen you outmanoeuvred, my dear. She obviously sees something she approves of. Good luck, Mr Drummond.'

'Well...' Fiona sucked in her cheeks as the wedding procession rolled away. 'It appears my new stepmother wants us to go for a walk.' She threw him a narrow-eyed look before turning on her heel. 'The gardens are this way.'

'Wait! Are you warm enough?' Angus had to take several long strides to catch up with her brisk pace.

'Fine, thank you.' She tugged her shawl tighter around her shoulders. 'How's Mhairi? Is she here too?'

'No, I came alone.'

'Pity. *Her* I would have liked to see.'

Neither of them said anything else as they made their way along several wide, bustling pavements filled with Christmas shoppers, across Princes Street and then on through the great wrought-iron gates of the gardens. The flower beds were empty at this time of year, but the lawns were still a frost-tinged green, and the large pine tree in the centre, decorated with brightly coloured ribbons and baubles, made a cheerful contrast to the dark silhouette of the castle looming on its black rock behind.

'This really is a beautiful city.' Angus stopped to admire the view of snow on a thousand glistening rooftops.

'Yes, it is.' Fiona threw a look over her shoulder. 'I consider myself very lucky to live here.'

'Aye, although I asked you once if you'd consider living elsewhere.'

'I remember.' She twisted her face to one side. 'Or at least, I think I do. I wondered afterwards if I'd imagined the whole conversation.'

'I know. I behaved badly that evening. *And* the next morning. If it makes you feel any better, I've regretted it every moment since.'

She didn't answer straightaway, a muscle working in her jaw as she turned back to confront him. 'I thought you were going to propose.'

'I was.'

'Then what happened?'

'It wasn't because I didn't care.' He put down his bag and removed his hat to rake his fingers through his hair. He'd thought about what he would say a hundred times on the journey but, now he was there, standing only a few tantalising feet away from her, he seemed to have forgotten every one of his carefully planned speeches. 'The truth is, I had no idea how rich you were.'

*'What?'* Her expression transformed with a look of outrage. 'And, now that you do, you've changed your mind again?'

'No!' He shook his head quickly. 'The opposite! All those days you were staying with us, I had no idea that you were an heiress. I knew you were a lady, but it was only after your father arrived that I found out how wealthy you were. Mhairi let it slip by accident.'

'Wait...' She opened and closed her mouth a few times as if she were trying to make sense of the words. 'I don't understand. You changed your mind about proposing to me *because* I'm rich?'

'Yes, and because of my stupid pride. I didn't want people to call me a fortune hunter like they called my father. I wanted to restore my family name and fortune on my own, without any help from anyone. That's why, when I found out about your fortune, I panicked.'

'I see.' Her brow furrowed. 'So, why are you here now? Nothing's changed, has it? Presumably you still object to being called a fortune hunter. What do you want, Angus?'

'A second chance.'

'Because?'

'Because I love you.' He advanced a step towards her. 'Fiona, you're the most unique woman I've ever met, with the strongest opinions and strangest taste in clothes, and I can't bear the thought of *not* spending the rest of my life with you. No matter what happens to the distillery or what people say, I want you more than any of that.'

'If you loved me then you wouldn't have let me go.'

'I made a mistake. I was a fool. Yes, I was afraid of what people might say. Of failing, too, of having history repeat itself all over again. But the fact is my mother loved my father. She never regretted a single day of their marriage or any of the money she lost. *I* was the one who let pride and fear of failure get in the way of what really matters. I shouldn't have. Our family name is as good as it's ever been, at least to the people who matter.'

She held onto his gaze, her own wide and pained. 'I thought that you changed your mind because of me. Because I was too forward and argumentative and vivid!'

'I love your opinions.' He lifted his hands tentatively to her face, cradling her cheeks between his fingertips. 'I want to hear all of them. I'm not saying we'll always agree, but I still want to know what they are. So what do you say, Fiona?' He tensed, waiting for her answer. '*Will* you give me a second chance?'

Fiona swallowed against a constricting sensation in her throat. She was vaguely aware of a choir singing Christmas carols in the distance, but she felt oddly detached from the world around her, as if her senses had all been numbed by the cold. She could barely even feel Angus's fingers on her face. Everything he'd just said ought to have made her heart soar, but if anything her spirits had sunk even lower. How could he just expect her to forget the way that he'd made her feel, the pain his rejection had caused?

'Angus…' She was surprised to hear her voice falter mid-sentence, as if it were someone else speaking. 'You hurt my feelings a great deal. And it's been a month since I left. Why come and ask me this now?'

'Because I couldn't get here any sooner. Your father was right about the weather. Your carriage had barely left before the snow started again. The trains stopped and I had to wait until the storm was over to walk.'

'You mean you've walked all the way from Aberdeenshire?'

'Not the whole way, but quite a big part of it.' One corner of his mouth tugged upwards sheepishly. 'I'm hoping that might work in my favour.'

'Well…' She blinked a few times, trying not to show

how impressed she really was. 'It's somewhat romantic, I suppose.'

'Just somewhat?'

'*Very.* But it's no use. I thought you were different from other men. Instead, you made me doubt myself and who I am.'

'I know. I'm sorry.' He leaned forward, pressing his forehead against hers. 'Tell me what I can do to fix things. Tell me how I can prove myself.'

'It's too late.'

'No, it isn't. The Fiona MacKay I know is one of the most determined, intelligent people I've ever met. She'll think of something.'

'I can't.'

'Yes, you can. *Please?*'

'No, I—' She started to pull away and then stopped, jerking her chin up as an idea struck her.

'What is it?' His eyes lit up eagerly. 'Whatever it is, I'll do it.'

'Do you remember that day at Pennan when you let me get drenched?'

'Yes.'

'Well...' She glanced towards the blue and gold sculpture of the Ross Fountain in the distance. Its four female figures, surrounded by mermaids, lions and walruses, seemed to beckon her. 'Get in.'

'Where?' He followed the direction of her gaze. 'Into the fountain?'

'It can't be any colder than the North Sea.' She folded her arms. 'You asked what you could do. This is it.'

'Right.' He strode straight off, not hesitating for so much as a second before vaulting over the wall and into waist-deep water. 'How's that?'

'Oh!' She put a hand to her mouth, part horrified,

part gratified as frigid water poured into his boots and over his breeches, soaking the ends of his greatcoat until it spread out like a cloak around him. As declarations went, it was very convincing. He had to be freezing, and yet…she drew her brows together…it still wasn't enough. Not quite…

'Well?'

'I'm thinking!' She looked around for further inspiration and then bent down, scooping up a snowball in her hand and pulling her arm back, earning herself a chorus of shocked gasps from the growing band on onlookers. 'How *much* did you say that you loved me?'

'Enough not to move!' He spread his arms out, unflinching as the snow hit him straight in the face.

'Sorry!' She winced. 'I was aiming for your chest.'

'That's a relief.' He shook his head like a dog. 'Is that better?'

'Much!'

'Can I get out now or do you want me to swim a lap?'

'You can get out!' She laughed.

'Thank goodness.' He waded back towards her, swinging his legs over the side of the fountain and drenching the surrounding pavement. 'What happened at Pennan will never happen again. From now on I'll make it my purpose in life to keep you warm, dry and happy.'

He squeezed out the ends of his greatcoat. 'I can't promise to make Meggie's a success, I can't promise to brush my hair every day or dress like a gentleman either, but I *can* promise that you'll never regret marrying me. I'll never make you doubt yourself again.' He closed his eyes briefly. '*Will* you marry me?'

'This is ridiculous!' A burble of laughter rose in her throat. 'We both look ridiculous! You wet and shivering, and me with half a peacock on my head.'

'I just told you, I don't care what anyone else thinks. All I care about is you. Now, will you put me out of my misery?'

'On one condition.' She looked at him seriously again. 'That not a penny of my fortune goes on your distillery. I don't want you ever accusing me of something as heinous as helping you.'

'Agreed. Does that mean yes?'

'Yes. Because I love you, too, Angus Drummond. *But…*' She put a finger to his lips as he moved closer. 'You can't kiss me here. There are people everywhere.'

'I know.'

'Some of them might be acquaintances.'

'Then they'll know that you're spoken for.'

'They'll think I'm being assaulted by a madman.'

'As opposed to an overbearing brute?'

'*My* overbearing brute. All right, one kiss—but don't expect to win arguments so easily after we're married.'

'Understood. Just promise me one thing in return.'

'What?'

'On our wedding day, I want you to wear the brightest, most dazzling dress you can find.'

'Oh, Mr Drummond.' Her lips curved as she leaned in for his kiss. 'You ought to be careful what you wish for…'

\* \* \* \* \*

## *Author Note*

My English parents bought a croft in Aberdeenshire in the mid-nineteen-seventies—a completely crazy thing to do when they were both working full-time and starting a family, but they claim they wanted a challenge.

Me and my sister were born there, and grew up surrounded by Highland cattle, chickens and a large number of cats. Back then, we could be snowed in and lose power and running water for weeks. My mum still tells stories about washing nappies in melted snow, and my dad has nerve damage in one leg from the time he walked home from work in a blizzard.

I've been back a few times since we moved away, and the landscape has changed a lot, but places like the beach at Aberdour are just as timelessly beautiful as ever.

By the way, the story of Jane Whyte, who lived close to the shore, is completely true. It's a little far east for whisky territory, but I decided to use artistic licence and steal a few miles.

The character of Mhairi—pronounced Varry—is named after one of my best friends at high school in Edinburgh, where we lived later. There were actually a couple of Mhairis, but I was one of what felt like a hundred Jenny/Jenni/Jennies, so I was jealous of any name that stood out. Since moving to England I've only met one other Mhairi—a student who told me she'd given up trying to correct people's pronunciation and went by Marie instead. So this story is for all the Mhairis or Mairis outside of Scotland, who are tired of spelling out their names.

By the way, there's a *very* bad pun in this novella. If you happen to know which movie was partly filmed in Pennan, I apologise, but I couldn't resist.

# THEIR SNOWBOUND REUNION

## Elisabeth Hobbes

To Team Reception.
An amazing group of women I'm lucky
enough to work with in The Day Job.

Dear Reader,

I began writing this story in early spring 2021, and as I write this author's note it is almost the end of May. To conjure up an atmosphere of snow, fog and ice in the middle of summer is a challenge, but as I look out my window toward the hills where this story takes place, they are so shrouded in gray cloud and driving rain that I can't even see the top!

I am so fortunate to live close to the gateway to the Peak District, where this story is set, and to revisit the setting of a previous book, *Redeeming the Rogue Knight*. I can't think of many places where I'd rather be snowed in.

My thanks as always go to my husband and children, who drove and walked around the area on numerous occasions with me, stopping to take photos of other people's houses and in some cases demanding we slow down on the road so I could wind the window down. The special tree is for A&A.

Thanks also to my editor Julia, who persuaded me to try the double challenge of uncharted territory of writing a novella and a Christmas book, and thanks for her great ideas of how to up the festiveness. As the season is nearly upon us, I hope you will enjoy meeting Amy and Anthony and discovering their story together as much as I enjoyed writing it.

I wish you the happiest of Christmases and the best this season can offer.

*Elisabeth*

## *Prologue*

Anthony Matthews was not there.

Amy Pritchard took off her gloves and loosened her scarf. Running up the hill from Priestclough village was impossible but she had walked as fast as she could. Nevertheless, the barren, sloping field covered with a sprinkling of December snow was empty. The solitary rowan tree which had been their meeting point for trysts since early summer stood alone in the centre, its lightning-split trunk visible from miles around.

It was hardly surprising. Amy was almost two hours late and the biting Derbyshire winds could chill a man to the bone within a quarter of an hour. She adjusted her hair, put back on her gloves then made her way along the hillside path to Windcross, the house where Anthony was staying with his aunt, Violet Chase.

Ready with a string of apologies and reasons for her lateness, Amy walked through the gates and was hailed by Miss Alberta Gough, Violet Chase's long-time companion. Miss Gough's arms were full of holly, which she always fashioned into wreaths.

She peered over the top of the pile at Amy. 'Miss Pritchard! We didn't expect to see you today.'

'I've come to speak to Mr Matthews,' Amy explained.

Miss Gough's face creased into a frown. She opened the front door and shouted.

'Violet, Miss Pritchard is here.'

Miss Chase appeared at a stride. She strode everywhere and did everything at the top of her voice. She was a woman in her fifty-seventh year, with steel-grey hair and a habit of dressing in China silks and smoking jackets.

'Good morning, Miss Pritchard. Your father hasn't yet accepted my invitation to the Christmas afternoon carols and mulled wine. Have you been sent on his behalf?'

The carol singing took place around an open bonfire in the grounds of Windcross on Christmas afternoon, lasting until dark, with mulled drinks and hot mince pies served. It was the highlight of what little social life Priestclough and the surrounding houses could offer.

'I am sure my father will gladly accept. However, that's not why I'm here,' Amy said. 'I was supposed to be meeting Mr Matthews at eleven, but my father insisted I transcribe some of the verses he wrote in the middle of last night, and his handwriting was dreadful. It took me far longer than I expected.'

'When the muse visits she does not care for the legibility of her inspiration,' Miss Chase said, shaking her head sympathetically. 'Your father should employ a secretary and not expect you to work all the hours in the twenty-four.'

She turned to Miss Gough who was hovering nearby, looking anxious. 'Berty, dear, will you go ask Cook to boil the kettle for tea?'

She turned back to Amy. 'My nephew left for Buxton at half past nine this morning in order to catch the eleven o'clock stage coach to Manchester.'

Amy's stomach plummeted. 'He was supposed to be staying until the twenty-second. Did he say why, or when he will be returning?'

Miss Chase pursed her lips. 'He said he does not plan to return for the foreseeable future. It was a rather sudden decision, from the way he threw everything into his valise.'

Amy reached for the door post, her strength leaving her. She turned her eyes to Miss Chase and felt tears spark in them, blinked them away and swallowed. 'Did he by chance leave me a note?'

'I'm sorry, he didn't. Are you all right, Amy? You've turned very pale. I'm sorry if this is a surprise to you. Would you care to take tea with me?'

Amy shook her head dumbly. 'Father will be expecting me for afternoon tea. I've already taken too long out of the day. Thank you for your time.'

Miss Chase patted her arm in the manner one might pet a dog. 'Don't mention it, dear. I can only apologise for Anthony's odd behaviour. I hope he will write and explain his conduct soon. Berty and I were only remarking on Wednesday that it was a pleasure to see you two getting on so well. We thought you had grown increasingly fond of each other over the past two years.'

'So did I,' Amy said, forcing a smile.

She returned the way she had come. At the fork in the steep path down the hill side she paused and looked in the direction of the lone tree. It didn't matter how punctual she might have been because Anthony had never been there waiting for her.

But why? She stood with her eyes closed, momentarily reliving the last time they had met two days previously. He had caught her from behind, wrapping his arms tightly about her waist, and had nestled his head on her shoulder as the snow fell about them.

'I wonder how many lives the tree has borne witness to. How many lovers? How many husbands and wives who bring their own children to visit it in turn? Just imagine that.'

'I don't know. It must have stood for fifty years at least,' Amy had replied.

'I'll wager none of them were as happy as we are,' Anthony had murmured, his lip tickling her ear until she'd squirmed and giggled. Then he had spun her to face him, kissed her until her head had spun and her lips throbbed with longing and had given her no reason at all to think his words weren't true.

She trudged home with a heavy heart.

Standing Stone Lodge smelled wonderfully of mincemeat and plum stuffing. Amy turned towards the kitchen to see what she could muster. However, her father called her into his study as soon as she closed the front door. Septimus Pritchard was standing in front of the window that opened onto the view over the village. The lodge was a little way up the hill, almost opposite Windcross, and he would have been able to see Amy returning home. Amy and Anthony had often joked that she could use Septimus's telescope to see Anthony waving from the tree field.

'I have been waiting for my tea to be poured.'

'Didn't John come?' she asked, referring to her father's manservant.

'Yes, but I sent him away. I wanted you,' Septimus said a trifle petulantly. 'No one understands me as well. I wanted to speak to you about the verses I gave you this morning. I have read your transcript and I must say I am disappointed. You rushed. You repeated one line twice and misspelled two of the Greek verbs. Your dear, departed mother would be most distressed to think she had left me with such an inadequate amanuensis.

'Goodness me child,' he added peering at her. 'Have you been crying? Your eyes are swollen most unbecomingly. Your face is a wreck. Tell me why at once.'

'I haven't, Father,' Amy lied. 'It's very cold outside, that's all.'

'Where have you been?'

'For a walk into the hills. I told you this morning, when you gave me the list of chores, that I intended to go out.'

'Yes, I thought you might have been visiting Miss Chase's young nephew.'

His eyes bored into Amy. Did he suspect they had become more than friends?

'I just wanted to walk before the snow fell too thickly.'

'An interesting young man, Mr Matthews. No money but an excess of ambition. I believe he hopes to secure a position on a Manchester newspaper. When I passed him in the church yard yesterday I mentioned an associate of mine from my youth who is in that line of employment. Has a daughter about your age. I'm sure Mr Matthews will do well if he gets himself in with the family.'

Amy pressed a finger to the spot between her eyes, not liking the direction her thoughts flew in. 'I'm sorry for the mistakes in the notes. I have rather a headache so, if you will excuse me, I shall retire to my room for a while and work on them later.'

Septimus frowned but Amy held his eye. Too often

she capitulated to his whims for the sake of a peaceful house, but now she knew she would be unable to concentrate. The turmoil in her breast could not withstand a lecture on Septimus's favourite subject: the poetry and wisdom of Septimus Pritchard.

'Very well. But pour my tea first and listen for the bell in case I need anything else. I sent Millie on an errand this morning and said she could take the afternoon to visit her mother. Incidentally, the cocoa you brought me at half past midnight was too thin. If I ask you for a drink at that hour, I am in need of something hearty. And you can be less stinting with the brandy.'

'Yes, Father. I'm sorry, Father.'

Amy poured a cup of tea from the pot on the small table beside Septimus then slipped out, resenting the fact that the housemaid was given time off that she herself was rarely granted. She sat in her parlour and began to work on her sewing. Every year she made red and green felt stockings for the youngest children at Netherclough School, to hang at the foot of their beds on Christmas Eve, but she could not concentrate on the task.

Her eyes filled with tears again and she felt hollow and cold. Miss Chase must be mistaken. Anthony would come back, or he would write to explain why he had suddenly left. There would be no letter before Christmas, so she would concentrate on enjoying herself as always.


But Christmas came and went. Winter turned into spring and spring to summer and there was no word from Anthony.

The final vestiges of Amy's optimism were shattered

by the announcement, eleven months later, of the engagement of Anthony Matthews and Henrietta Barton.

'I pride myself on the match as I made the introduction,' Septimus remarked, cracking his breakfast boiled egg into two halves that reminded Amy of the way her heart currently felt.

Septimus for once noticed Amy's anguish. Her father rarely showed interest in anyone or anything that was not to his own advantage, and that he should assist Anthony in such a way was too cruel a twist of fate.

'Did you have hopes in that direction? Never mind, my girl. Trust me, you are better off. He could not have kept you in the manner I do, and I could not do without you to assist me. After you have eaten, find me the volume of Tacitus on the third or fourth shelf. I have a notion to write a narrative ballad concerning the Batavian Rebellion.'

He left the table, leaving Amy to obey. She dropped her head in her hands and wept, wild despair and grief building inside her. She would not have cared how Anthony kept her. She had always known she would have a generous dowry, and when she inherited Standing Stone Lodge she would have brought more to the marriage. Septimus would have had to learn to do without her and rely on his servants or himself.

Perhaps he was right and Amy's destiny was to remain at her father's side.

She wiped away the tears and went to the library in search of the book, determined to put Anthony Matthews out of her mind for ever.

# Chapter One

*Fifteen years later*

'Will you tell me how you heard of this position, Mrs Munroe, and why you are interested?'

The solicitor, sitting in the chair which had once been occupied by Miss Chase, stared at Amy.

'I am an old acquaintance of Mrs Brookland, the wife of the church warden in Priestclough. She wrote to me telling me of Miss Chase's death and enclosing the advertisement seeking a housekeeper for Windcross.'

'You know the area a little?'

Amy smiled. 'A little. From a long time ago. Nothing worth mentioning to your employer. I am currently residing with my late husband's cousin in Glasgow but at the end of September she plans to live by the Italian Lakes for a year or two. Such opportunities as this, with a generous wage and accommodation, will be few and far between. It seemed as if the stars were aligning.'

The solicitor did not appear interested in Cousin Jean's Italian adventures. He studied Amy's letter again. 'You have been widowed now for one and a half years? Allow me to offer my condolences on your loss. As well as general housekeeping, you will catalogue the belongings of the late Miss Chase so an inventory might be compiled and death duties calculated accurately before my client, Mr Matthews, can take possession of the house. Do you feel you have the ability to fulfil the position?'

Amy's stomach jerked at the mention of Anthony. If she was to accept the position here she must not allow the ghost of Anthony Matthews to rise after so long a slumber.

'Before my marriage I acted as a secretary and housekeeper for my father. After my marriage I performed the same role for my husband. The notion of actually getting paid to carry out this task is appealingly novel.'

The solicitor grinned, showing a rare sign of humanity. Emboldened, Amy asked the question that had been troubling her. 'May I ask, what is the likelihood of coming face to face with my employer?'

Any concern she had that Anthony Matthews would link the then twenty-four-year-old Amy Pritchard with Mrs Napier Munroe, widow of a Scottish botanist, was slight in the extreme but she had no desire to see him.

The solicitor looked slightly confused by the question.

'I believe it highly unlikely Mr Matthews will ever occupy this house. He inherited Windcross from his aunt unexpectedly and his work as the editor of a newspaper keeps him in Lancashire. If you would like a moment to consider, I will summon the maid to bring you tea in the Garden Room.'

He pressed the small button on the wall beside the desk. In theory this ought to have rung a bell in the servants' hall. In practice it stuck halfway. Amy concealed a smile. The bell had done this for as long as she could remember but Miss Gough had showed her the knack.

'Perhaps wriggle your finger in a circle to loosen it,' she suggested.

The solicitor gave her an odd look but did as she suggested. Sure enough, the sound of a bell pealed along the corridor.

'Well done, Mrs Munroe.' The solicitor flashed her a second genuine smile. 'I believe it is fate that you should come and work here as you know the ways of the house.'

Amy's humour abandoned her. Of course she knew the ways of the house. Even after Anthony had left, she had visited Miss Chase and Miss Gough three or four times a year until Septimus's death when Amy was thirty-two. The only times she had not been included in gatherings had been on the three occasions when Anthony had brought his wife to stay and Miss Chase had tactfully not extended the invitation to the Pritchards.

Even so, she was not prepared for the torrent of emotions that assailed her as she stepped inside the airy Garden Room. This had always been her favourite room when she'd paid visits in happier times. In summer it was cool. In winter the fire in the deep stone hearth warmed it.

The golden September light showed it at its best now. Amy swore she could smell the freesias and lilies that had once filled tall vases at each side of the double doors to the garden. Little had changed in the house since Amy had last entered it over seven years previously. She wandered around the room, brushing her fingertips over the white painted windowsills and furniture which now stood covered in dust sheets.

She trailed her hand across the back of the moss-green velvet love seat that stood in an alcove beside the fireplace and a quiver passed through her fingertips, travelling up her arm. She had multiple associations with that particular piece of furniture and a sense of melancholy overwhelmed her. Here she had first felt the stab of attraction. Here she had first spoken to Anthony. Here, after they had crept away from a summer croquet tournament, he had first dared to press his lips to hers. Here he had hinted that he had an important question to ask her when they planned to meet on that fateful morning.

She found herself shaking. She had endured and conquered the pain of Anthony's rejection, and for many years had not given a second thought to him. Now, back in the same room where she had first met his gaze, the emotions flooded back, dizzying her with their intensity. Her throat grew tight and she pushed her knuckles against her lips, as if that would obliterate the memory of a softer touch.

'Fifteen years have passed, Amy,' she said aloud. 'Become mistress of your emotions.'

After perhaps a quarter of an hour had passed, the secretary entered the room.

'Have you reached a decision? I would like to be able to write to my client by the evening post.'

Amy sipped thoughtfully from the Japanese painted tea-cup that Miss Chase had loved. Everything made logical sense. She was a widow with few resources. Although most of the house would be unused, she would have her own bedroom and sitting room as well as permission to walk in the gardens. The salary was generous and the workload light. Her fellow staff would be a husband and wife as gardener and cook, along with one maid of all work who would come in daily from the village.

'I will take the position,' she answered.

'Good. Mr Matthews will be very pleased to hear it. When will you be able to begin?'

'If Mr Matthews is agreeable, I will move here on the first of October.'

'I'm sure that will be satisfactory, Mrs Munroe. As I said, he does not intend to visit the house, but he is desirous of affairs being put in order as soon as possible.'

Amy held out her hand to the solicitor.

'Thank you for your time. I'm sure I shall be very happy working here.'


Amy's life was indeed highly satisfactory. Windcross was within reach of several invigorating walks, down to Priestclough village or along the ridge via Upperclough, to give excellent views of Derbyshire and Cheshire. Buxton, with its arcade of shops, was close. Her work was not particularly taxing and the small staff she oversaw took her instructions willingly.

When December arrived, Amy started to get the first pangs of melancholy. She had visited Windcross for most Christmases she could remember, as Miss Chase had loved the season. Naturally her mind returned to one particular Christmas, but she did not want to think about the heart-breaking fortnight after Anthony's unexpected departure. That was the worst Christmas she could recall.

Instead she forced herself to be cheerful.

'We should decorate the house for Christmas,' she remarked to Mrs Carey, the cook. 'There should be a tree with candles in the parlour and garlands wound around the stair banisters.'

'There's little point with no family here,' Mrs Carey

replied with a sigh. 'I only came here when Miss Chase was in her last years and too ill to receive visitors. In my previous post in Bradford, I would have spent weeks preparing puddings and cakes and pies. It hardly seems right that a house this grand should have no celebrations.'

'Do you like Christmas, Mrs Munroe?' asked Mr Carey, who was warming his feet by the cast-iron range. 'I always thought the Scottish were a dour race.'

'I'm not Scottish,' Amy reminded him. 'It's true, though, that Mr Monroe never paid much attention to what day it was. I would have to pull him away from his treatises on highland grasses or diagrams of thistles even on Christmas Day. Though when I did he enjoyed himself.'

A notion seized her, bringing with it the promise of sugared almonds and glittering candles.

'I intend to decorate my sitting room with garlands even if the rest of the house is bare. This will be the first year I have complete control over how my house looks and I shall do as I please.'

'And I'm sure I can bake as many pies as Mr Carey will eat,' laughed Mrs Carey.

On the twentieth of December, when Amy was installed in the study working through the accounts of rents to be paid in January, the first and bills to be settled, Kitty, the maid, knocked on the door, bringing a telegram.

The communication was brief, wasting no words. Amy read it twice then laid it down and poured herself a strong cup of tea from the big brown pot. She drank it in one go, then picked up the sheet again.

There was no mistaking the contents or the author.

*Mrs Munroe,*
*Trust employment and inventory progress sat-*
*isfactory.*
    *Visiting Priestclough on 21st December to pay*
*respects at aunt's grave.*
    *Will visit Windcross to discuss any matters*
*arising to date.*
    *Light luncheon required.*
*Anthony Matthews, Esq.*

Amy laid down the letter again. Anthony was coming here tomorrow. The solicitor had assured her he
had not intended to visit, and now he would be there
the following day. She could not escape meeting him.

She stood and paced around the room, twisting her
handkerchief between her hands. Would he care that
she was living there? Would he be indifferent? Angry
at being deceived about her identity? Most probably
he would not mind that she was living in his property
and would not terminate her employment when she had
made such good progress on the inventory.

She had laid to rest her memories of the time she
had spent with Anthony, but now the full extent of his
perfidy hit her like a physical blow, and she was filled
with indignation. He had been a coward at the time, too
ashamed to end their association in person and vanishing from her life. She had an entire day to steel herself and would have the advantage of foreknowledge
over him.

The following day dawned cloudy, with the smell of
snow in the air. A thick frost covered the trees and lawn,
turning them into silent, ghostly figures, and the six
inches of water in the ornamental pond was frozen solid.

At eleven o'clock Amy heard carriage wheels crunching on the gravel. In the study, she ran a final eye over the ledgers. Not that anything was out of order, but she thought it best. She remembered Anthony's penchant for doing everything thoroughly.

Everything.

She shuddered as an unexpected bubble of desire popped in her belly. Anthony had been the first person ever to kiss her and at the time she had not appreciated how single-minded his approach had been. Every ounce of concentration went into his kiss, as if their lips were the only thing of consequence in the world.

When Amy had married Napier, she had been disappointed to realise how his kisses paled in comparison. But then, Napier had asked her to marry him and Anthony, despite every impression that he'd intended to, had not.

She walked to the door. Her mouth was dry but her hands clammy.

*Control yourself,* she whispered. *An hour or two and it will be over.*

The coachman opened the door of the Clarence and out stepped a tall man wearing a grey silk top hat, under which Amy could see dark brown hair with a slight wave to it. His overcoat of grey wool was cut close and emphasised his slim frame. An orange woollen muffler concealed his lower face. His head was bowed as he stepped down onto the frost-hardened gravel, but Amy knew that his eyes would be light brown with flecks of coffee.

He looked up and frowned, then reeled as if a great blow had been dealt to him.

'Amy? Is that truly you?'

Amy felt a rush of anger. How dared he appear

shocked when he had dealt her such a crushing blow as to sever all contact and leave without a word or good-bye?

This was the man she had given her heart to. The man she would have joined her soul and body to in marriage. She'd believed her devotion had been reciprocated but had been wrong.

She determined to make the interview as short as possible. She would not mention the past and, if Anthony dared to raise it, she would greet any comments with the disdain they merited.

## Chapter Two

Anthony hated travelling by coach. In his youth he made every possible journey on horseback but now he was forty and accompanied by two children, and all the paraphernalia that followed them, so had no choice. Rose, aged seven, was a hearty traveller who had her nose pressed against the glass, giving a running commentary on the people and places they passed. Oliver, at ten, had his father's more delicate stomach and sat back against the seat with his eyes closed, humming Christmas carols to himself.

Anthony let both children do as they wished, remembering journeys as a child when his mother and father would argue from the instant the door closed over the best way of teaching Anthony to master his travel-induced nausea. His parents argued over practically every decision, not just on journeys, but the combination of the urge to vomit, the cramped vehicle from which he could not escape and their pointed remarks had etched a deep aversion to arguments on Anthony. Even as an adult, having to broach a difficult matter with a colleague or friend could cause his stomach to churn unpleasantly.

Anthony ran his tongue nervously over his lips. He had always been a guest at Windcross, and it felt unnerving to be returning as master of the property. He could not get used to the change in his material circumstances and he was half inclined to simply ignore the property, wait until the housekeeper had finished the inventory and sell the house.

He had loved Windcross—partly for the respite from parental squabbles—but intermingled with his pleasant memories were many sad ones. His last visit had been the day of Aunt Violet's funeral. Before that he had not visited for three years, blaming his work. Before that he had forced himself into exile when his love affair with Amy had ended so abruptly.

He closed his eyes and drifted back to the wonderful summer he had spent there, half-grieving and half-glad of his memories. Where was Amy Pritchard now? Violet and Alberta had never spoken of her in his presence. She had left Priestclough shortly after the death of her father, by all accounts, and of that Anthony was glad.

Or wasn't.

He changed opinion on that fact frequently, depending on whether he was pleased for Amy that she had found freedom or bitter that he himself had not been enough to lure her away from her devotion to Septimus.

The rocking motion of the Clarence had increased as it had made its way down the winding roads and made Anthony feel sick.

That was nothing to the sense of nausea which enveloped him when he came face to face with the woman standing on the doorstep waiting to greet him.

His first impression was of severity. A black dress. Hands held loosely at her sides. Looking up, he noticed her hair before her face—thick coils of auburn that sat brushed against pale cheeks.

Then he saw her face and confusion swept over him. Mist descended over his mind and he found he could barely utter a coherent sentence. At first he thought his eyes were playing cruel tricks on him. After all, he had spent half a journey remembering Amy Pritchard and the times he had spent with her here.

'Amy? Is that truly you?'

'Good morning, Mr Matthews.'

The punch to his sternum as he realised his eyes were not deceiving him temporarily stole the power of speech from him. Her eyes met his levelly, shining with the same bold intelligence that had bowled him over the very first time they had met. Warmth spread beneath his collar despite the bitter wind. Even older, she was still beautiful, and his body reacted in the same way it always had.

He could not afford to react. He had to master himself.

'What are you doing here?'

Too brusque. He mustn't let the resentment show. Mustn't reveal the deep trench of hurt that opened up again at the sight of the woman who had dismissed him, without even having had the courage to do it to his face.

'I'm sorry, that was rude,' he said. 'I believed you had left the area. I am here to see my housekeeper. Are you visiting Mrs Munroe?'

Amy laced her fingers and pressed her two thumbs together—the old mannerism that betrayed any hint of nervousness—and her eyes flickered.

'I am Mrs Munroe.'

'No. No, that's not right at all,' Anthony snapped. 'Mrs Munroe is a widow of some advanced age from

Scotland. My solicitor told me so after he employed her on my behalf.'

Amy's eyes filled with the fire that had once had the power to make Anthony her devoted acolyte. Her fine brows rose into a pair of Roman arches.

'I take exception at the description of *some advanced age*. However, to your solicitor I suppose any woman over twenty-one is practically elderly. I am Mrs Munroe, and my husband was Scottish. He is dead, therefore I am a widow from Scotland.'

Anthony looked her up and down, not caring that it was the height of rudeness. She was dressed in a high-necked gown of black with black buttons from the waist—still alluringly narrow—to the collar. The dress was plain, save a fringe of black crepe where the bodice joined the skirt. At her throat she wore a black velvet ribbon with a pendant of Whitby jet.

Widow's weeds, sure enough.

The blood drained from his legs, leaving him a husk.

'You married?'

It shouldn't matter. Their romance had ended long before she'd become another man's wife, but he couldn't suppress the surprise in his voice. He hoped she didn't hear the hurt her words caused him.

'I did. My husband passed away almost two years ago. He was older than I was and his heart failed him.'

'My condolences,' Anthony murmured automatically, thinking how often he had been the recipient of those words himself since the death of his wife, Henrietta, five years ago.

'Papa! Papa, can we come out now?'

'Papa, I'm cold.'

'Papa I need a drink.'

'Rose keeps pushing me!'

Anthony turned his attention back to the Clarence. Dash it all, seeing Amy again was enough to make Anthony forget his own children!

'Your telegram didn't mention children,' Amy said.

'I was saving money,' Anthony explained, perhaps a little more defensively than necessary. He'd always had to be careful with money and his imminent change in financial circumstances had not changed that. Amy nodded in understanding.

'Of course. Shall we go inside? I have instructed Kitty to light the fire in the study, which I have taken the liberty of using for my cataloguing work. If your children are cold they are welcome to make use of my own sitting room. Mrs Carey is preparing lunch for twelve o'clock.'

She spoke briskly, her tone a reminder that this was a business call, not social. Amy Pritchard had run her father's household with complete proficiency, ensuring the poet had had no mundane worries to interrupt his creative flow. She clearly devoted the same talents to running this household.

'Thank you. Children, you must get out and come inside quickly into the warm. I don't want you catching chills.'

Anthony opened the door of the coach. It was starting to snow. Only a flake or two, fortunately, but the weather was considerably more wintery in the hills. The children climbed out and Anthony's throat tightened with adoration that had not altered since the day they were born. The children were unaware of their father's devotion, and both gazed up at the house.

'Is this our house, Papa? It's like a castle...' breathed Rose.

Anthony met Amy's eye. They exchanged a smile

that Anthony was pleased to note seemed a little more genuine on her part.

The original grey stone house was over a hundred years old. It was two storeys and double-fronted, but seventy years after construction the owner had built a wing on one side. Now it was an L-shaped building with a hexagonal tower room elevated above the vertex. Aunt Violet had used the tower to house the souvenirs of her myriad travels.

'I thought the same the first time I saw it as a child,' he told his daughter. 'It will be ours, though I'm not sure we will ever live in it.'

The children made noises of disappointment. Anthony ignored them and followed Amy through the front door.

He had misjudged her. Believed she had loved him. Believed their frequent talk of weddings and married life had indicated she would accept his offer. But she had refused even to meet him in person to hear his proposal and it had pained him more than Amy could ever possibly know. If he had loved her less than he did, he might have disobeyed her instruction never to mention it again and pleaded with her to explain her abrupt change of heart. Even though it had broken his heart, he had obeyed her plea and left that very morning.

He looked around the hall, feeling discomposed. It took him a moment to realise what was troubling him: there were no Christmas decorations.

Windcross at Christmas had always been a joyous occasion. Aunt Violet and Miss Gough had insisted on every room being festooned with garlands, baubles, branches of holly and candles. In the alcove beside the staircase there would always be a fir tree of the variety Prince Albert had made fashionable—it being a source of indignation to Miss Gough that Queen Charlotte's role had been overlooked. In his memory, they were there, so it was with disappointment that he noted their absence. It did not feel like Christmas here.

A streak of grey and white appeared from the landing. It flew down the staircase and passed between Anthony's legs. It caused him to both forget his dark musings and break into a parody of a dance in order to avoid trampling on it.

'A cat!'

Amy turned back and realised what was happening. She scooped the animal into her arms with a repeated sucking of her teeth that was obviously meant to signal affection. The cat—a tom Anthony decided, on looking into its eyes—settled over her shoulder and gave Anthony a haughty glare of possessiveness. Rose discarded her doll and threw herself towards the animal.

'Don't touch it,' Anthony commanded. 'It could be mad, or worse, and it probably has fleas.'

Amy gave him a sharp look. 'Cornelius is completely clean and perfectly safe for a child to touch.'

'Father won't let us have a pet,' Oliver said. 'He says they may cause harm.'

Amy frowned. 'Nonsense. An animal will only cause harm if it thinks it may receive it in return. Here, young Master Matthews, hold your hand out with the palm down and tickle him behind his ears like this.'

She demonstrated but, before Oliver could follow her instructions, Anthony spoke out.

'Mrs Munroe, I will thank you not to contradict me regarding my wishes for my family.'

'Of course, Mr Matthews, please accept my apologies. I assure you, though, the children will be perfectly safe playing with the cat as he is an old and well-mannered gentleman.'

'Ple-e-e-ase, Papa,' Rose wheedled.

Anthony reluctantly allowed Amy to pass the cat into Rose's waiting arms and the look of joy on his daughter's face was almost enough to quench his worries.

Amy smiled but it looked forced. 'I am sure you would like to begin our interview as soon as possible so that you may be on your way at your earliest convenience.'

She obviously wanted rid of him and that suited Anthony to the ground.

'You're right. Shall we proceed?'

He followed Amy through the familiar hallway and along the corridor into Aunt Violet's study. Fashions had changed since he had last seen her. The silhouette had become narrower and the waist was lower. It suited a short woman like Amy much better than the wide skirts of her youth. Her figure was still excellent, with a straight back and narrow waist.

He'd wrapped his arms round that waist so many times that the undersides of his arms tingled at the memory. He flexed his fingers to rid himself of the sensation.

'Would you prefer tea or coffee, Mr Matthews?'

He asked for tea and watched as she wiggled the button for the bell.

'It still sticks, I see,' he observed, giving her a smile. She merely nodded then took a seat on the adjacent corner rather than opposite. Three leather-bound books were placed beside each other. Amy began speaking the instant she was seated, leaving Anthony no time to converse.

'In this ledger I have all the accounts containing the

weekly expenditures since I took charge of the house. The other is income from the land and two cottages which are rented out. The green journal is my inventory so far of your aunt's belongings, with notes I have taken the liberty of making. I believe you will find everything in order but, if you wish me to leave you to peruse them in private, I will of course be glad to.'

Glad to leave his presence, Anthony thought. Even as she spoke her hands were moving to the arms of her chair and she was leaning slightly forward, as if preparing to rise. Yet again he was hit by the impression that she really did not want to spend time in his company.

It stung. Whatever imagined slight had caused her to break off their relationship, it was unfounded. Out of sheer bloody-mindedness he sat back in the chair, drawing the closest ledger towards him.

'I am perfectly happy for you to remain here in case I need to query anything.' Realising as he said it that it sounded insulting to her, he added, 'But I'm sure I won't.'

He took his spectacles from their case in his pocket and put them on. This indication of fading eyesight was a recent enough development for him to still feel conscious of it. He glanced at Amy, though why he cared what she thought was beyond him.

She tilted her head to the side and gestured to the case. 'I find it takes me three attempts to thread a needle nowadays,' she said.

The confidence was presumably intended to commiserate with him, but it merely made Anthony feel old. He opened the ledger and gave a cursory glance over the columns and rows written out in a neat, slanted script. Examining the finances was one of his reasons for being here, but he found he had little interest in doing so while he was so acutely conscious of Amy's cool gaze on him.

A knock on the door heralded the arrival of tea. The maid deposited the tray on the edge of the desk and left with an efficient bob. Unasked, she had brought two cups. Anthony gestured to them.

'Will you join me, Mrs Munroe?'

Amy poured.

'Lemon or milk?'

'Have you forgotten?' he asked.

She pursed her lips. 'Your tastes might have changed.'

Anthony added a lump of sugar to his cup and helped himself to two slices of lemon from the dish. He offered the tongs to Amy.

'No, thank you.'

She poured milk into her cup and took a sip.

'*Your* tastes have changed,' Anthony remarked. 'You used to take your tea like I do. In fact, it was you who first taught me how pleasant it was.'

She gave him a sharp look. 'You misremember. It was my father, not I. He insisted that tea should be drunk sweet with a slice of lemon.'

'My apologies,' Anthony said. 'It is a long time ago. I'm sure I misremember all sorts of things.'

He hadn't meant the comment to sound as biting as it did, but Amy stiffened. She put her cup back in the saucer, which she held in her left hand, elegantly balanced on her fingertips.

'I started drinking mine with milk as a tiny act of rebellion against my father.'

Anthony grinned then grew serious, wondering why she had felt the need to rebel against such an inconsequential matter.

'What are you doing at Windcross, Amy?' he asked.

She looked surprised, her fine brows rising. She took a sip of tea and put her cup back in the saucer again. When she spoke, she kept her eyes on it, staring intently.

'I needed employment.'

'Why do you need employment?'

Amy looked up from her tea. Her face was hard, her eyes challenging him to press the point. It was an aspect of her character he had never seen in her youth.

'Mr Matthews, you are my employer, and as such are entitled to know some of my affairs, but not all. I must decline to answer you.'

Anthony dropped his gaze first, though he would never tire of staring into Amy's eyes. She'd had no cause to be hard when she was younger, and seeing coldness directed at him hurt much more than it should after so long. With a stab of his heart, it struck him that the hardness was directed at the world in general.

Her circumstances must have altered drastically if she was now required to take up a post as housekeeper. Septimus Pritchard had lived in a modest house, as he said befitted a poet who cared nothing for the material pleasures of the world, but his table had been laden with the best produce Derbyshire could supply, and he had kept his own carriage and four servants. Amy would have been a rich woman on his death and should have been independent.

Anthony imagined her late husband burning through Amy's inheritance before leaving her destitute. At the time, he'd tortured himself with the idea that she had rejected him because he had little wealth and no career to speak of. He should feel at least a measure of triumph that she had gambled on snagging a husband with better prospects than Anthony had had and lost.

Instead all he felt was an unexpected surge of protectiveness towards her. She looked defensive and Anthony wanted to defend her.

'My apologies. I didn't mean to pry. Please tell me, though, why Windcross in particular?'

'I wished to return to Derbyshire after living in Scotland for so many years. I saw the advertisement you had placed.' She leaned forward and fixed Anthony with another penetrating look. He found himself leaning forward to her, the old habit of sharing confidences and intimacies coming back to him unsettlingly easily. Her eyelashes fluttered and she sat a little straighter.

'I know you must find it strange, and I offer my apologies for the surprise I obviously gave you. I was assured by your solicitor that you would never visit the house and that we would not come face to face.'

Anthony sat back. 'You specifically asked that?'

'I did not believe it would be wise for either of us. The past...'

She pressed her lips together, whitening them in the process and concealing the fullness. Anthony's stomach lurched. He'd kissed those lips so often that, despite not having thought about Amy for years, he swore he could remember the exact curvature and the scent of her skin.

'And yet here we are,' Anthony said.

The fire was starting to thaw the chill from his bones and he was feeling more like himself. He could face the thought of his second objective, which was walking down the valley to the churchyard to visit Aunt Violet's grave. Weary of the awkwardness, he pushed himself to his feet and piled the ledgers one on top of the other. He would take them away with him, read them at his leisure and have them posted back in the new year.

'Though we do not need to be any longer. If you would show me where my children are, I shall give them a tour of the house until lunch is ready. You may go about whichever of your duties you see fit.'

He walked past her out of the room, and once in the freshness of the unheated passageway he leaned against the wall, heart pounding.

It struck him only at that moment that he might have misinterpreted Amy's eagerness for their meeting to be over, and it was in fact her guilt that caused her to wish him gone. She must have felt some stab of conscience at having jilted him without even having had the decency to speak to him in person. That could have resurfaced now they were finally face to face. He had been the injured party, so it felt deeply unfair that he felt as drained and shrivelled as a child's India rubber balloon.

## Chapter Three

The snow began to fall heavily over lunch. Anthony and the children ate in the dining room while his coachman joined Amy and the Windcross staff at the large table in the servants' hall. 'Hall' was too grand a word for it, really. When the house had had a full complement of staff, this would have been where the female members spent their evenings. Now it housed a table big enough for eight to eat around and four cosy chairs by a fireplace.

The coachman, a native of Matlock named Samson, was gloomy. 'I didn't like some of these hills coming up and it won't be good in snow going down. If we aren't careful, we'll get stuck and the horses will catch a chill.'

'I'm sure Mr Matthews will be eager to leave as soon as he has eaten,' Amy assured him. She studied her chicken soup. He had seemed as ill at ease as she had been but, now their awkward interview was concluded, she felt relief and a little pang of sadness for the past that had never happened.

Rather than leaving immediately as Amy expected, after lunch Anthony expressed his intention to go into Priestclough and visit his aunt's grave in the churchyard. Priestclough would be accessible for now, but it was common for the village to be cut off at this side of the valley.

'Shall I tell Samson to ready the Clarence?'

Anthony looked out of the dining room window which had an aspect over the hills. The snow had begun to fall thickly and was settling on the lawn and drive.

'I think I'll walk and let Samson warm himself a little longer. He's got quite a drive ahead of him for the rest of the day. There used to be a path from the back gate of the gardens that led to the village. Is that still there?'

'It is.' Amy looked away. They had frequently walked together along it in happier times. She wondered if he was remembering that too because he gave a little cough and turned to the window.

'Rose. Oliver. I want you to pay your respects too. Hats and gloves on quickly.' The children sloped off, grumbling slightly at the thought of going out in the cold. Anthony turned back to Amy.

'Mrs Munroe, I wonder if perhaps you would care to accompany us and pay a visit to your father's grave at the same time?'

He couldn't really want her to join him. He was only being polite but his consideration was touching. However, she had no desire to visit her father's grave.

'Thank you, but no,' she said quickly.

'Of course.' Anthony's jaw stiffened. 'I shouldn't presume to take your time or direct your activities. No doubt you have other things to be doing.'

Amy's afternoon was free. She had devoted the entire day to her employer's visit. He would undoubtedly attribute her refusal to her not wanting to spend time with him. Although the thought of walking with Anthony down the path that had brought so many happy moments made her sad, that was not her main reason for refusing.

If only Anthony knew that the sight of Septimus's elaborate headstone was a knife to Amy's guts, reminding her of his selfish vanity. The grand headstone in a prominent place had been paid for before Amy had discovered how little money she had inherited. The time for intimacies was long past and she had no intention of sharing the true reason with him. She didn't wish to part with a bitter taste between them, however, so thought of a concession.

'Would the children like some mincemeat tarts to take with them in the coach? I can have Mrs Carey make up a basket.'

Anthony's eyes softened. 'Thank you. That's very kind. If it is not too much trouble.'

'Not at all. Your aunt had seventeen jars of mincemeat in the pantry so Mrs Carey has been indulging her love of Christmas flavours by using up the preserves.'

They faced each other, the atmosphere awkward. Anthony thrust his hands into his pockets. 'Right! I should be going.'

He left the room and soon Amy heard the front door closing. She walked to the window and saw the three of them picking their way gingerly down the gravel path to the bottom of the garden. She spent the next hour in the kitchen, drinking tea with Mrs Carey and making up the promised basket of pastries. When the grandmother clock in the hall chimed three, she began to grow slightly anxious for their whereabouts.

The walk down to Priestclough should take no more than twenty minutes at a brisk pace. Coming back up could take double, but two hours was excessive to stand at a grave, speak a few words or a prayer and return. The snow was now falling thick and fast and the sky was grey, shrouding the hills in white. Anthony knew the area, having visited so frequently, but the snow could make the hills treacherous and most of his visits had been in spring or autumn.

The first thing she knew of their return was a hammering on the front door. Kitty rushed to open it and swirls of snow followed them into the house and began to melt on the rug. Anthony stamped his feet, leaving more snow, then hugged Rose to him. The child was shivering and looked close to tears.

'That was harder than I expected.'

'You've been such a long time. I was getting worried about you,' Amy said.

'Were you?' His eyes creased at the edges, creating fine lines.

Amy's stomach swirled as violently as the snowstorm. Was that wrong to admit?

'Come in and get warm. Kitty, put the kettle to boil and tell Mrs Carey to heat some milk for the children. Mr Matthews, we have brandy in the kitchen, or whisky in the dining room, if you would prefer a glass to tea.'

'We don't have time for that.' Anthony brushed snow from his shoulders then turned to Rose and vigorously started to shake the hem of her cloak, sending more snow flying. 'We have a long journey ahead of us and we need to get off the hills before dark.'

He might as well not have spoken as the children were already rushing into the dining room and stretching their hands out to the fire.

'If you have a long journey, that's all the more reason not to leave before getting warm,' Amy said. 'At least give the children something hot to drink before you go.'

'Very well,' Anthony said. 'In which case, I will take

a whisky. I assume it is the remainder of Aunt Violet's Lochnagar?'

Amy confirmed the provenance and Anthony helped himself to a generous measure from the decanter in the lacquered *chinoiserie* cabinet. While the children drank their milk, Anthony paced around the room restlessly, occasionally glancing out at the worsening conditions.

Amy watched from the doorway, her eyes following Anthony, however much she might try to look elsewhere. He was still lean, though had the beginnings of a slight paunch to his belly that suggested too many good luncheons and too little exercise. His beard was closely trimmed around a jaw that was still sharp and a smattering of grey matched the colour at the side of his temples. He was still a fine-looking man, and she was surprised that a flame of desire managed to ignite beneath the indifference in her heart. She felt nothing for him. Nothing at all. She would not allow herself to start now.

Anthony caught her eye. She looked past him quickly, and at the window, embarrassed to have been caught staring. She hated to think he might realise she still felt anything, even a slight acknowledgement that he had aged well.

'I don't think the snow is going to stop,' she remarked.

He shook his head. 'My timing was dreadful. I felt obliged to visit Aunt Violet's grave, as I have not visited since her funeral, but I did not consider the elements. I think in future I shall arrange to coincide with the day she passed away.'

'You will be coming back?' Amy's stomach clenched.

Anthony's eyes flickered briefly before meeting Amy's again. 'Not frequently, I imagine. Once matters of probate are settled, I shall most likely sell Windcross. Are you content to continue working here until then?'

The visit had been full of awkward moments and in truth she wanted nothing more than never to set eyes on him again. She struggled to grasp at the detachment towards him that she had cultivated, but it was harder now he was standing in front of her, showing consideration for her wishes. Matters should be concluded within a year, and if she only saw him again on the anniversary of his aunt's death she could endure that.

'If you are happy to continue employing me, I am happy to stay,' she answered frankly.

He looked relieved.

'I shall, naturally, notify you when the house is to be sold so you can make whatever arrangements you need to. That is, regarding your future position. I don't know—'

'Thank you, I'm sure you will give me more than adequate notice,' Amy interrupted. When Windcross had new owners, that would indeed raise the issue of Amy's future, but she would not worry about that now, and that was not Anthony's concern.

He held out a hand and she shook it. It was the first time they had touched in almost fifteen years but the weight of his hand and the warmth of his skin was disconcertingly familiar. When she took her hand away she consciously had to not curl her fingers into her palm to feel the place he had touched her.

As the Clarence drove away Amy caught a last glimpse of Anthony as he turned his head and stared out of the window. His face was inscrutable, but Amy assumed that he was as relieved to have the meeting over and done with as she was. She went back into the study. Kitty was busy tidying away the tea things and waving a duster over the desk top.

'So that's Mr Matthews, is it? Not a bad looking man, for all that he's old. My mum used to wait at table here when old Miss Chase was alive and she said he was fine looking. My mum said he got sweet on a young lady when he visited but nothing ever came of it.'

Amy banged the chair down abruptly. 'Kitty, you should not talk of your employer in such a way,' she snapped.

Kitty looked taken aback. Amy rarely had to raise her voice to the girl, who was turning into a very adequate maid. Kitty mumbled an apology and scurried out with the tray. Amy sank into the upholstered chair that Anthony had occupied. She felt drained after holding her composure in check during the visit and her resilience was diminishing.

Anthony clearly had not been sweet enough to follow through with his idle talk of marriage. He hadn't even had the courage to say goodbye in person when he had left Windcross. The mystery of what had so suddenly changed his affections had gnawed at her for years. She had done nothing personally to warrant it, she was certain. She had concluded that a poet for a father-in-law was not enough of an incentive for an ambitious news journalist. Thank goodness he had never married her and discovered her financial situation once it was too late!

She closed the door of the study and left. Anthony had taken the ledgers, and until he returned them in the New Year there was no need for her to be in there. It was almost Christmas, and Amy was determined to fill her time with pleasure and not dwell on the past that had never been. She had spent one Christmas fifteen years ago mourning Anthony and was determined that she would not do it now. He would be out of her mind just as he was out of her sight.

The late afternoon was Amy's favourite time of day. The settling snow muffled all sounds from outside, and her sitting room was cosy and comforting after the trials of the day. She settled by her fire with a plate of the mincemeat tarts and her work basket of ivy leaves and green calico to make Christmas garlands. She hummed carols to herself as she cut long strips and pinned the leaves to the fabric, and gradually her spirits began to lift. More than ever she longed for colour, brightness and company. She couldn't arrange the company but she would decorate all the rooms she would venture into. The house would not look as festive as it had in Miss Chase's day, but Amy would do her best.

Less than an hour after Anthony had departed, the agitated neighing of horses punctured the stillness and Kitty burst into Amy's sitting room.

'They're back, Mrs Munroe. The coach has come back. Something must be wrong.'

Amy dropped her garland into the work basket and hurried through the house. True enough, the Clarence had returned and was coming to a skidding stop in front of the door.

Anthony climbed out before Samson had time to descend and open the door. He was bareheaded and his muffler was wrapped tightly around his face. The two men had a low-voiced conversation. Samson shook his head and Anthony clapped the coachman on the shoulder. It was now dark but, from the light that beamed from the hallway, Amy could tell that both men were soaked from ankle to knee and Anthony's heavy over-coat had mud smeared over one side.

'What's happened?' Amy asked.

Anthony looked at her with weary eyes. He loosened the muffler.

'A large branch has come down across the road just before the turning up to Sternside Farm. We tried to move it, but it was too heavy.'

He leaned into the coach and ushered the children out.

'I helped,' Oliver announced, his eyes full of pride, which reminded Amy of his father.

'I would have done too if Father had let me,' Rose added, frowning.

Amy moved towards the children, arms wide. 'Come inside. You look half-frozen.'

Anthony shot her a grateful look as the children scurried past and into the glow of the hallway, where Kitty was waiting. He shivered but remained standing beside Amy.

'We tried the back lane down into Priestclough, but the snow was too thick.'

Samson was stroking the horses. He looked over his shoulder. 'I'm sorry, Mr Matthews, but I wouldn't risk the horses.'

'Even if we had, I suspect that by now the road out the other side into Cheshire would be too treacherous in the dark. We had no alternative but to wait and return,' Anthony reassured him. He looked back at Amy. 'Mrs Munroe, I very much apologise for the short notice, but it seems we have no alternative but to spend the night here.'

Amy swallowed. Now he said it, it seemed inevitable that would always have been the outcome, and hearing Anthony apologise for wishing to sleep in his own property was odd.

'Of course,' she said. 'I am afraid none of the beds are made up, and the bedrooms have no fires lit, but if you will give me half an hour I can have them ready for you.'

'There is no hurry,' Anthony said. 'I don't intend to retire to bed at this hour. For now, I would like to get the children warm and dry. How long will it take to heat the drawing room?'

Amy thought a minute and frowned. 'No one has used that room since your aunt died, and the large window makes it cold even when the fire has been burning all day. My own sitting room is smaller and I have a fire lit already. If you permit the children to join me in there, they will warm through much quicker.'

Anthony's tight jaw relaxed. 'Thank you, Mrs Munroe. I have no objection at all. If you would be kind enough to take them there, Samson and I will stable the horses. Tell me which room you will put me in, and once we're done I will change into dry clothes. Fortunately, we have a trunk with us, as we have been staying with relatives this past week.'

'The room you used to stay in, I suppose,' Amy said. 'I'm afraid it will be very cold at present, though.'

'I don't mind shivering for a few moments longer,' he said, giving her a smile that was almost a grin and signalled that he was reviving his spirits. 'Now, the children are waiting, and you are starting to turn blue yourself. Get back into the warm!'

He joined Samson and the two men began to unhitch the horses. Amy turned her attention to the two children and ushered them inside.

'Oliver, Rose, please come along now with me.'

She led them down the passageway and into her sitting room.

'Oh! How cosy!' Rose exclaimed. She ran to the mantelpiece where Amy had tied dried flowers and sprigs of holly. 'We have nothing like this in our house. It looks like a Christmas card.'

Amy smiled at the praise. She rarely had visitors. 'Well, hopefully you will be home tomorrow when the big branch is moved, and you can put up your decorations then. It won't be too late.'

Oliver shook his head. He was a serious boy and Amy suspected there was more of his mother in him. 'We never put decorations up.'

'Oh.' Amy pursed her lips at the unexpected insight into Anthony's domestic arrangements. That didn't seem like the man she recalled who had spent one Christmas out gathering baskets of holly to decorate the entrance hall and who had been a firm champion of mistletoe. Oliver's next words both explained the mystery and pulled the rug out from beneath Amy.

'Not since Mamma passed away, we don't.'

'I don't remember ever having decorations,' Rose said.

'Of course not, silly. You were only a baby,' Oliver replied with all the contempt that three years' seniority could bring.

Amy felt for the edge of the chair to support her. Anthony was a widower. She hadn't known. It hadn't even occurred to her to consider why he was travelling with the children and no wife. He wore no mourning garb, but a quick calculation of Rose's age told her the event must have happened at least five years ago, so he was long past the length of time a man was required to display outward signs.

She settled the children on the sofa by the fire and left them briefly to give orders to Kitty and Mrs Carey. She returned to find them inspecting the room. Oliver had found the last mincemeat tart and was looking longingly at the plate, while Rose had discovered the ivy garland and was brushing her fingers over the leaves.

'They're so pretty.' She cooed.

Amy looked around for something to occupy them. She picked a volume of *Tales from Shakespeare* by Charles and Mary Lamb that she had owned and loved since childhood.

'Shall we have *The Tempest* or *The Winter's Tale*?' she asked with a smile. 'Both are appropriate for the weather. Or perhaps *Twelfth Night*, as that is almost upon us. It was always my favourite to read around Christmas.'

The children settled on *Twelfth Night* and Amy began to read it aloud. They all became so engrossed in the story of Viola and Olivia that Amy lost track of time, until a knock at the door announced Anthony's arrival.

'Please come in,' she called.

The door opened and Anthony ventured across the threshold with all the trepidation of an Athenian about to enter the labyrinth. He had changed into a pair of fitted black trousers and tailcoat, along with a stiff-collared white shirt and a black, silk waistcoat with a subtle pattern of dark grey embroidery.

Amy had never seen him dressed so formally and he looked breathtakingly handsome. She felt her cheeks flood with colour and rose to her feet, stepping towards him a little clumsily. He stopped opposite her and for a moment they regarded each other. She felt twenty-two again, seeing him for the first time.

'Mrs Munroe, is something wrong?'

Anthony furrowed his brows and finally Amy found her voice.

'I'm sorry, Mr Matthews, but the meal I have asked cook to prepare won't live up to your attire. It will be a very informal affair. Glazed kidneys, stewed brisket and swedes, followed by spotted dick.'

Anthony glanced down at himself and wrinkled his brow, and a small line appeared down the centre between his eyebrows. 'I make no assumptions, Mrs Munroe. Unfortunately, it was all I had at my disposal that was clean enough to wear.'

'Papa was at a Christmas ball last night at my aunt Rosemary's house,' Rose broke in. 'It was so exciting! Aunt Rosemary allowed us to watch over the banisters for the first two dances. Papa danced with a lady dressed all in white, with red hair just like yours, then another who wore green.'

'That's enough, Rose,' Anthony said firmly.

The girl looked downcast. Her eyes lost a little of the sparkle that they had shown. Clearly this was the most exciting thing she had ever seen.

'It sounds wonderful,' Amy told her. 'Those gowns sound beautiful.' She glanced at her own black dress and felt a pang of envy.

'If you enjoy being paraded in front of half a dozen marriageable women,' Anthony muttered under his breath.

Amy caught his eye and he became engrossed in adjusting his sleeve. Rosemary was Anthony's older sister. She had made an excellent match with a minor member of the aristocracy who had an estate outside Bakewell. Apparently, she was matchmaking her widowed brother, and he did not seem happy about it.

'I'm sure dinner will be perfectly pleasant,' Anthony

said. 'I assume it is your meal we will be sharing? Will there be enough? I would not want you all to go hungry.'

'Oh, yes,' Amy hastened to assure him, 'There will be plenty. Mrs Carey always makes enough.' She paused, considering he might think his employees extravagant or wasteful with the budget he gave them. 'Though she is thrifty, and I have a small appetite.'

'Do you, now?' Anthony said, frowning. 'So you do not consider I am starving you with the allowance?'

'Not at all. You are a most generous employer. None of us could complain in the slightest.'

He acknowledged her words with a brief nod. 'All the same, I feel inspired to write an editorial encouraging all employers to ensure their staff eat suckling pig and lemon posset each night, just in case they have to entertain their employers unexpectedly.'

He smiled and Amy returned it. He was very appealing when in good humour.

'And are you happy with your situation here?' he continued. 'Is this room pleasant enough?'

He looked around the sitting room with interest. His eye fell on a painting hanging over Amy's writing desk and he stiffened.

'You still have that,' he murmured, taking a step towards it.

The picture in question was a spring scene of Windcross from the hills opposite. Priestclough village nestled in the bottom of the valley. In a field below the house, a small couple stood hand in hand beside the distinctive rowan tree that had been split by lightning. Amy had painted it on an excursion with Miss Chase, Anthony and other friends the second year he had visited. The final spring that they had spent together.

'I saw no reason not to keep it,' she said defensively.

'It was one of my better pieces. I was pleased with the colours.'

'No reason not to, as you say,' Anthony said crisply. 'If you will excuse me, I have some letters to write before dinner and shall retire to my study. Might I impose on you to keep the children here for the time being?'

'Of course,' Amy answered.

Anthony left and she returned to reading to the children. She glanced up at the picture, unsurprised that it had caught Anthony's eye. The figures standing under the tree were herself and Anthony, added to the painting at his request. The place was where they'd met frequently and should have met on that December day when he left.

As she brought *Twelfth Night* to its happy, if contrived, conclusion, Amy idly wondered whether she would have the courage to broach the subject of his desertion with Anthony, but knew deep down she would not. What would be the objective? Knowing why he had not come would make no difference now and would make the evening awkward.

Better to let that door remain closed.

## Chapter Four

Morning brought bad news. Anthony woke early, initially disorientated by the weight of unfamiliar blankets, but gradually he recalled he was at Windcross. His pocket watch showed the time as half-past seven. Throwing back the window drapes, he discovered the snowstorm had continued overnight, long enough to bury the wheels of the carriage. It did not bode well for the journey home.

He dressed in the clothes from yesterday that were now dry and found Samson and Mr Carey in the kitchen eating warm bread rolls. Amy was nowhere in sight, which he had to admit was a relief. Her presence was unnerving, throwing up happy memories of times that had promised a future together. He had not made the connection until Rose had described the ball that he had asked auburn-headed Miss Roth to dance first without knowing why. Now he wondered if her hair, so like Amy's, had been the stimulus.

Mr Carey stood as he entered. 'Morning, sir. Are you looking for Mrs Munroe? My wife has taken her up a pot of tea. She usually comes down by eight.'

'No, it is you I was looking for. I want to investigate the state of the road.'

Anthony helped himself to a roll and took a bite without butter. Warm and chewy, it improved his mood and gave him the resolve to step out into the snow drifts.

Mr Carey fetched an axe and together the three men walked along the road to the fallen branch. What would ordinarily have been a brisk twenty-minute walk took over an hour as they had to pick their way through untouched snow that was crisp on top but gave way, so the men sank down to mid-calf. The tree branches were heavily laden and the Derbyshire hills were beautiful. An artist who chose the subject for a Christmas greeting card would sell them in the hundreds, but the conditions filled Anthony with a sense of foreboding. He was right to feel so, as they discovered the branch, fully six feet long, was now buried beneath snow, creating a barrier.

Mr Carey gave it an experimental kick and reported it was frozen fast. 'Even if we could get that out from the snow drift and manhandle it from the road, you don't want to risk trying to drive the carriage through the snow, sir. When we're stuck here, we're stuck.'

It was a gloomy pronouncement and they returned to Windcross despondently. They were all shivering and soaked to the knees. Amy was waiting in the doorway of the boot room with a look of concern on her face that smoothed away as she saw them approach. She was holding a large blanket, which she handed to Anthony.

'I've asked Mrs Carey to heat some brandy to make hot toddies for you all, and there are boiled eggs and porridge waiting for you in the dining room.'

'You wonderful woman!' Anthony exclaimed warmly as the scent of cinnamon, honey and brandy reached him.

He clasped her hands. They were much warmer than his and the heat made his fingers tingle, as if he had plunged them into boiling water. Amy's eyes widened and her lips became a full bud of surprise, the sight of which caused Anthony's heart to thud and sent blood thrumming through his nether regions.

He cursed himself inwardly. Slight shame caused by the stirrings of arousal aside, he had forgotten for a moment that this was not the old Amy, and his words had been too personal. He let go of her hands and stepped back.

'I mean, thank you, Mrs Munroe.'

She took his overcoat and disappeared down the passageway to her sitting room. Someone had brought Anthony's evening dress trousers downstairs and they were hanging over a chair. He gratefully changed out of his wet ones and made his way to the dining room.

Breakfast was waiting on a hot plate beneath silver domes in the centre of the table. As well as the boiled eggs and porridge there were slices of cooked ham, more of the excellent bread rolls and a pot of strong coffee. Oliver and Rose were already eating. Anthony helped himself, brushing aside Rose's scattered fragments of eggshells.

'Mrs Munroe said you went to unblock the road. When will we be going home? Can I walk in the garden before we leave? I want to look at the frozen fish pond,' Oliver said.

Anthony took a swig of coffee. 'I am afraid you will have all the time you wish to look at fish ponds. The road is blocked and will not be accessible until the snow melts.'

There was a firm knock at the door and Amy entered.

'Mr Carey has told me about the situation with the road,' she said. She glanced from Anthony to the children and back at him, with a questioning look in her eyes. Had they always been so green, Anthony wondered, or were they made more brilliant by the black she wore that gave them nothing to compete with?

'I was just explaining to the children. Please, join us. Would you like some coffee?'

He stood and pulled out the chair beside his then, once Amy had sat down, he poured her a cup. She added a generous quantity of cream but again ignored the sugar.

'Mrs Munroe, how long will the snow last?' Oliver asked.

Amy glanced at Anthony again and raised her brows questioningly, clearly checking with him before answering. He nodded encouragement.

'Who can say? Winter in these parts can be hard. It could thaw by tomorrow morning or last a fortnight.'

'Will we starve to death?' Rose asked, turning wide eyes on Anthony.

'Of course not, my pet.' He scooped her up into his arms.

'Rose, your father is right. The larder is well stocked with preserves and pickles. It might not be the most exciting Christmas fare, but you won't go hungry.' She gave the girl a kindly smile. 'Mrs Carey and I are planning to make a ginger cake today, all ready for Christmas. If your father permits it, you might help us.'

Once again, she looked to Anthony for approval.

'Of course,' he replied. 'That's very kind, isn't it, Rose? Say thank you to Mrs Munroe.'

Rose beamed and mumbled her thanks. Amy smiled warmly at the child and a little flame ignited within Anthony. Jealousy too, that he hadn't managed to inspire that warmth in his direction. Then she looked over

Rose's head, bestowed the same smile on Anthony and his legs went weak.

'We should have stayed at Aunt Rosemary's home,' Oliver muttered. 'I could have played with her puppies. She had five black and white ones, and said I might name one, but Papa insisted on leaving.'

His words were directed to Amy but the complaint was clearly aimed at Anthony.

'Thank you, my boy. You can stop your rudeness,' Anthony warned, but Oliver continued.

'He didn't want to have to dance with Miss Moore again but I don't know why. She was very pretty and Uncle William wanted you to marry her.'

'Oliver, I said *enough*!'

Anthony rarely had to speak sharply to the children, but Oliver was spitting out his personal affairs in front of someone who was a complete stranger as far as the boy was concerned.

Amy not being a stranger made it far worse, in Anthony's opinion. He glanced at her but she was buttering a bread roll, tactfully ignoring the argument. He gave Oliver a stern look.

'I think your breakfast is finished. Go back upstairs and make sure your room is tidy. I will ask Kitty to unpack your clothing, as we will be staying longer than expected.'

The children left. Anthony sighed and refilled his cup.

'I'm sorry for Oliver's behaviour. He's a good boy, but he's young for his age, and says whatever nonsense comes into his head.'

'Is your sister matchmaking?' Amy asked. She looked him straight in the eye and he found the urge to unburden himself.

'Completely without my consent and quite by ambush.'

'Was Miss Moore the redhead in the white dress?'

'No.' His cheeks grew warm, taken aback that Amy had remembered that detail. He folded his arms and grimaced.

'I was led to believe the event I was invited to would be an intimate family gathering to celebrate Christmas, not a ball that included every eligible woman in her husband's extended family.'

She wrinkled her brow sympathetically. 'The children mentioned last night that their mother had gone to her rest. How long have you been a widower?'

'Six years,' Anthony said. 'Henrietta died of scarlet fever in the year of the bad outbreak.'

'I'm very sorry for your loss,' Amy said.

Anthony acknowledged her words with a slow tip of the head. 'The grief has eased over the years, naturally, but I still think of her very fondly. She was a remarkable woman.'

'I'm sure she was. I can imagine the sort of woman that…' Amy's eyes flicked away. 'Actually I don't think I can. I'm not sure what sort of woman you would choose to marry.'

A bitter taste filled Anthony's throat as the hurt of rejection long buried bubbled to the surface. Amy should know, as she had been the first example. Part of what had drawn him to Henrietta had been a similar sweetness in manner to Amy. That, and having a father who owned the newspaper he had been hoping to build his career writing for. It was cynical but he had hesitated for long enough before allowing himself to grow close to Henrietta, finally concluding that, if he could not marry the woman he adored, he would marry one he was fond of, who could offer other advantages.

'She was pretty and charming, accomplished and intelligent,' he said. 'I've always liked intelligent women and those who know their own mind.'

Amy's lips tightened and Anthony regretted his words. She had known her own mind. Unfortunately for Anthony, it had apparently not involved marriage to him.

'Do you really have enough food for all of us?' he asked, hurriedly changing the subject to a more practical and less contentious matter. 'I wasn't sure whether you were just comforting Rose—which was kind of you, by the way.'

She thought for a moment, her face growing serious. Anthony took the opportunity to study her while she was distracted. She had the slight beginning of lines at the side of her eyes and corner of her lips, but it looked as though they had been born from repeated humour rather than frowns. She was no longer the youthful beauty who occasionally flitted through his memories, but she was still remarkably handsome.

'You never visited your aunt in one of the worst winters, but every home in the Peak District expects to be cut off once or twice a year. The kitchen is not stocked as extensively or elaborately as it would be if the house was open but, if you are happy to eat plain food, we have enough to see us through a week or two of bad weather.'

'I hope we will not be trapped here that long!' Anthony exclaimed. The prospect of enforced leisure did not appeal, and he could imagine Oliver's and Rose's displeasure at the thought of spending Christmas without the gifts that would be waiting at home or any of their amusements.

Belatedly realising how rude and ungrateful he'd sounded, he added, 'Only because, since Henrietta died, the children and I have spent Christmas quietly. We are used to being at home with only ourselves for company. As far as food goes, I'm happy to eat anything, and the children have plain tastes. After a week of rich dishes at Rosemary's house, last night's steamed pudding was a rare treat.'

'You might not say that once you've had the same pudding at lunch today and dinner tonight.' Amy gave a faint smile then raised her brows and grew serious once more. 'Your children did remark that your house is not decorated. I remember you used to enjoy helping your aunt and Miss Gough hang the holly wreaths when you were staying here.'

The children had told her that! He remembered walking into Amy's sitting room on the first evening after dressing in a chilly bedroom and being enveloped in brightness and warmth. It had felt like an embrace. The kitchen too had transported him to happier times, with the scents of spices and orange peel. He hadn't realised the children minded the lack of such things at home.

'Henrietta used to decorate the house. The year she died, it did not seem appropriate or important to hang garlands and baubles. We never started again.' He bit his thumbnail thoughtfully. 'Perhaps I have been inconsiderate.'

He stood and pulled Amy's chair out to help her rise. She turned and their eyes met. Her hand rested on the back of the chair and her fingers brushed against his. A flicker of emotion deep in his belly caught him unawares, though he could not put a definite name to what he felt. He gave a cough, using his hand to cover his mouth as the excuse to move it away from Amy's. His shirt was sticking to the small of his back despite the temperature in the room being cool, bordering on chilly.

'Mrs Munroe, I am going to change and bathe. Would you arrange some warm water to be sent to my room, and for a fire to be lit in my study?'

It felt deeply wrong to be giving Amy orders. He was unable to do it without making it into a request and almost apologising for the inconvenience of asking.

'I shall spend the morning in the study reading through the ledgers. I might as well make use of the time, and it will save me having to take and return them.'

'Of course, Mr Matthews. Will the children be joining you there or shall I light another fire in the drawing room?'

Anthony pursed his lips. If they'd been at home, Oliver and Rose would have had their own bedrooms full of toys, or be supervised by a governess. Here there was none of that. He floundered and looked at Amy uncertainly. 'What do you advise?'

'I said before that Rose is welcome to join us baking in the kitchen,' Amy said. 'Oliver is also welcome, or he can help Mr Carey chop logs if he prefers a more boyish activity.'

'If it truly isn't a nuisance to you,' Anthony said gratefully.

'Not at all. After all, my employer has given me leave to take a holiday until the New Year, as he will be examining the ledgers.'

The half-smile crept back onto Amy's lips so that she seemed almost playful, and for just a moment she was the laughing girl he had fallen in love with again, giggling over private jokes while the older generation

walked ahead. She gave him a slight curtsy, and left
Anthony shaking his head in bemusement.

There had been glimpses of warmth, such as when
they'd spoken about the children, but whenever either
of them referred to the past he froze, and the air of awkwardness between them was at times as thick as a snow
drift outside. He could only imagine the unease if he
dared to refer directly to the hurt she had caused. His
parents' turbulent marriage had given him a natural
instinct to avoid confrontation, so shutting himself in
the study for as long as he was condemned to be here
was the safest option.

He went back upstairs. Windcross was an odd old
building. The staircase led to the centre of a corridor,
with bed and storage rooms in both directions and on
either side of the corridor. Anthony's bedroom was at
the end, where the original building met the new wing.
Opposite his door was the circular staircase leading up
to the tower and adjacent, in the end wall, was a plain
door. This door separated the family of the house from
the servants whose rooms were all in the later addi-
tion. It struck Anthony as he thought about the layout
that Amy's room was beside his, separated only by that
door. They might as well have been separated by the
Great Wall of China.

He stared out of the window, willing the snow to melt
and set him at liberty. He unearthed his clothes from
the travelling trunk, bathed and changed into a pair of
comfortable, dry trousers and a warm waistcoat. When
he returned to the study, the fire was blazing and he
discovered a fresh pot of coffee waiting for him.

He settled behind the desk and opened the first ledger. It was Amy's record of Aunt Violet's property, and
he spent a fascinating hour reading some of the pecu-

liar objects his aunt had collected over the years, all detailed in Amy's neat script.

*Six teaspoons with carved handles representing apostles*
*A green jade cylinder with rounded ends, possibly Chinese, use unknown*
*Five lace collars from Bruges*
*Assorted glass kugel balls from Germany, purple and green, in the shape of bunches of grapes*

These last objects Anthony remembered from Christmases gone past, when Aunt Violet had hung the heavy baubles on the fir tree where they caught the firelight. It would be nice to see them again and would help make Windcross more festive, as they would doubtless be spending the day there. There was no way of acquiring a tree, and it was too much to expect the whole house to be as inviting and bright as Amy's small sanctuary, but if it was at least a little festive the children would enjoy the day more, and Anthony would feel satisfied that he had made the best of the situation.

All the accounts were in order and Anthony couldn't have been more satisfied. The only thing that gave him a slight moment of unease was where Amy had recorded the weekly food consumption. As he had already seen, the diet of the servants was plentiful but plain. Remembering the lavish meals he had eaten at her father's table, he couldn't help wondering if she missed those days. Was her slim figure a sign of malnourishment or the legacy of her mother? Anthony had never met Mrs Pritchard, who had died when Amy was twelve, leaving Amy to become chatelaine of her father's house.

Anthony forced himself to stop feeling sentimental.

The life he would have offered Amy would have been humble in comparison to the manner her father had raised her in. Starting out as a young writer, he'd earned barely enough to keep himself. It was little wonder she had thought better of their relationship. Now their situations were reversed, and his good reputation as a newspaper journalist was increasing yearly. He wondered if she regretted the choice she had made.

His children's voices blasted his quiet contemplation as their feet thundered past the doorway. The morning had nearly ended and it would be lunchtime before too long. Anthony looked out of the door to see the children vanishing into the Garden Room. Rich scents of nutmeg and sugar wafted from the kitchen, filling his brain with festive memories. He inhaled deeply, closing his eyes.

Rose ran back and threw her arms around him. 'We baked a mincemeat cake and a ginger cake. Now we're going to learn to play Snapdragon!'

She ran off again. Anthony heard a discreet cough. He looked round sharply and realised with a start that Amy was standing in the kitchen doorway.

'Were we making too much noise, Mr Matthews? I do apologise.'

'No, not at all,' he assured her. 'I must commend you on the way you are running Windcross, Mrs Munroe. I doubt I could have found a better pair of hands to place it in. I should apologise for my reaction when I first saw you yesterday. I was unprepared to discover you working for me, when once...'

*When once we might have been husband and wife.*

The unsaid words hung in the air between them. He couldn't resent her for it but it made him sadder than it should have, after so long.

He swallowed. 'I was thinking about what you said

earlier regarding decorations. The house should be brighter and more welcoming. As we will very probably be spending Christmas here, decorating the house would give the children an occupation. Your sitting room looked so festive. I wonder if I could trespass on your time and good nature a little longer to assist them? Do you remember where the glass baubles were?'

'Of course.' She beamed at him, the first smile of absolute pleasure he had seen on her face. 'We'll start immediately after lunch. I'm sure we can promise you quite a transformation by dinner.'

'Thank you,' Anthony said, imagining the bright glass baubles hanging from the picture rails on ribbons. The thought of such festivity prompted him to add impulsively, 'Perhaps you will consider joining us to dine tonight? So you can appreciate your efforts.'

He feared she might refuse and his mind spun dizzyingly back to the moment of her rejection. It still hurt, even after all this time.

Instead she gave him a shy look, tilting her head slightly to one side. 'Thank you. I would like that.'

His frame relaxed. 'Good. Now, I will spend the rest of the day writing. I have a mind for an article about the state of the roads and the need to ensure travellers can reach their destinations.'

Amy smiled again. 'I'm sure it will be very persuasive. I remember your account of the Lancashire cotton boycott. It was inspiring.'

'Did you read that?' His cheeks grew warm at her words. He remembered the piece, of course. His description of the meeting where mill workers had refused to process cotton picked by slaves had been the article which had caught the attention of the senior editors at the *Stockport Gazette*. He and Amy had been separated for six years by then, and to know he had been in her thoughts even slightly made his throat tighten.

Her eyes filled with fire. 'Of course. I thought it was a wonderful article. What those workers did to bring about a boycott against the products of slavery in America cannot be underestimated. You wrote with such passion that no one reading your words—or your account of theirs—could fail to be moved in support of abolition.'

'Thank you, Amy. That is all a writer could ever hope to hear.'

Her eyes widened and he realised in his enthusiasm he had called her by name rather than title. 'I'm sorry. I was forgetting myself.'

He looked into her eyes and saw a strange watchfulness. 'But may I call you Amy from now on? To address each other so formally feels wrong.'

'Of course you may. I agree. It is unsettling to me too,' she said quietly. 'Now, I will leave you to your work and see you at lunchtime. Goodbye… Anthony.'

She walked after the children, leaving Anthony with the sound of his heartbeat thundering in his ears.

# *Chapter Five*

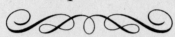

Hearing her name on Anthony's lips made Amy burn brighter than the berries on the holly bushes that grew beyond the garden.

*Don't begin to care for him again*, she cautioned herself as she followed the children into the Garden Room.

His reaction to his sister's matchmaking had made his views on remarriage perfectly clear and, even if he had been keen on the idea, Amy would not be his first choice. He hadn't wanted her when he'd been an ambitious young man and to all outward appearances she had been wealthy. He would most certainly not want her now she was older, and so financially strained she needed to work, and relied on him for bed and board.

Still, their conversation filled her with pleasure. She had caused him to reconsider his indifference to Christmas decorations. She told the children of his suggestion and was greeted with a mix of excitement and incredulity.

'Do you mean Father wants us to decorate the house for Christmas?' Oliver asked.

'Truly?' added Rose. 'But what with?'

'Well, you know I had begun making ivy garlands

last night,' Amy told them. 'We could finish those. There is a box of musical scores with half the pages missing that I put into the cupboard upstairs. We can make lanterns and paper chains with those to hang up, and there are very pretty baubles. If we wrap up warm, we can go and get some sycamore branches and gather some holly from the hills now it isn't snowing. They will look nice in here.'

She gestured to the large vases.

'I like this room,' Rose said.

'So do I,' Amy agreed. 'It was always my favourite.'

After lunch Anthony returned to the study. Amy and the children dressed warmly. Rose twirled in circles in the hallway in her pine-green coat and cried out, 'Decorate me, I'm a Christmas tree!'

Oliver and Amy laughed and told her that, yes, she did look like a tree. Amy's mourning coat was warm, but black felt too sombre, so on impulse she added a scarf of dove-grey threaded through with silver that had been a gift from Cousin Jean. It was the first touch of colour she had worn since Napier's death.

They set out, with Amy carrying a large flat basket and secateurs. Singing Christmas carols as they walked, they joined the footpath beyond the gate and tramped through the deep snow down the old path beneath the garden. The holly bushes had grown wild and before very long they had filled the basket. With Oliver's help, Amy broke off some small sycamore branches and he carried them back with a serious expression. They returned through the gate leading from the hills to the garden.

'What's through that archway?' Oliver asked, pointing to the overgrown rose trellis that led to the lawn in front of the Garden Room.

'There is a fountain and pond,' Amy said. 'There aren't any fish, but would you like to see?'

She led the children down the path. It was slippery with snow and all three of them had to clutch onto each other to stop falling over, causing more laughter. Out of the corner of her eye she saw a curtain twitch in the house but paid it no mind.

The water in the large, circular pond was only two or three inches deep, not even coming up to the stone lip, and had frozen solid.

'Do you think we could skate on it?' Oliver asked. 'Are there any skates, Mrs Munroe?'

'There might be some in the shed,' she replied after a moment of consideration. 'We could look tonight.'

'Father will never let us do that,' Oliver grumbled.

Rose shook her head. 'He will if Mrs Munroe asks him. She persuaded him to let us decorate the house, after all. He does anything she asks.'

Amy hung her head, glad of her deep brimmed bonnet to hide the streak of scarlet that flared across her cheeks.

'Well, I am going to try sliding on it now,' Oliver said.

Before Amy could object, he clambered over the lip of the pond and started to take careful steps. After a few, he grew more daring, skidding his feet and moving in ungainly slides. He looked at his audience with an enthusiastic grin that reminded Amy of Anthony in his youth. She applauded.

'Oh, me too. I want to try it!' Rose exclaimed.

She didn't have the chance because at that moment Anthony appeared, striding down the path with his face like thunder. He was coatless, wearing only his waistcoat and shirt. His study overlooked the garden and he must have been distracted by the noise.

'What on earth are you all doing out here?' he bellowed. 'You could drown! You'll get soaked or freeze to death. Go inside at once, children.'

Amy stared at him, astounded at the fury in his voice.

'The ice is solid, and in any case it isn't deep—' she began.

'It doesn't have to be,' Anthony interrupted. 'They could break a limb or fall and concuss themselves.'

'We wouldn't,' interrupted Oliver.

Anthony rounded on him. 'You know better than to be reckless, my boy,' he said. His face had gone ashen. 'Why are you even out of the house in this weather? How far have you been wandering?'

'Only to the path beyond the gate and the first turning down to Priestclough. We were gathering holly and sycamore to decorate the house,' Amy explained. She lifted the basket and inadvertently caught hold of a holly sprig. She gave a small cry that was more surprise than pain as the pointed leaves pierced her palm and let it fall.

'You're not even wearing gloves,' Anthony exclaimed. He shook his head and left her, following the children back inside.

Amy took a couple of deep breaths before she picked up the basket and made her own way back, but it did little to quell the turmoil she felt. Her eyes stung with impending tears. She had no idea what had caused Anthony to be so alarming in his behaviour. She had never heard him raise his voice. He'd always told her he'd hated the sound of arguments since being a young child.

She put the basket on the table in the boot room and went into the passageway. Anthony was standing in the doorway, his arms folded and his face stern. He turned to go as she entered but she called him back.

He wavered and she recognised the hesitancy in him.

'Don't walk away. For once, tell me what the matter is. Anthony, I don't understand.'

'Mrs Munroe, why did you take my children out of the grounds and down a hill in this weather? Why, by all that is sane, did you let them climb into a fountain?'

'We went to gather greenery—I told you.' She folded her arms. 'You wanted me to decorate the house for Christmas and now you are angry at me for finding the means.'

His face grew incredulous.

'I meant use some of Aunt Violet's baubles and a handful of extra candles! I didn't want you to go out in dreadful weather and get yourselves soaked to the skin. You could all have been lost in a blizzard.'

'What blizzard? The sky is clear.'

He grimaced. Amy chewed her thumbnail. 'If I thought the children would have come to any harm, I would have made them stay at home. I wouldn't do anything to put them in danger.'

'Then doubtless you'd have set out alone and needed rescuing,' Anthony remarked, rolling his eyes.

'Rescuing?' Amy laughed, despite his fury. 'Anthony, have you forgotten how well I know these hills? You're behaving as though I was setting out to the wilds of Antarctica.'

He gestured to her folded arms. 'You succeeded in hurting your hands standing in the garden.'

'Only slightly.'

Without warning he took hold of her hands and held them between his, rubbing vigorously at her chilled fingers. 'These are so cold!'

He turned her palms upwards and ran his thumbs lightly over the small red holly pricks. He lifted them to his face and peered, then stared at her over the top of them. 'No damage, fortunately.'

'I told you so.'

She'd expected him to release her when he'd finished his ministrations, but he kept hold of her hands, with his thumbs settling in the centre of her palms. It had been too long since anyone had touched her like this and she had become unfamiliar with the warm, enveloping largeness of a man's hands. The heat travelled up through her wrists, sparking something inside her she hadn't felt in years. She licked her lips nervously and watched as his eyes widened. She jerked her arms away, unnerved by the awakening hunger growing in her breast.

'I'm a grown woman, not a child, and I know these hills well enough to keep away from anywhere dangerous.'

He scratched his beard and gave her a rueful look. 'You must excuse me. I worry too much about the children. That's no excuse for getting so irate, I know. You should take off your wet coat and get warm by the fire.'

Amy turned to walk to her sitting room, but Anthony caught her by the sleeve and shook his head.

'The study, I think. The fire is larger there and I confess to being slightly indulgent with the logs. It will warm you through much quicker.'

He slipped his hand through the crook of her arm and guided her in the direction of the study, keeping her close to his side. Amy let herself be led. A blanket of warmth enfolded her as she crossed the threshold. There was more: a scent layered over the wood smoke that had the spiciness of sandalwood and an edge of pepper. It took her a minute to realise it was Anthony's cologne. His day spent in the study had imbued it with his presence, eradicating the trace of Amy's lemon balm toilet water. Her cheeks grew hot immediately. She fumbled for the buttons on the front of her coat, but her hands were still cold and a little clumsy.

'Let me help,' Anthony said.

He eased the buttons through the embroidered loops of cord and unwrapped the scarf.

'It's pretty,' he said, running it through his fingers. 'You must be able to leave off full mourning soon.'

His hands continued down the buttons and lingered at her waist. Amy had forgotten in the years since they had been apart how large his hands were. She glanced down. He spread his hands around her with the thumbs at the front grazing the top of her hip bones and the fingers spreading behind.

'I used to be able to almost circle your waist,' he murmured.

A small flame of embarrassment flickered into life at her thickening shape.

'That was so many years ago.'

She didn't know why she felt the need to excuse her ageing. He looked down at her, his lips curving into the lopsided smile that had first caught her eye all those years ago.

'You're still more shapely than many women a decade younger. Trust me, I've danced with enough of them over the past week to make an accurate comparison.'

Amy pressed her lips together. His words were too intimate, and the thought of him with his arms around young women sparked an emotion that was too close to jealousy for her liking. It felt dangerously as if not a day had passed since last he'd held her in his arms. She stepped back out of his reach and, as she did, a small crease furrowed his brow.

'You used to be more accepting of compliments,' he remarked. 'Did your late husband not endow you with many?'

'He was not a man of many words,' Amy admitted. She narrowed her eyes. 'Though when he did speak them it was a guarantee they were sincerely meant, and therefore were twice as treasured as if they had tripped off his tongue like rose petals.'

The crease deepened in Anthony's forehead. He turned away and walked to the walnut and ash globe in the corner of the room which concealed bottles of brandy and whisky. He poured two measures, brought them both back and handed one to Amy.

'I can't help but feel criticism in your words. Was I too effusive with my compliments so that you doubted their sincerity?'

After so many years, Amy should have been immune to the painful memories of his sudden departure. She had been for long enough, but the varnish on her shield seemed to be cracking. It seemed, disconcertingly, that the longer she spent in his company the more the old wounds were opening.

'I do not wish to be teased about the past,' she said sharply. 'I'm not sure what you hope to gain from it. An admission that your words moved me or that they hurt me?'

'That they meant something to you at all,' Anthony said quietly.

'I...' Amy sighed and passed a hand over her brow. The snow had melted, leaving droplets of ice water on her hair. The dampness on her fingers grounded her. 'What are you hoping this line of conversation will prove?'

He shrugged and dropped his head. 'Honestly, I'm

not sure. Perhaps an admission that the way we parted was not ideal.'

'Of course it was not ideal,' Amy snapped. She lifted her head and glared at him. 'It was far from ideal, but what arrogance or insecurity is it that you must have confirmation of the power you had over my heart? I don't understand it.'

'Don't you?'

His eyes flashed, riveting her to the spot with such intensity that she inhaled audibly. He looked down again at the drink in his hand and muttered, 'Is it so incomprehensible I should want to know that our time together meant something to you?'

How could he doubt it? Was that the reason he abandoned her? That he'd believed she was not sincere in her love? She wasn't sure whether to be angry or sad. Either way, she did not want him to realise the effect his words were having on her equilibrium, so she answered in as even a voice as she could summon.

'Yes, it did. And I trust you would answer the same?'

Once again his eyes met hers, only now they were creased and wary.

'Yes. I would.' He abruptly drained his glass and deposited it on the desk. 'You're right. I shouldn't have asked. This is why it is better to avoid talking. We must spend the next few days together and opening old wounds would be unwise if we don't want the time to be uncomfortable. Will you be joining us for dinner, as you said?'

'If you are still happy to have my company,' she answered, the 'have to' stinging. She picked up the glasses and left him.

Oliver and Rose were waiting for Amy outside her sitting room.

'Is Father angry at you?' Rose asked.

'Not at all,' Amy assured them. She ushered the children into her room. 'He was worried for your safety.'

'He behaves as if we are both babies,' Rose grumbled with all the indignation of a child not long out of the nursery.

'That's because he loves you.'

'It's because Mama died,' Oliver said. 'We are all he has. I do wish he would marry someone else and he might be less anxious. And less grumpy.'

'And less sad,' Rose added.

Amy turned her attention to the basket of holly, spreading it out on the table. Hearing such frank but intimate accounts of Anthony felt intrusive, and she had the sense that he would not be comfortable with his children sharing their assessment of him, but her heart jerked painfully at Rose's words.

'Let's make him happy by decorating as we promised,' she said. 'We'll start with the dining room, as he'll see that first.'

The afternoon was delightful. Amy taught them to make paper chains by cutting and gluing strips of paper. The children were full of chatter and excitement as they finished the ivy garlands and cut stars from the music sheets. Whatever Anthony's indifference to Christmas or perceived sadness, it was clear his children were well loved and loved their father back.

They moved into the dining room and hung their work proudly from the picture rails and window frames. Amy pinned the stars to the curtains and laid sprigs of holly along the mantelpiece. When Anthony approached the room at dinner time Oliver was standing sentry to cover his eyes with Amy's scarf before he entered.

Rose guided him inside and Amy removed it. He looked around in wonder then applauded.

'Well done, children. I'm not quite sure it merits your wet boots, but it looks very festive.'

The children ran and hugged him. He smiled at Amy over their heads. 'Well done, Amy,' he said quietly.

His voice was warm, as was the expression in his eyes. Amy stepped towards him, forgetting briefly that she was not a welcome part of the communal embrace. She stopped and Anthony held out a hand to her, inviting her into the family circle.

She took it and a lump filled her throat. She wanted to be part of this warmth. Seeing Anthony and his family threw the reality of her solitary existence into harsh daylight. She had once dreamed of a future with him at her side, of the children they would have, the home they would make. She had no children or family and never would. For the short time over Christmas, would it be so wrong to pretend that this life was hers?

The evening continued to be merry. Dinner was a curry of mutton followed by apple Charlotte. When coffee arrived, despite Oliver's pleading for a cup, Anthony sent the children to play in the drawing room, promising to join them shortly for a game of spillikins.

'Do not play Snapdragon without us,' he commanded. 'I don't want the house burning down.'

'Will you stay and take a cup with me?' he asked Amy.

'I'll stay gladly but coffee keeps me awake until the small hours,' Amy said. Anthony poured his cup and moved to the small sofa beside the fire. Amy hesitated before joining him, taking her half-finished glass of wine. The sofa was an old-fashioned piece of furniture, straight-backed and small. It was designed for two occupants but there was not much space between them.

'The room looks beautiful. Thank you for helping the children,' Anthony said.

'Why did you get so angry at me taking them out?' Amy asked.

Anthony shifted on his seat, simultaneously twisting the cup in his saucer.

'I can tell you're uncomfortable talking about it,' Amy said. 'You always did shy away from things that made you uncomfortable.'

'Did I? I suppose you're right. It's a bad habit, isn't it? I blame my parents for instilling such a hatred of arguing in me.'

'We can all blame our parents for a number of things, but we can't let them follow us for ever. Still, this afternoon you didn't, so that was good.'

His eyes were warm. Amy could have looked into them for the rest of the evening, studying the colours.

'I don't want to hold them back or make them feel obliged to me. But the first moment I laid eyes on each of them they became my most valuable treasures. And of course Henrietta—' He broke off and looked into his cup.

'She always suffered from bad chests in the winter, and summer colds, and she was fearful of the children inheriting her weaknesses. Naturally I acquiesced to her wishes to keep the children protected, and when she died I felt it was my duty to continue. Perhaps I have been too rigorous.'

They faced each other and their knees brushed together. Neither of them moved. The moment should have felt awkward, but they were both in good humour, and Amy felt completely at ease in Anthony's company.

Anthony grinned faintly. 'Do you remember the fashions when we were young? You ladies in your vast crinolines needed a seat like this for yourselves. Whoever thought that was a sensible garment?'

'You men seemed to admire them well enough, from the compliments you gave us,' Amy retorted, returning the grin. 'Mind you, that is the case for every new style. It's impossible to know when you mean it and what it is you think you should say.'

Anthony's eyes grew serious. 'I meant every compliment I ever gave you, Amy. I couldn't write poetry like your father and I know my words must have seemed dull in comparison.'

'Is that what you thought? I never found anything you said dull, and I most certainly didn't want you to be like my father.'

Was that why he had left? Was it possible he'd thought he was inadequate in comparison to Septimus? Had Septimus himself suggested that?

They stared at each other, saying nothing until Anthony gave a gentle cough.

'I should go to join the children. They will be waiting for me, and most likely by now quarrelling and threatening to stab each other with the spillikin sticks.'

He stood and made a small bow. 'Goodnight, Amy, and thank you again for what you did with the children today. You have given me lots to consider.'

Amy watched him leave. Lots to consider, he said. Anthony was not the only one. Her brain was whirring like a zoetrope and she could feel the shape of some revelation just out of reach. Whatever the reason, she suspected she was coming closer to discovering it, if only she could tease it out without causing distress to herself or Anthony.

# Chapter Six

Amy had indeed given Anthony much to think about. Her voice had been so cold when she'd talked about her father that he could scarcely believe she was the woman who had so warmly praised him in her youth.

Anthony recalled how she had not wanted to visit Septimus's grave when he had offered. He had initially believed that had been to avoid his company, but perhaps there was another reason. It worried him that she had been speaking falsely through her smile all those years ago, and if her devotion to her father had been a lie, then what else had been?

His first concern was a more mundane one, however, and as soon as he had finished breakfast he found Amy. She was upstairs in the tower room sorting through a wicker basket. She was noting the contents in her ledger and that tugged at Anthony's brain, though he couldn't for his life have said why.

'Do you think I should let the children skate on the fountain?' he asked.

'Yes, I do,' she replied without hesitation. She closed the lid on the basket. She beamed at him.

'If you intend to, then do it today. The air smells warmer, doesn't it, and the snow might start to thaw.'

Amy put her hand on his arm. 'I'm so pleased you changed your mind. I think there are skates in the back of the barn. Shall we go and look now while it is still light enough?'

He held an arm out but, instead of taking it, she gestured to her gown. 'I should fetch my coat. It's cold, even though the sun is shining.'

'Of course.' He lowered his arm, feeling a little foolish. 'I shall do likewise and meet you in the yard.'

The barn was old and built of stone. Dark, musty and filled with colonies of spiders. Amy and Anthony spent a good few minutes coughing before Anthony had an idea. He returned to the house, spoke politely with Mrs Carey and a few moments later re-joined Amy, carrying tea towels.

'Here, wrap this around your face. Tie it at the back like this.'

He secured his own then held one out to Amy. She took it. As her hands went behind her head, he was filled with a burning need to touch her and see if it invoked the same tremors that he'd unexpectedly felt when he had helped with her coat buttons.

'Let me help,' he said. She turned obediently around and he took the cloth from her hands, brushing against her fingers in the process. Sure enough there was the same frisson of longing that constricted his chest and made his heart beat faster. Her hair was neatly plaited and wound into a low knot on the nape of her neck. He knotted the ends of the tea towel above it, recalling days long ago when he had been permitted to kiss the soft skin of her neck and wind his fingers in the auburn braids that had hung in loops to her shoulders.

She was wearing a fresh, lemony scent that made Anthony dream of spring afternoons, even in the depths of winter. He wondered what she would do if he leaned forward and pressed his lips into the downy hollow at her hairline.

He blinked to banish the image as a shroud of melancholy clutched at him and finished his task. Amy turned and they looked at each other over their makeshift masks. Even with only her eyes visible he could tell she was amused at what they looked like.

'I'm afraid I haven't begun to explore the barn,' Amy apologised. 'I've catalogued much of what was in the bedroom and started on Miss Chase's collections.'

'I know. I read your inventory.' Anthony dragged a box into the light and opened it. 'I wish I had known my aunt in her younger days. She seems to have been quite the explorer.'

'I remember admiring her immensely. She was very intelligent and independent. I wanted to be like her when I was young. My friend Beth and I used to make up tales of her travelling around the world, with princes and sheikhs falling madly in love with her, and breaking their hearts when she left them.'

'Is breaking hearts something you aspired to?' Anthony asked.

'No. I would not readily wish a heartbreak on anyone.' Amy bowed her head. She dragged over an old trunk and knelt beside Anthony. When she next spoke, her voice was exceedingly bright. 'I don't know why there will be skates, though, because I can't imagine your aunt ever skating. She seemed far too dignified for that.'

'My sister used to when we were children,' Anthony

said. 'Not on the fountain, but the pond at Sternside Farm.'

'I don't remember you coming here as a child,' Amy said.

'Quite often. My mother decided early on that she would cultivate the relationship with her sister, as Violet was childless and unmarried, in the hope we would receive a small legacy in her will. It seemed quite mercenary to be so calculating—my father certainly thought so and it was yet another reason for them to argue—but I genuinely enjoyed Aunt Violet's company. Being unmarried, she had no one to argue with, besides Alberta, so it was more peaceful at home, where my parents seemed to find a reason for conflict in any situation.'

Amy put back the contents of her box—half a croquet set—and closed the lid.

'Mercenary or not, it is better to have a true estimation of a person's expectations. Just imagine if you had fostered the relationship only to discover there was no money to be had. How disappointing that would have been.'

Anthony wrinkled his brow. Her words were troubling, and he had a horrible feeling he had stumbled upon a clue for her rejection. Was that why she had so abruptly changed her mind about marrying him? He had not been rich enough then to keep her in the standard she'd been used to. At the time he had been planning to ask for her hand, he'd only been beginning his career and had not made his name, much less a fortune.

He vaguely recalled a conversation regarding investments on a lunchtime picnic that had included Septimus Pritchard. The wealthy poet might have persuaded his daughter that Anthony was not a horse to back. Well, she had gambled and lost, if that was the case.

He looked her in the eye.

'I certainly didn't expect to inherit Windcross. It was a common assumption that my aunt would leave everything to Alberta, who had been a loyal companion, but she died a year before Violet.' He closed his own box. 'You would have hated me if we had met during childhood. I was an abysmal boy. Not at all like Oliver. I would probably have pushed you in the lake or pulled your ringlets.'

'And I would have told your aunt and had you whipped, so you would have hated me,' Amy retorted. Her eyes grew serious. 'You don't hate me now, do you? When you arrived and saw me, you looked so furious.'

Anthony glanced down at his hands so Amy didn't see the burgeoning emotion growing within him. How could she ever think he hated her? Even when her treatment of him had been so unexpected, his primary emotion had been pain at losing her.

'No. I don't hate you. It was a shock to see you there. I could wring my solicitor's neck for not asking for your history.'

'I doubt I would have taken the position if he had,' Amy said. 'I hoped we would never meet. I'm sorry you didn't have more warning to prepare your emotions as I did.'

She looked down at her hands and then gave him a bright smile that he noticed did not quite reach the corners of her eyes. They looked hazel and green in this light, and the shadows lent them a serious expression. Unconsciously he leaned towards her and, as his mind caught up with his body, he realised with a start that he had been preparing to kiss her.

He straightened up. From the way Amy pressed her

lips together, he suspected she had noticed. What he could not tell was whether she would have resisted.

'I think we need to talk about what happened years ago, but not here or now,' she said.

'I agree, especially not in a cold, dark barn.' Anthony stood and brought over another box and opened it. 'Success!' he cried. 'I think there must be a dozen skates here, although I'm not sure how many are pairs. Some of them are in bad condition.' He tipped them onto the floor and they clattered into a heap.

'Look,' Amy said. 'Some of the straps are still in place. The leather hasn't perished in the slightest. I am sure we can use them.'

'We?' Anthony asked.

Amy picked up a pair of blades that looked the right size for her boots. 'I skated once or twice with Napier when we stayed in Glasgow and it was such fun. We can't let the children have all the ice to themselves, can we?'

She laughed at the expression on his face, which he knew must be showing his reluctance. 'Surely you want to test the ice yourself to see if it will bear your weight to ease your mind?'

If Napier Munroe had taken Amy skating, Anthony would not refuse. He gave her a grin. 'As always, you argue in a way that leaves no room for contradiction. Yes, we will try it. I'll ask Mr Carey to clean off a pair for each of the children.'

He selected a pair of skates the same size as his boots, stood up and held a hand out. 'Come along, then, Amy—lead me to my doom.'

'Now?'

'Why not? You are here, I am here, neither of us

have any pressing tasks. Let's seize the moment before I change my mind.'

Amy's smile slipped away. 'No, I would not want that to happen.'

Her voice was quiet and rang a warning bell in Anthony's head. He wondered if she was thinking back to the time when she had so abruptly changed her mind about marrying him. Did she regret it now? And, if so, how long before she had regretted it after they had parted?

'Let's go and try the skates before the air gets too warm and begins to melt the ice,' he said.

There had been another slight snowfall while Anthony and Amy had been in the barn and they emerged under greyer skies. The footsteps left on the path to the fountain from the previous day were slightly covered. He offered her his arm and, even though there was little chance she would slip, she took it.

The way his heart thumped was disconcerting. A further suggestion of her perfume as she leaned against him prompted another organ to awaken from its slumber. It had been far too long since he had climaxed in the company of a woman, rather than alone, and he grew hot at the thought of it, despite the bitterly cold air. He wondered if Amy missed spending the nights in her husband's bed, though he doubted Munroe, at twenty years her senior, would have been a very energetic lover.

'What are you thinking of?' Amy asked.

He jumped a little guiltily. 'Why do you ask?'

She gave him a measured look. 'Your eyes have the faraway look which always suggested you were deep in thought, and you sighed.'

'No particular reason,' he answered, unsettled at her perceptiveness.

He turned his face to the sky, glad of the occasional flurry of snowflakes to cool his cheeks. Snow had settled on the raised edge of the fountain. Anthony brushed it off and they sat beside each other on the cold stones.

'Give me your foot,' he said, holding out the skates. She obeyed and he pulled her leg onto his lap to steady it as he buckled the blades onto the bottom of her boots. The pressure of her leg on his sent ripples through his thighs directly to the most intimate parts of him as he imagined those legs intertwined with his own. If he didn't get control of himself, he would not be able to stand, much less skate!

His fingers fumbled slightly at the buckles on the straps.

'Shall I do yours?' Amy offered.

He shook his head. 'No, but you can help me stand when these are on my feet. I find it impossible to believe anyone could balance on such things.'

She laughed. 'Once you get your balance, you will be perfectly fine. See.'

She stood, wobbling slightly, and throwing her arms out to balance. Anthony reached out to steady her, taking hold of her hands. She smiled down at him.

'We'll help each other.'

'Yes, we should,' he replied. Together they managed to get Anthony standing. Amy took a hesitant step over the edge and into the fountain. She skated into the middle of the ice, hips swaying enticingly, then back to the edge.

'It holds my weight,' she said. 'Come join me.'

Anthony needed no second invitation. He clambered onto the ice. His leg skidded and he wobbled slightly, performing an unintentional turn. Amy put her hand into the small of his back.

'Stand up straighter and bend your knees. Let me show you.' She held herself erect and lifted the front hem of her skirt slightly so Anthony could see her feet. She pushed one foot away so that she glided over the surface then beckoned to him with both hands.

'Now you come to me.'

Anthony gave an experimental kick, swayed and somehow managed to edge forward. He gripped onto Amy's outstretched hands, closing his fingers tightly around hers. She squeezed back and though they were both wearing gloves, and not even an inch of bare flesh had touched, it sent a frisson of longing coursing through him. Her eyes widened and he realised he was not alone in feeling the pull of desire.

'That's right,' she said. 'The more you do it, the easier it will become. Try to go from one side to the other. You can hold the fountain if you find yourself stuck midway.'

Anthony regarded the fountain sceptically. The basin was in the shape of a conch held by a rather pert young woman who seemed to be struggling to keep a toga on, revealing rounded buttocks and the hint of breasts.

'Which bit exactly do you propose I cling on to?'

Amy's answer was a deep-throated chuckle that sent sparks flying over Anthony's scalp and down his neck.

'I'll go first,' she said. She moved with grace over the ice. Anthony watched her go, again transfixed by the way her hips swayed from side to side. Every woman should skate to look her best, he decided.

He edged his way across the ice, ignoring the indecent nymph and instead focusing on reaching Amy. She was waiting with arms open in case he fell. Though he had found his balance, Anthony took the opportunity to take her around the waist and draw her to him. She reached her hands to his shoulders.

'Is that how you would have held the fountain?' she asked, grinning wickedly.

'It seemed a waste when you were so close,' he murmured.

She gazed up at him, her eyes wide and knowing.

'I'm glad you were forced to stay here,' she murmured.

She licked her lips, perhaps intentionally, perhaps unconsciously, but if so she was clearly thinking the same thing that was going through his mind. To kiss her in the way he wanted to would be to risk opening his heart too much, but he could not bear to be this close and not steal one moment. He lowered his head and brushed his lips over her cheek. She lifted her hand and brushed her fingers across his jaw, leaving a trail of searing heat.

He kissed her again, this time on the mouth. She responded by pressing her lips to his.

It was not what Anthony would describe as a passionate moment, but the soft, slow kiss was enough to inflame him and tie his stomach into knots. That she had not refused sent his heart soaring.

Far too soon, however, she pulled away. 'This isn't a good idea' she murmured.

'Probably not,' he agreed. 'I don't regret it, though.'

Amy shivered and rubbed her hands over her arms.

'Are you cold?' he asked.

'Very. We should either carry on skating or return to the house.'

There was a third option. Anthony could hold her tightly and warm her with the heat of his body. He wanted to so badly but did not know how she would react.

'We should go back and give the children the good news that they will be able to skate later.'

They sat on the edge of the fountain and removed the skates then walked back to the house side by side. The narrow path had, in the past, given them the excuse to walk arm in arm, and Anthony wondered if Amy was as acutely aware of the slight gap between their bodies as he was.

'Would you mind if I come back to Windcross again?' he asked as they reached the front door. 'More than just to visit Violet's grave?'

She looked amused. 'It is your house. I have no authority to deny you a visit.'

That wasn't what he had asked, and she must have seen something in his expression because she touched his arm and added, 'Nor would I want to. It would be good to see you again before you sell Windcross.'

That idea didn't seem so appealing now, but Anthony could hardly afford to keep two establishments.

'I'm glad. The children like it here. I'd like them to see it in summer. That's always so beautiful, isn't it? Are you happy to keep working here?'

'Of course.'

He took a deep breath and smelled snow on the air. It did not look as if they would be leaving today or tomorrow, but he discovered that he did not care in the slightest.

## Chapter Seven

The children were delighted with Anthony's news that they could skate. Amy watched as they both squealed with delight and hugged their father.

'Now, you must promise me you will be careful,' Anthony said. 'We will go this afternoon when the weather starts to turn colder again. In the meantime, I shall go with Samson and Mr Carey to see what the road is like. We will begin trying to clear our path to freedom. Oliver, would you like to come with us? A strong young man like you would be a great help.'

Amy watched as the boy almost doubled in stature. His smile was identical to his father's. Anthony clasped him by the hand.

'Then we shall meet in the boot room in a quarter hour and gird our loins to break down the obstructions. We will soon be free of the tyranny of the snow. Amy, Rose, will you wait for the return of your heroes and supply us with cocoa and biscuits?'

Rose had been about to throw a tantrum from the look on her face, but this important task nipped that in the bud. She glowed and assured her father she would. Anthony winked conspiratorially at Amy over Rose's head. Her heart fluttered. He'd always had the power to charm and seemingly it didn't matter about the age of his target. He left, and both children turned to Amy.

'What did you say to him? I know it must have been you, Mrs Munroe,' Oliver said.

'And he called you Amy too. Is Papa going to marry you?' asked Rose.

Amy's joy evaporated.

'I don't imagine so. He doesn't want to marry anyone, and if he did there are many richer and younger women than me.'

'Yes, but he likes you, I can tell,' Oliver said.

'And you like him too, don't you, Mrs Munroe?' Rose asked.

Amy's cheeks began to burn. She couldn't disagree, not after the kiss and the way Anthony had held her. But, even if he did like her, what did she have to offer him?

'Marriage takes more than just liking someone. You have to be suited in so many ways. When you are older, you will understand.'

She clapped her hands briskly. 'Now, Oliver, you must go and help your father, and we shall go ask Mrs Carey to begin baking.'

Anthony and the men returned in good spirits within two hours. They all stood in the kitchen, warming themselves by the range while Rose walked round with a tray of ginger snaps.

Anthony bit into one with enthusiasm then addressed the room. 'We dug out the snow from around the branch. It won't take much effort to move it once the weather gets a touch warmer.'

'The wind is changing and coming from the east,'

Mr Carey said. 'I think we'll have no more snow by tomorrow.'

'So you could be home for Christmas after all,' Amy said.

Anthony shook his head. 'No. Whether or not it thaws, I want to stay here. Our house will be cold and the thought of just myself and the children doesn't appeal as much as it did.'

He took another biscuit and walked round the table to stand opposite Amy. 'If you are happy to have our company, we would love to have yours. *I* would love to have your company.'

Her pulse sped up. His eyes were intense, and she might have been reading more into his words than he'd put there, but it sounded almost as though he was courting her again. He wanted her company. Inch by inch they were pulling down the wall between them. They might be friends again. In time, could they mean still more to each other, as they had once?

'Yes, I would like that very much.'

Over his shoulder Amy could see the children nudging each other and whispering. Anthony followed the line of her gaze and frowned.

'Children, what is the matter? Are you not happy to forgo your gifts for a few more days so we can spend time in company?'

'Of course, Father. We are perfectly happy,' Oliver said, casting a meaningful look at Amy.

'We only want to make sure we get to skate before the weather changes,' Rose added.

'I promised you, didn't I? And you know I keep my word,' Anthony said. 'Now, be off with you and leave me to talk with Mrs Munroe.'

The children ran out, whispering under their breath.

Anthony turned to Amy. 'I have a recollection of some old toys that used to be kept in my room. Skittles, a box of tin soldiers and suchlike. Do you think you could find them? I would like to give the children something to surprise them on Christmas morning.'

Amy readily agreed. An afternoon of searching unearthed a large travelling trunk that contained not only the soldiers but also a spinning top and a couple of books. There was also a leather-bound box, which Amy discovered was a travel writing slope. The glass inkwell was crusted with residue, and a pen nib had become wedged in the hinge, but otherwise the condition was good. The compartment beneath the blotter contained a collection of letters bound together with string, all addressed to Anthony. They must have sat there for a number of years.

She reached for them then drew back her hand. They were not hers to open, but it gave her an idea. Rose and Oliver were not the only ones who would receive a surprise on Christmas morning. She would present the box and letters to Anthony then.

She took the writing slope to her own room then went in search of Anthony. She found him in the study, reading by the fire. He gave her a warm smile as she entered. He'd removed his jacket and was clad in his waistcoat and shirt sleeves with his collar loosened. He looked completely at home. Again, she caught a hint of his woody cologne, and her eyes drifted to his throat, which she suspected was the source of the scent. Her husband's torso had been hairy, but she imagined Anthony would be smooth, and caught herself wondering how different the sensation would be to run her hands over the firm curves of his chest.

'Your father's poetry,' he said, displaying the slim

volume, though she had not asked what he was reading. Thankfully he had interpreted her staring as curiosity.

'He inscribed this volume to my aunt. I don't think I fully appreciated it at the time, but his writing is most… singular. He uses some very bold similes.'

Amy suppressed a smile at his tact in choosing his words.

'Now that he is dead, I can admit my father's poetry was not to my taste. I like happier subjects, than the epic suffering and deaths of mediaeval queens and barbarian kings. Sadly, the literary world agreed, and his final work, *Lupercus and Veleda*, did not receive any praise. I doubt you will find a copy of that here.'

Anthony removed his spectacles. He peered at Amy slightly as his eyes adjusted to the change. 'But you always spoke in such high terms of him. I found your devotion quite laudable.'

She gave him a pitying look, wondering if she was destroying a long-held assumption that women always felt what they said. 'Of course I did. I was a loyal daughter.'

'And his muse, of course,' Anthony said.

She burst out laughing. 'Wherever did you get that idea? If my father had any human muse, it would have been my mother, but in truth he laid all claims of his genius at his own door. I would never have been as presumptuous as to suggest such a thing, and if I had done he would have corrected me most firmly.'

'But I thought—' Anthony began. He broke off and shook his head, looking slightly puzzled. 'Never mind. I might be misremembering. It was a long time ago. Did you meet with success?'

She put the toys on the table, along with a second

box of glass Christmas baubles painted with holly and mistletoe.

'Perfect,' he said. He picked up the spinning top and gave it an experimental twist. It rolled in a half-hearted manner then fell off the table and came to a stop at Amy's feet. Anthony bent and picked it up.

'I never could get the hang of those.'

He put the spinning top back down on the table.

'No wonder you never perfected it if you stop after one try,' Amy said.

'How many attempts at failure should a fellow make?' He looked at her with his head on one side.

Amy picked up the top and whip and sent it whirring across the table in a rapid arc. She raised her brows. 'Eventually the effort will be rewarded.'

Anthony frowned, then laughed. Amy joined in, feeling as if the years had never happened and they were as close as they ever had been. Teasing him like this, her heart felt lighter than it had done in a long time. She spun the top with a flick of the wrist. It whirled off the table and this time they both bent to pick it up. Their eyes met as they were doubled over and for a wild moment of excitement Amy thought he was about to kiss her. He picked up the top and rolled it between his fingers.

'I suppose I always did give up rather easily. It is a fault I should try to correct.'

Amy put the spinning top back in the basket along with the other toys. Anthony handed her the whip. As she took it from him, he took her hand.

'Is there anything you want for Christmas? A brooch or trinket of some kind? Earrings, perhaps? My aunt had some beautiful pieces. You should see if anything catches your eye.'

It was a generous offer but what her heart wanted was not to be bought. Anthony's hand on her wrist had sent shivers through her and ignited thoughts of kissing and more. She missed being touched, and would forgo every jewel in the world to be held by a man who wanted her.

'I couldn't do that,' Amy answered.

'Why not?'

'I would be defrauding the estate. Everything needs cataloguing before it can be disposed of.'

A determined light filled Anthony's eyes. 'The estate can go hang. If you find something you want, tell me. Everything in this house will be mine before too long. I would give you it then, so you might as well have it beforehand. If there is anything within my power to give you, I will. I would like to.'

Amy swallowed. She knew what she wanted from Anthony: the same thing she always had. It was becoming clearer with every passing moment they spent together, but that had never been within his power to give. For whatever reason, he had been incapable of giving her himself.

'Thank you. I will consider it. And now I had better go. Tomorrow is Christmas Eve, after all, and Mrs Carey and I still have lots to prepare.'

The skating was a triumph. Anthony declined to repeat the experience, but the children shuffled around in a slightly ungainly manner, while Amy was more assured. To Oliver's annoyance, Rose was the better of the two. Sensing there was about to be a fraternal outburst Amy offered him her hand.

'Come skate with me, Oliver. I will help you.'

'Can you do that?'

'Of course she can,' Anthony called from the side. He had taken up a post on the edge of the fountain. 'Amy taught me this afternoon. She can do anything.'

'In that case, I will,' Oliver said. He held her hand and together they made three slow journeys around the perimeter. When they returned for the third time, Anthony was standing waiting on the ice.

'Now, Oliver, it's my turn to command Mrs Munroe's attention.'

He held out a hand.

'Papa, you look like you're going to dance,' Rose giggled.

'Perhaps we are,' said Anthony. 'Mrs Munroe, would you do me the honour of dancing with me?'

He moved his arms into the position for a waltz. Heart beginning to pound, Amy pushed herself closer, slightly faster than she'd intended, and banged into him, with her chest against his. Her breasts cushioned some of the impact and she was acutely aware of the throbbing in them that resulted. Anthony made a strange noise in the back of his throat. It sent a shiver through her, much in the way she imagined a small creature felt when alert to a more powerful one nearby.

She looked into his face and saw the same hunger there that she felt within. She caught the scent of Anthony's cologne and inhaled unconsciously. She licked her lips and his pupils widened. He lowered his head towards her. For one, dizzyingly thrilling moment she thought he was about to kiss her, but then he must have recalled they had an audience, because he straightened up.

'I'm not sure people are made for dancing on ice,' she murmured.

'Perhaps not.'

A gust of wind blew. Rather than scraping at Amy's skin, it caressed her cheeks, warmer and gentler than it had done for days. 'The weather is changing. It's going to get warm, as Mr Carey predicted. The ice will begin to melt.'

'Then we had better make the most of the time we have.' Anthony took her in his arms and began to step slowly on the ice, leading her through the steps. She had to do nothing more than remain upright and hold onto him. The thin blades felt precarious but, with Anthony holding her, she had no fear she would fall.

'I'm tired of skating. I want to go build a snow man,' Oliver said.

'You would do better to master the task you have started,' Anthony told him, glancing briefly over his shoulder before returning his attention to Amy.

'I don't want to. I might ask Samson to fight me with snowballs,' Oliver replied.

'Very well, off you go. I shall stay here a little longer,' Anthony said. He looked gravely at Amy. 'I've spent too much of my life giving up on things too soon. I intend to change that and see things through until I am satisfied with them.'

Amy's skin fluttered. The children might only think he was referring to skating, but she suspected a double meaning. Was he hoping to resume their previous intimacy? She was being foolish to allow herself to care about him again. She could tell herself it was purely physical attraction she felt but she knew that her heart was in danger of becoming his again. She dropped her hands, doing her best to ignore the look of confusion on his face.

'I think we should all go back before we get cold.'

Anthony put his hands to her shoulders and rubbed them down her arms. 'Are you cold?'

'Not yet, but I am anticipating that event, and would rather prevent than cure.'

She skated to the edge of the fountain and sat down. Anthony remained where he stood, his face pensive. He was not the only one who could speak in layers and she could see he was musing on hers.

# Chapter Eight

The children raced ahead to build a snow man, leaving Amy and Anthony to walk back together. Anthony took his time, linking arms and holding her close. He almost risked putting his arm about her waist, but that was too intimate in front of the children, who he suspected were keenly watching the pair of them.

They had created a small mound by the time the adults reached them. Amy applauded and pointed them in the direction of the coal shed to find suitable eyes.

'Did you never have children of your own?' Anthony enquired.

'No. We would have been delighted but it never happened in all the years we were married. We never found out why.'

'I wasn't sure. Your husband was older, you said.'

Amy burst out laughing. 'Napier was twenty years older than me, not fifty. Our intimate life was highly satisfactory.' She tilted her head to one side and gave him a coquettish look. 'Did you imagine that he was too old to enjoy the marital act?'

Anthony's jaw tightened. He had been hoping Amy's marriage had been chaste but clearly he was wrong. The idea of another man, even one now dead, making love to her made his flesh prickle unpleasantly. He knew such unwarranted possessiveness was a poor show, but he couldn't help himself. Amy stepped closer to him. He could feel her breath on his cheek and it made his throat constrict.

'Do you suppose ten years from now you will have no interest in making love?' she asked.

'I haven't given it too much thought,' Anthony lied.

'Really?'

Amy gave him a measured look that suggested she recognised it for the falsehood it was.

'And what of you?' he asked.

She smiled. 'Oh, perhaps I shall be like your aunt and take a series of lovers.'

She laughed, presumably to show she wasn't being serious. Anthony joined in but inside his stomach was tightening unpleasantly. He'd lost Amy once and now, being with her again, he found the idea of letting her slip away again unbearable. Anthony wondered how much she still mourned her husband and what would happen if he decided to court her after her period of official mourning was ended.

Would she reject him as she had once done, now she had no other means of support? Would he ever truly believe that she wanted him for himself, not what he could offer? More crucially, did he have the courage this time to pursue her anyway and risk getting a broken heart for the second time?

Though the topic of her marriage had arisen in dark circumstances, Anthony finally had an excuse to satisfy his curiosity. He burned to discover what Amy's husband had been able to offer her that he had failed to, even though his pride was most likely to get a bruising.

'Will you tell me about him? How did you come to meet and marry?'

'Napier attended my father's funeral. He had been a junior master at the school my father briefly taught in. He was a botanist and needed a secretary to keep his notes and write them up. When he learned that I was in need of employment, he offered me the position.'

This was unexpected. He had assumed Napier had been the cause of her poverty.

'Why were you in need of employment? Your father had no other beneficiaries, did he?'

'There was nothing to inherit. My father was deeply in debt. When he died I had to sell the house and we had barely enough to cover the death duties. I was left with a legacy from my mother of twenty pounds a year, which was not enough to live on.'

Anthony felt relief wash over him. He'd initially been crushed to discover Amy had married after rejecting him, but now he understood it had been necessity, and not until after her father had died. It was a little mean-spirited of him, but his self-esteem grew, knowing it had not been a better man than him who had enticed her to break free of her obligations to Septimus.

He held his arm out for Amy and they began to walk back towards the house. His senses felt heightened. He was acutely aware of all the places their bodies touched and where the spaces were. Amy was taller than Henrietta had been, and not quite as delicate. He didn't feel the same urge to shelter her as escorting his wife had incited. The feelings that Amy aroused were more primal. He wanted to carry her to his bed, tear off the severe mourning dress and make love until they were both incapable of moving or speaking.

Unaware of his erotic fantasies, Amy carried on speaking.

'Fortunately for me, Napier's research was interesting. I learned a lot about Highland grasses and thistles. I could regale you for hours if you are ever short of something to fill your evening. Napier and I got on well, and after six months he concluded that keeping a wife was just as easy and more advantageous than paying bed, board and wages for a secretary.'

'How romantic,' Anthony said drily.

He considered the timings. Septimus Pritchard had died in March 1863 but Amy had not married Napier Munroe until the autumn. Henrietta had died in May. That meant there had been a period of five months where they would both have been free to marry. If Anthony had returned to Priestclough during that time and tried to court Amy again, would she have been open to his proposals? How different their lives might have been if he had done so.

Amy rolled her eyes at his clumsy jibe. 'He was, in his own way. People talk of the Scots as being dour, but he was anything but. If he had been a serious man, I could never have married him. We celebrated Christmas, Hogmanay, Burns Night…'

Was that a tilt at him for his lack of Christmas cheer? Probably not, but he felt it all the same.

'I'm glad your husband made you happy,' he said.

Amy's eyes grew grave. 'He was a kind man and I was very fond of him.'

Sentiments very similar to Anthony's feelings for Henrietta. Anthony opened the front door and allowed Amy to pass before him. The children's coats and boots lay in a heap by the staircase and the sound of a riotous game of some kind echoed along the corridor from the sitting room. Anthony winced, as there was a thud that sounded like a ball rebounding off the door.

'Oliver and Rose are both fine children,' Amy said. 'They are a credit to you and your wife.'

Anthony bowed his head, feeling slightly guilty about where his imagination had previously taken him. He had given little thought to Henrietta over the past few days and now he was imagining undressing Amy.

'We only had a few years together. I'm not sure Rose even remembers her mother. It appears neither of us were very fortunate in our marriages,' he observed.

'Don't say that,' Amy responded. 'We were both fortunate to find people who cared for us and who made us happy for the brief time we had them. Don't you agree it is better to have loved and lost than never to have loved?'

'In principle, yes,' Anthony agreed. 'Loss never goes away, though, does it?'

'Exactly,' Amy agreed quietly.

'I think the children have had enough of our presence. Will you join me in the Garden Room for coffee?' Anthony asked.

She accepted with a smile and they walked side by side down the hallway. Anthony hadn't been in the room on this visit, but he recalled it from years gone past. The room was at its best during the morning, but the large windows gave enough light that it was a welcome place to sit.

'Wouldn't it be lovely to see this room full of guests?' he said. 'Do you remember gatherings Aunt Violet used to have?'

'I do.' Amy trailed her hand along the back of the sofa then walked to the window and sat in a basket chair. 'It was in this room we first saw each other, of course. One of Miss Chase's garden parties. I was sitting right here and you brought me a cup of fruit punch.'

Anthony pulled up a stool and sat beside her, feeling like a courtier at the feet of his empress.

'Not quite the first time. I passed you in the garden half an hour earlier. You were walking towards me and gave me the most radiant smile. I felt as though the sun had exploded. Fortunately, I realised before I made an ass of myself that you were smiling at my aunt. When I saw you sitting in the love seat alone, I almost wrestled the punch from the vicar so I could give it to you. Then when I did you gave me the same smile.' He lifted her hand to his lips. 'I knew in that moment I was a lost man.'

'I remember feeling the same. I sipped the punch and couldn't take my eyes off your lips. I was imagining them in place of the cup, you see.' Her cheeks dimpled. 'I don't think I ever confessed that.'

'No, you didn't. And I never confessed that once you had finished I took the cup and refilled it, so I could drink from the same one your lips had been on.' He shook his head and gave a slight laugh. 'We were so young. Now look at us—an old pair.'

'I don't feel old,' Amy said. 'Even when I get to your aunt's age I hope I shall still enjoy life.'

She sounded wistful and Anthony was filled with a desperate sadness for her situation. To be widowed and financially dependent was a struggle for a woman.

He couldn't help himself any longer. He turned to Amy and took her by the shoulders, moving round so he was in front of her.

'Amy, I have to know something. I keep wondering what might have happened if I had returned between the death of my wife and your marriage to Napier.'

'I don't know,' Amy whispered. 'You would have discovered me practically penniless, and doubtless my appeal would have been diminished.'

'The prospect of your inheritance was never on my mind,' Anthony said. 'Besides, I would have been richer and might have been a better prospect myself. Once enough time had passed to let the hurt fade, we might have become friends again.'

'We might,' Amy agreed quietly.

Anthony opened the door and held out his hand for Amy to pass. 'And has enough time passed now?' he asked.

'So that we might become friends?'

'Unless you would like to become my lover,' he suggested daringly, thinking back to her supposedly flippant remark. 'If you intend to have a series, I would rather be at the front of the queue.'

He'd rather be the last, and the only one. If he thought she was serious, he would get down on his knees and ask for her hand in an instant.

Her eyes grew wide and he thought he had made a horrific mistake. Then she threw her head back and gave a long peal of laughter.

'Oh, Anthony, I am almost tempted to accept. I have missed the way you made me laugh. Will you excuse me? I need to go speak to Kitty about her dusting.'

He held a hand out and helped Amy to her feet. She brushed down her skirt. The plain black mourning dress now looked detestable. She should be wearing bright colours.

'Why did you come back here after Napier died?' he asked.

'This area is my home. I had to live somewhere and it was the first place I thought of. My father's house was sold when he died, so I couldn't return there, and in truth I didn't want to.'

She lifted her head, a portrait of dignity.

'Please don't pity me, Anthony. My life is not what I imagined it might be, but I am making my own way in the world and am happy to be doing so. For the first time in more years than I can recall, I am beholden to no one.'

'I don't pity you,' he said, truthfully.

He watched her go, his mind a tumult of emotions. By God, he wanted her. He'd settle for being her lover but that seemed too precarious a position. She had doubted his devotion all those years ago. That had become abundantly clear.

He walked through the house, his eyes roving over the transformation that had taken place in just a couple of days. Now surfaces were covered in decorations, baubles sparkled on strings and the holly that had caused their argument was wound into wreaths and hung in front of the mirror in the hall. It looked so welcoming and he had Amy to thank for it.

He had an idea now of a gift for Amy to show he cared for her.

On Christmas Eve he woke up early and dressed warmly. He set out as soon as it was light to begin preparations. He first visited Sternside Farm, where his arrival was greeted with pleasure by Mrs Gregory, the farmer's wife.

'How wonderful to see you, Mr Matthews. Nobody expected you here for Christmas.'

'I didn't expect to be here myself,' he admitted. 'I've come begging food. Mrs Munroe would be content with mutton stew. However, I think we should dine on better than that.'

'I'll see how I can oblige as soon as my husband gets home from the upper fields,' she answered. 'And if it isn't too bold, will you be having carols?'

'Carols?' Anthony asked.

'On Christmas afternoon. Everybody in the neighbourhood used to love your aunt for doing it. Even in the last years, when she was too frail to leave her bath chair, everyone would gather round the Garden Room doors and sing so she could hear.'

Anthony gave her a warm smile. 'I didn't know that. How kind of you all. As to this year, I hadn't thought of it. I didn't intend to be here and it seems too late to plan.'

'Nonsense,' Mrs Gregory said. 'Nobody needs elaborate food, but if that's the worry I can bake a pie and Mr Gregory can bring a pot of beer or three. All we need is a brazier or two to warm ourselves and good company. That's what makes the occasion special.

'Yes, it is,' Anthony agreed. 'I think that's a wonderful idea.'

He left with the promise of a goose and returned to the house. For the first time since Henrietta's death, he was anticipating Christmas with a heart full of excitement and joy.

He found Mrs Carey in the kitchen and broached the proposed party with slight trepidation. He need not have worried, as she was overjoyed at the prospect of carolling visitors, forgetting herself and clutching at Anthony's hands.

'I'd be delighted to bake some good Yorkshire parkin. This house needs people in it, especially at this time of year.'

Anthony asked for a plate of sandwiches, plenty of

hot coffee and cakes to be sent to him in the Garden Room. He handed her a list of his other requirements.

Mrs Carey ran her eyes down the list. If she had thoughts about what he was planning, she kept them to herself.

'You won't find strawberries anywhere at this time of year, Mr Matthews, but I think I have a bottle of preserved cherries in the larder if you can make do with that.'

'Thank you. Please don't trouble Mrs Munroe with any of this. She doesn't need to know what I am doing. If she asks my whereabouts, tell her I am working.'

'Of course, Mr Matthews.' Mrs Carey bobbed a curtsy then her eyes twinkled. 'I happen to know Mrs Munroe is partial to sugared almonds and I have an un-opened box in the cupboard.'

Anthony had not mentioned Amy but there was no point pretending.

'Thank you, Mrs Carey. I'll take them now.'

He located the sweets in question then went to the Garden Room. Smiling to himself, he shut the door and set to work.

# Chapter Nine

One of Amy's pleasures in life was a cup of tea in bed before she had to face the day. Cornelius the cat padded up from his place at her feet to sit on her lap. She scratched him in his favourite spot behind the left ear until his eyes closed and he rolled over, pressing his head into her palm.

'Despite how I've talked to Anthony, you're the only bedfellow I'm likely to have,' Amy told him.

Anthony's lover...

She was almost certain he had been joking when he'd suggested it, based on her retort about Aunt Violet's youth, but what if he hadn't been?

If she had agreed, would she now be lying in his bed or he in hers? She hugged herself, imagining that the arms around her were his. She trailed a fingernail along her arm and up to her collar bone. Even over her thick, wool nightgown the pressure made her shiver. She'd worn lace and satin to bed on her honeymoon, thin enough to feel Napier's hands through the fabric. Was it so wrong that she yearned for intimacy after more than a year of widowhood?

She brought in the jug of hot water left by Mrs Carey

and washed. Standing naked by the sink, she looked down at herself. She was happy with what she saw. A little sagging around her belly, slightly more dimples on her thighs than there had been a decade earlier, but nothing to be ashamed of or that would repel a man. She wondered what he liked and how different it would be to her married lovemaking.

She brushed out her hair and wound it up. Her period of deep mourning was over. The scarf had been a start but there was no reason for her to wear such austere black any longer. When spring came, she would buy a dress in grey or lilac.

She crossed her bedroom with an optimistic spring in her step and a light heart, which was immediately disrupted when she discovered the children waiting outside her room.

'We can't find Father,' Oliver said. 'Do you know where he is?'

Rose actually peered around Amy to look inside her bedroom, though Amy suspected the girl didn't understand the implications of what she was doing.

'I've only just woken up. Perhaps he went out for a walk?'

Mrs Carey provided the solution to the puzzle. 'He's in the Garden Room. He went out along the road early to try and clear the snow. Then he came back, asked for coffee and said he wasn't to be disturbed.'

Amy smiled at the children. 'There you are. He is just busy working in the Garden Room. He hasn't got lost or anything to worry about.'

She did worry, however. The dining room felt empty without his presence as she and the children ate toast and honey for breakfast. She heard him ring the bell and walked swiftly to the Garden Room door, only to find Kitty had arrived first and was already fulfilling his request for coffee. Amy intercepted the tray and knocked on the door to deliver it herself.

Anthony partially opened the door and stuck out his head. His smile became a touch less warm when he realised who was standing there.

'I asked Kitty to bring this,' he said. He took the tray from Amy's hands.

'I know, but I thought I would come and say good morning,' she replied. 'The children were asking where you were. Is anything the matter?'

She stepped closer but he retreated a little into the room and nudged the door shut with a foot.

'Everything is perfectly fine, but I have a lot of urgent work to complete, so I would be grateful if you were to keep them occupied. Do you mind taking charge of my children, Amy? It is a rather large favour and not part of your terms of employment.'

'I don't mind at all. They are very pleasant company,' she assured him.

'I'm glad you think so. Now, I must get on. Good day, Amy.'

He closed the door before she even had time to reply.

She returned to her sitting room and began to sketch a picture of the frozen fountain and four figures. She intended to give it to Anthony and the children the following day as a memento of their visit, but perhaps Anthony would not want to be reminded of it. She laid down her pencil and bit her thumb. He couldn't have urgent work today. It was Christmas Eve and she knew from having talked to him that he had a little leisure time. The only conclusion she could reach was that he had turned cold on her overnight. It had happened before, of course, and then there had been no warning or explanation, but this time she would not let him leave without one.

Anthony remained ensconced in the Garden Room for the entire day. The children ran around the garden to look in through the windows, but when Amy followed to bring them back, she discovered Anthony had put the curtains across and not even a crack of light was visible.

'Is he angry?' asked Rose.

'He doesn't often become angry, but when he does he goes out walking, so I don't think he's angry,' answered Oliver.

'That's when he's sad,' Rose corrected. 'Don't you know anything?'

'Sometimes it is hard to tell the difference. Especially for adults.'

The children both looked at Amy as if she had said something foolish. Perhaps to their minds it was.

She sent the children inside to stamp off the snow from their boots and she lingered a moment. Part of her yearned to enter the room despite Anthony's command that he was not to be disturbed. Over the days he had spent at Windcross, he had eased into the Anthony she had first fallen in love with—laughing with her, spending time talking and finding excuses for small, intimate touches. Even admitting he had missed out on his children's Christmas. This sudden cloistering was pitiful to see.

While she was standing and thinking this, the curtains twitched and she looked up to discover Anthony standing in the window, the curtains pulled back around him as though he were an actor about to take a bow. Their eyes met and his lips twitched into a bright smile.

'Spies never find anything to their favour.'

His voice was muffled through the glass, but there was a touch of humour in it. 'Why are you here?'

'The children were concerned,' Amy told him. 'They think you're angry or sad.'

'Only the children?' Anthony asked.

'No. I am concerned too,' Amy replied, looking him directly in the eye. She gestured to the window. 'All this secrecy when yesterday you appeared so content. What has changed since our last conversation?'

Anthony pursed his lips and his expression became grave. Remembering his aversion to broaching difficult matters, Amy suspected he had hidden himself away to avoid speaking to her.

'I won't press you to answer, though I wish you would,' she told him gently.

'Tell the children I am neither angry nor sad. Tell them all will be revealed before too long. I hope that will satisfy your concerns too.'

'Not really,' Amy said. 'It merely suggests that as always you are in hiding rather than confronting something.'

Anthony shook his head. 'As you know, that is my greatest fault. Now, go back inside where it is warm and curb your interest if you can.'

He pulled the curtains back round him with a flourish. Amy walked around the garden rather than return to the house. The temperature was milder and the snow was starting to melt in patches where the sun was bathing it. She wasn't cold, but she felt chilled inside. Anthony's behaviour suggested he was not in a melancholy or anxious state, so what was the mystery? She glanced back to the house and found Anthony was at the window again, watching her. He winked and Amy's stomach rolled over. His wink had always managed to excite her, and back then she had welcomed it. Now it felt dangerous.

She was becoming too attached to him again. The suggestion she might become his lover now seemed a cruel taunt. She had first made the joke, but it didn't seem funny now. He could have any woman he wanted when he chose to marry so why would he choose a penniless woman when he had rejected her before without knowing how poor she was?

The mystery of what Anthony had been doing was finally solved at dinner that night. He emerged in time to eat but closed the door behind him and forbade anyone to enter.

'I have left clutter everywhere and it must not be put into disarray.'

That explained it. Even on Christmas Eve he could not take himself away from work. After dinner, however, he went straight back into the Garden Room, only to reappear ten minutes later at the door of Amy's sitting room.

'Mrs Munroe, might I have a word with you please? Not in here, but in the Garden Room. There are some things in there I would like you to help me clear up.'

'Of course.' Amy followed him obediently along the corridor. Anthony held the door open and gestured for her to pass through. She walked in, expecting to see piles of paper or journals, but what awaited her left her speechless.

He had lit a fire which made the room glow and, to add to the effect, candles flickered in candelabras on every possible surface. He must have raided Mrs Carey's supplies and emptied every box. Tree branches and sprigs of holly stood in the large ceramic plant vases in front of the windows, and from the boughs hung small paper stars. The glass baubles Amy had found hung from a larger branch that stood beside the piano. They caught the candlelight and sent rainbows dancing off the walls.

It was magical. A winter fairyland.

She turned back to the door to find Anthony standing watching her, a tender smile on his lips.

'Happy Christmas, Amy.'

She put her hands to her mouth, quite overwhelmed with astonishment. Of all the things she had imagined, such a sight—that Anthony had been engaged in such an activity—had never crossed her mind.

'I'm afraid I couldn't find a fir tree so I had to hack a couple of branches off something. It might be a sycamore or oak. I'm not very good at naming trees.'

She turned to him with a smile that held back the tears she felt forming in her eyes. 'Anthony, it's beautiful. Is this what you were doing all day? I thought you were working.'

'I was. Working on this.'

He approached her slowly, seemingly nervous.

'I wanted to give you something for Christmas and to thank you for welcoming us so warmly. We descended on you and expected you to accommodate us. Then I complained when you tried to make the house Christmassy.'

'You didn't want Christmas at all,' Amy reminded him.

'No, but the children did, and when you tried to give them one I stamped my feet like the worst child of all.'

'Shall we bring the children in to show them?' Amy asked, starting to walk to the door. Anthony reached for her hand and held her back. She looked down at their linked fingers. 'Tomorrow. But this room is for you.'

'Me?'

'It always suited you being in here and I want you to enjoy it for a while in peace.'

He turned her hand upright and lifted it to his lips. Her palm prickled with the anticipation of being kissed, and when the kiss came he parted his lips, pressing the fullness of them onto the mound at the base of her thumb. His breath was hot on her hand and sent bolts of lightning shooting up her arm.

'I want us to enjoy it together. Will you dance with me?'

'There isn't any music, with no one to play the piano,' she pointed out. Even as she said it she was drawing closer to him.

'Do we really need music, you and I?' he murmured.

He walked to the centre of the room and put out his hand.

'Take my hand if you will, Mrs Munroe, for the polka is about to begin.'

Laughing, Amy put her hand in his and the other on his shoulder. Anthony put his hand on her waist. Their eyes met and Amy stopped breathing as desire thumped her fully in the sternum. He felt it too, she suspected. If he kissed her she would willingly let him.

Anthony cleared his throat. 'It has been a long time since I have sung anything aside from Sunday hymns. You must forgive me for the cacophony I am about to unleash.'

He tapped his feet rhythmically four times and then began to sing.

'"Here we come a wassailing…" Something, something… "Trees…green…"'

As he sang, he began to dance Amy around the room in a lively jig. She couldn't help but laugh. He only knew half the words, it appeared, but he had the tune, and his liveliness was infectious. They galloped around in a mad circle, dancing a form of jig with no particular steps, feet skipping, jumping and twirling until Amy was breathless and laughing.

'Love and joy come to you…' Anthony sang.

He stopped dancing abruptly, causing Amy to bump up against him.

'Love and joy,' he repeated. 'What more can any of us ask for?'

'I can't think of anything,' Amy answered quietly.

'Can you pick a song now?' Anthony asked.

Amy thought for a moment then began to sing *Silent Night*. Her voice was a little thin, and she already knew that by the time she reached the high notes she would struggle, but Anthony took up the tune with her. He wrapped his arms around her, closing the space between them, and began to waltz.

The dance fitted to the rhythm of the song closely enough and they moved slowly in time. It was an intimate moment, with their bodies held together as Anthony guided Amy around the room. It seemed entirely inappropriate to be dancing so intimately whilst singing about the birth of Christ, but Amy didn't care. Supported in Anthony's arms and dancing around the room, guided by the firm, assured pressure of his frame, she felt entirely at peace.

She gave up cautioning herself not to fall in love with Anthony, aware she was already much too far down that path to draw back. They had moved closer to the warmth of the fire and Amy's cheeks began to burn. She gazed up and found Anthony looking down at her. He reached out a hand and led her to the rug.

'I thought we might have a picnic.'

He walked to the furthest corner and returned bearing a silver tray that held a bottle of wine, two crystal glasses and two silver bowls. He filled the glasses and held out one to Amy.

'Sauternes. A Christmas gift from my sister and brother-in-law's cellar. It's a mature one, judging from the colour.'

Amy looked at the wine. The liquid was a deep, golden yellow that reminded her of honey. She licked her lips, aware that Anthony was watching her.

'Your good health,' he said.

They drank. The wine was sweet but sharp and delicious. It caressed her throat on the way down and warmed her belly.

'I have these too,' Anthony said. He showed her the contents of the bowls. One contained cherries that Mrs Carey had bottled in sugar syrup and which glistened tantalisingly in the firelight. The other contained sugared almonds.

'Mrs Carey told me you liked them,' Anthony said.

'You asked her?' Amy had been relaxing and now she sat up, tense. 'Does she know what you planned? What will she think?'

'Mrs Carey thinks you deserve a treat. A respectable woman such as she is certainly wouldn't imagine anything unseemly is going to happen.'

'And do you imagine anything unseemly is going to happen?' Amy asked, curling her lips into what she hoped was a beguiling smile. He answered with one of his own.

'I find myself teetering on hope and dread from minute to minute. I wouldn't dare let my imagination run so wild.'

As he spoke he captured a cherry on a teaspoon and held it out towards Amy. She leaned forward, closed her lips over the cherry and took it into her mouth, keeping her eyes on Anthony. Anthony's eyes widened and his lips parted. Amy picked up a second cherry between her fingers and held it out to Anthony.

'They're good. Try one.'

He leaned forward and parted his lips. Amy placed the glossy orb between them then sucked the remaining syrup from her fingers. She had barely finished when Anthony leaned forward and kissed her.

She had been hoping he would, but his impulsiveness still sent a thrill through her. He tasted of wine and cherries: summer flavours that seemed out of place in the depths of winter but, oh, so right. She kissed him back, mouth open to savour the taste of him and to feel the firm pressure of his lips and the heat of his mouth.

They clutched at each other and fell down onto the rug, lying together.

It wasn't how she'd remembered Anthony's kisses. In the days of their youth, Amy had always been slightly reserved, holding back lest she forget herself and go beyond the bounds of acceptability, and Anthony had been guided by her wishes. Now there was no chasteness to the kiss. They had both developed new rhythms and skills, long practised with their respective spouses. Finding a way to accommodate this and adapt to a new person took a few moments. Their hands were as fierce and exploratory as their mouths, stroking and kneading, firm and gentle, fingertips and palms.

It was exciting. A new world of possibilities and pleasure ready to be discovered.

Anthony drew away, breathing heavily.

'Amy...' He ran his hands through her hair, which had begun to slip loose from its knot. 'You have no idea how I've longed to do that.'

'Yes, I do.'

He laughed and pushed himself up on one elbow, lying stretched out to face her. She smiled up at him and put her hand to his chest, spreading her fingers wide to feel the shape of his muscles. He inhaled sharply so she moved her hand further down. He caught her wrist and shook his head.

'You've been a wife, Amy, so I don't need to skirt around delicate issues for fear of shocking your maidenly senses. If your hand keeps travelling downwards, I imagine you know what effect it will have on me.'

'Would that be so bad?'

'Yes! No. Yes...as we can't act on it.'

Amy leaned over him and took a sip of her wine, brushing up against him. She'd already felt the hard bulge of his erection when he had rolled close and it was still apparent that he was as highly aroused as she.

'Why not?'

He reached for his own wine and knocked the whole glass back in one go.

'If I made love to you, what would it mean? What would you want it to mean?'

Amy put her glass down beside her. 'I don't know,' she admitted quietly. 'Yesterday you talked about me becoming your lover. Were you joking?'

Anthony shuffled himself more fully upright. 'I don't know. I don't think I would want a mistress. It would feel wrong.'

'I'm not sure I care about God's laws or society's morals,' Amy said.

'Nor do I,' Anthony said rapidly. 'I mean it would feel wrong only being your lover, when once I had imagined you being my wife. I loved you so deeply back then, before I had really experienced life as a grown man.'

He twisted to face her and put his hand to her cheek. 'I think it would take very little for me to love you madly again, and if I did I would not be content until I knew you would never leave me. Dare I hope?'

The admission that he was falling in love with her was the most romantic thing Amy could recall anyone saying to her.

'Yes, you can dare,' Amy replied, covering his hand with hers. 'We are both changed and grown, and maybe this time we can work out our differences rather than running from them.'

'Maybe this time we can,' Anthony agreed.

From across the valley came the faint sound of bells.

'It's Christmas Day,' she said.

'Happy Christmas, Amy,' Anthony said. He gathered her into his arms and kissed her again. It was not the hot, frantic kiss of passion needing to be unleashed, but was tender and loving, implying optimism and new beginnings.

It was the best gift she could have received.

## Chapter Ten

Anthony woke with a sense of elation in his heart. He had not anticipated his plan meeting with such success and the sight of Amy's face as she beheld the Garden Room would stay with him his entire life. She had glowed brighter than all the candles combined, but when he had told her he could see himself falling in love again he had lied. He was already there.

Oliver and Rose were already awake and running about the dining room in a state of high excitement. Amy was sitting at the table with a cup of coffee. She looked up as Anthony entered the room and gave him a smile that sent his heart racing.

'Good morning, Mr Matthews.'

He helped himself to porridge from the tureen, added a spoonful of honey and then joined her.

'I hope you slept well,' he asked.

'Eventually,' she answered, with a smile that made her eyes dance.

'As did I,' he replied. They had retired to their respective beds—much to both of their reluctance—at one in the morning. Anthony had lain awake for another hour at least, revelling in the sensations Amy's kisses had aroused in him. He doubted she would ever know how hard it had been not to surrender to her suggestions of lovemaking, which had been doubly thrilling, as she'd been so enthusiastically frank about her desires, but from the curve of her lips he might be wrong.

'We need to talk,' Amy said.

'About last night?' He stirred sugar into his coffee, concentrating on the swirling liquid. His habitual aversion to conflict arose. If she was going to tell him it had been a mistake, he didn't want to hear it.

'About what happened years ago.'

Anthony raised his eyes. Amy was looking intently at him. 'I suppose we do,' he agreed. 'But not today. Let's enjoy Christmas.'

'You keep putting it off,' Amy said. He could almost feel the frustration radiating from her. It was unfair of him, as she must be desperate to unburden herself, but he could not quite let go of his inclination to avoid conflict.

'Tomorrow, I promise.'

The morning involved a trip along the snowy footpaths to Priestclough to attend the church service. The sky was clear and the snow was turning to slush. The roads would be clear by the end of the day, Anthony estimated.

His appearance was greeted with surprised delight. The vicar welcomed him heartily, and various other parishioners old enough to remember Anthony from his youthful visits smiled and nodded. One or two shot covert glances at Amy, though she appeared not to notice anything out of order. It struck him that, while he had left the area, Amy must have been left to endure gossip about why their romance had come to such an abrupt end. He wondered how many of the villagers knew her reasons for breaking with him.

Anthony walked around, issuing invitations to pay a call to Windcross later in the afternoon for carol singing.

'Another surprise,' he told Amy. 'Mrs Carey is baking more pies and mulling wine.'

She laughed and slipped her arm through his. 'You really are intent on making Christmas perfect.'

After the service, Anthony and the children walked to Aunt Violet's grave. The children, already fidgety after the long sermon, were not best pleased and trudged along.

'Why do we need to visit this?' asked Oliver.

Anthony looked at him reprovingly.

'This is my aunt's final resting place,' he said, slightly embarrassed at his children's behaviour in front of Amy. 'You should be respectful of her memory. It is thanks to her generosity that we now own Windcross and are wealthy.'

'Does that mean we can have our own carriage and horses?' Rose asked, brightening. 'And my own horse to ride?'

'Isn't the carriage yours?' Amy asked.

Anthony laughed. 'The Clarence isn't mine. Good grief, do you think a writer for a provincial newspaper can keep a coach and pair of horses as well as a coachman?'

'I thought… I assumed…' Amy tailed off.

'It belongs to my sister. Samson is in her employment,' Anthony explained.

'They have no arms on the door.'

'It is her private carriage. She very generously loaned it to me so that we could return home, on the understanding that Samson would be back with his family for Christmas. Poor man. I feel he has been very hard done by.'

'Poor man, indeed. Let's return home. Mrs Carey will be starting to cook dinner and I would like to offer any assistance.'

Amy looked away and Anthony felt a flicker of nausea growing inside him. He looked at her surreptitiously. Had she only been interested in him because he appeared wealthy? They really must have the conversation at some point, but now was not the time nor place.

'Wouldn't you like to visit your father's grave while we are here?' he asked, giving the children a stern eye to ensure they didn't protest.

'Yes, I suppose so,' Amy said, a touch reluctantly, Anthony thought. They walked around the church yard until they came to Septimus Pritchard's ornate headstone.

*Poet of this parish*

The vanity struck Anthony as hilarious, as if Pritchard had fancied himself as a Priestclough laureate. Amy found nothing amusing in the grave, however. She stood in front of it with her hands neatly folded in front of her and her face expressionless. Whatever communion she was making with her father was private. She must have felt devoted enough to erect the unsightly monolith, even though she had been left penniless as a result of it.

'I'm sure your father would have been happy with a plain stone, but it is to your credit as a daughter that you chose this.'

Amy turned to him, her placid eyes now burning. 'It was not my choice. He left instructions in his will that the stone was to be paid for out of the estate. I have tried not to mind too much, and I hope that if he is looking down from paradise he is content with it.'

She fiddled with her gloves and glanced in the direction of Windcross. 'We should go before the weather changes.'

She turned and walked swiftly away.

The sky was cloudless, and conditions could not have been better, so that was just an excuse to leave. Anthony walked alone while Amy and the children marched ahead, singing. He could tell they already liked her. She would fit into their lives perfectly, a place where she always should have been. If she wanted him, of course.

The children had no reservations about anything. They were thrilled with the presents Amy had found and the ones gifted by their aunt. Even more, they adored the Garden Room, which Anthony showed them as soon as they had eaten the lunch that had been waiting for them. He had removed the evidence of the picnic and only the memories of his evening with Amy lingered. Once the children had been given their gifts, Amy pulled out an old, leather-bound box and held it towards Anthony.

'It's a poor thing to do to return a man's property to him and call it a gift, but while I was cataloguing some of your aunt's belongings I found this writing box. I saw that the letters were addressed to you. They must have been there for the past fifteen years at least.'

The letters. Anthony felt sick. Amy smiled at him but Anthony couldn't smile back. His face felt frozen.

Amy's brow creased. 'I haven't read them, if that's what you think. I only looked at the envelopes themselves. Anthony, what have I done wrong?'

He ignored her question and opened the box. There on the top was the letter that had broken his heart. He remembered now how he had tossed it into the box, scarcely able to believe the contents. It would have been the first thing Amy had seen when she'd opened it so she could not even claim ignorance of what she was doing.

'A strange gift to remind me of my darkest moment,' he agreed. His voice was tinged with bitterness.

'Papa, what's wrong? Don't you like the box?' Rose asked.

'The box is perfectly lovely,' Anthony replied. His instinct to flee the tense atmosphere rose up and he would not deny it.

'Children, play with your toys. Enjoy the remainder of your day. I shall be back later before the carollers arrive.'

He plucked the letter in question between his fingers. He screwed it in his fist, stood and left the room. He bundled on his outdoor boots and coat and strode out of the house, slamming the door behind him. Walking at speed, with his head bowed, he took the path leading down to the village but at the fork turned to the right and along the narrow path to the flat field with the split tree that he had most recently seen in Amy's painting.

He hadn't gone far before he heard Amy's voice calling his name. He turned and looked back along the path to see her making her way gingerly towards him. The ground was treacherous and once or twice she slipped and had to throw her arms out wide to regain her balance. Seeing it happen, Anthony's muscles tensed, and if he had been closer he would have flung his arms round her to prevent any injury befalling her.

He had intended to walk out his distress but he stopped by the forked rowan where they had so often sat together. Amy slowed her pace and picked her way towards him. By the time she was there, he had opened the letter and was staring intently at the contents, barely seeing the words.

'Anthony, will you please explain what on earth is going on?' Amy said.

'Why would you seek to raise ghosts at this time? Were you not satisfied with my promise to talk tomorrow?'

'Anthony, I don't understand what you mean,' Amy protested.

'Did you think I wouldn't care about the contents? Or perhaps you thought that now I could look back and laugh with you at the way you treated me?'

He held the letter out towards her. She stared back, her brow still wrinkled. Anthony swallowed, tasting bile in his throat.

'Do you not even recognise it? After you scrawled the note that broke my heart did you simply go about your day?'

Once again she frowned. 'I have no idea whether you would have kept anything, Anthony, because I don't know what it is you are showing me.'

'Your letter!' he exclaimed. 'The one you wrote to me and sent via a maid instead of coming yourself.'

'I have never written to you in my life!' Amy exclaimed. 'Show me.'

She held out her hand and he gave her the letter. He watched as she read it, her eyes moving rapidly over the lines. Anthony knew them by heart, even after all these years.

*Mr Matthews,*
*I know you are expecting my presence this morning, but please accept this note in my stead. I anticipate already the question you wish to put to me and I find I lack the courage to answer to you in person.*

*Should we meet again soon, I ask you as a friend not to let those words pass your lips. I entreat you never to mention this correspondence to me directly or obliquely. My duty is to remain at my father's side. If I have inadvertently led you to believe my feelings towards you are anything other than of warm, neighbourly friendship, I humbly apologise.*
*Yours in friendship,*
*Miss Pritchard*

She raised her eyes and Anthony was shocked at the bleakness in them. She had turned pale, her porcelain skin becoming alabaster.

'Anthony, I never wrote this.'

'What?' He stared at her, dumbfounded.

'This isn't my handwriting.'

She held it out towards him between her thumb and forefinger, as if it was distasteful even to hold. He took it from her and looked at it. The matter that had been nagging at the back of his brain finally jumped up and yelled for his attention. He had seen countless examples of Amy's writing in the ledgers she had been keeping. It was neat and slanted, not this looping, girlish handwriting with a flourish to the signature.

She was telling the truth.

'Then who did?' he asked.

She closed her eyes, pressing her lips together until they became a thin, scarlet streak against the paleness of her skin. She looked fragile…a sculpture carved from ice. Anthony remained silent, not daring even to breathe loudly in case he caused her to shatter. When she opened her eyes, they were full of fury.

'I think it was my father.'

Anthony's legs turned hollow. He leaned back against the tree.

'The morning we were supposed to meet here. When I hoped you might propose to me—'

'When I was going to,' Anthony cut in.

She looked desolate and Anthony wished he hadn't spoken.

'All morning my father was fussing around and finding me tasks that prevented me leaving to meet you. He had some almost illegible night scrawlings that he insisted I transcribe urgently. I remember it clearly.' She lowered her eyes. 'I've never forgotten a single moment of that day. I couldn't refuse or explain to him why I was so desperate to leave. By the time I was free and I arrived here, it was past twelve and you weren't here. I decided you had given up waiting and returned to Windcross.'

Anthony reached for her hand. She had come to meet him. She would have accepted his proposal. His stomach twisted with a violence that was physically painful. 'I didn't know.'

'No, I don't expect you did.' Amy's voice hardened. She tore her hand free from Anthony's. 'I walked to Windcross, only for your aunt to tell me that you had left shortly after nine. You never even went to meet me.'

'I thought it was what you wanted me to do,' Anthony protested. 'The letter clearly said not to contact you.'

He tried to take her by the shoulders but she squirmed free roughly.

'How could you think I would ever write something like that? Did you believe my love so flighty? For shame, Anthony!'

She started to cry, tears spilling down her cheeks. The

sight tore Anthony to shreds. He reached out a hand, but she drew back, as if he had threatened to slap her.

'I loved you so deeply that the letter left me devastated.'

Amy let out a cry of anger. 'But that love meant so little that you did not even try to discover why I might have done such a thing.'

'I thought that you had sent the letter,' Anthony said.

'It didn't occur to you to even meet me and try to ask why my affection had altered over the space of a weekend?' Amy asked. 'You didn't even try to change my mind. You just walked away.'

'I obeyed the instructions I believed were yours. Amy, try to understand. I was doing what I thought you wanted. I was broken when I left.'

'Don't pretend it was to respect my feelings,' Amy scoffed. 'You never liked conflict and you took the easiest path.'

He looked at her bleakly, unable to answer in the face of her all too accurate judgement. She shook her head then walked away, back in the direction of Windcross. Anthony leaned against the tree and put his head in his hands.

He felt weakened by the knowledge of how badly he had done by Amy, and how much his propensity to avoid conflict had lost him fifteen years previously. He had wronged her both in thought and deed all those years ago, and it was little wonder she was furious with him. If he did not act now, then he would be in danger of losing her again before he had even truly won her.

When the slush began to penetrate his boots and his feet resembled ice blocks, he trudged back to the house. He slipped inside quietly and stood in the hallway. The house smelled deliciously of roast goose, and steamed plum pudding but Anthony had no appetite.

Oliver and Rose were still in the Garden Room. He could hear their laughter, and from the way they quarrelled he could tell Amy was not with them. He could not face re-joining them until he had spoken to Amy. He knocked on the door of her sitting room but there was no answer. He was about to leave, assuming if she was there she was choosing not to answer, but decided that he would no longer take the easy option. The room was empty and chilly because Amy hadn't bothered to light the fire. She had been expecting to spend the day with Anthony and his family, after all.

He made his way to the kitchen, expecting to find her with Mrs Carey, but she was not there.

'I haven't seen her since you all came back from church this morning,' Mrs Carey answered, to Anthony's question. 'Her room is up above so I'd have heard if she went up there. The floors creak something terrible. I hope she's back soon, as the family from Sternside Farm will be coming soon.'

Rising panic made Anthony's skin crawl. He didn't care about the visitors, but if Amy was not in the house where was she? He had assumed she would return to Windcross but what if she'd taken the other fork in the path and had gone down into Priestclough? From his memory, she had not been wearing her stout boots. If she attempted to walk that way, she would become cold very easily.

'I'm going to search for Mrs Munroe,' he told Mrs Carey. 'If she returns, please don't let her come looking for me or we'll be going round in circles.'

As he put on his coat and warm scarf for the third time that day and set off at a pace, it occurred to him that going round in circles was all he had ever done.

## Chapter Eleven

Amy was only halfway down the path into Priest-clough when she realised she had made an error. Her feet were frozen and her hem was heavy and sodden. She had been so anxious to follow Anthony and see what was wrong with him that she hadn't even changed into her boots, and her soft shoes had been ruined within a few hundred yards. It made walking almost impossible, but she shivered and pressed on.

She could not decide whether she was angrier at learning her father's cruel duplicity or at Anthony for believing it and not having had the courage to face her. Rage gave her the tenacity to carry on and she arrived at the church yard hot and out of breath. Once she sat down she would start to feel the cold, but for now her temper kept her hot.

The church was deserted. No doubt the vicar was in the rectory enjoying his Christmas goose before even-song.

Amy stood in front of her father's grave and glared at his headstone. Never had she despised him more than now, and the carved slab was the perfect illustration of why.

'I hate you,' she spat.

It felt good to finally voice it.

'I. Hate. You.' She repeated it more forcefully.

A foot crunched on the gravel somewhere to her left.

'And do you hate me also?'

Anthony.

Amy turned slowly around. He was muffled in his coat and scarf, and his face was red, as if he had been exerting himself. He was bareheaded and his hair was messed up. He raked his fingers through it, tangling it even more.

'I don't know,' she answered. 'I'm disappointed in you.'

'I'm disappointed in myself,' he said. 'I'm furious. I hate myself. The younger me, I mean. I hate him. If it were possible to travel back into the past, I would give the younger me a sound kicking.'

Amy laughed softly. 'Save your shoe leather for my father and kick him for me too. He is responsible for our estrangement.'

'No, he isn't,' Anthony said. 'Oh, yes, he put the barriers in our way, but I chose not to disassemble them. I could have come to meet you, but I didn't.'

'You were doing what you thought I wanted,' Amy said.

Anthony shook his head. 'No, I was doing what was easiest for me to do.'

'You would not have found me there anyway,' Amy pointed out.

'In which case I should have marched to Standing Stone Lodge and knocked on your door until you admitted me. As you did when I was not there to meet you.'

He rubbed his forehead and stepped closer to Amy.

'I told myself that I was doing your bidding by leaving without speaking to you, and I am very convincing when I set out to be. I convinced myself easily enough, and that lessened the hurt I felt, but I know it was an excuse. I didn't want to face you. I couldn't bring myself to, knowing how fragile my grip on my emotions was. I would have broken down and wept.'

He gave her a wry smile. 'I did weep, in fact, but only in the privacy of my room.'

He sounded more wretched than Amy could remember him being. She shivered and Anthony frowned.

'You're freezing. What on earth did you think of, walking all this way down here in your shoes?'

'I didn't want to go back to the house straight away. I wanted to rage at my father.'

Anthony unwound his scarf and wound it around Amy's neck. It was warm and soft, and smelled of him and the cologne he wore. She buried her face in it.

'Thank you.'

'It really is the least I could do,' he said. He grimaced. 'The absolute least.'

'You came to find me,' she said. 'Why?'

He put his hands on her upper arms and looked into her eyes. When she did not pull away, he drew her closer.

'For once in my life, I was determined not to walk away from a situation and an uncomfortable conversation. How could your father have been so cruel?'

'I think I understand why. He wanted to keep me from marrying. He would have had to provide me with a dowry and certain money I was entitled to upon my marriage. There was no money, thanks to him trying to maintain a lifestyle his poetry could not support, and the scandal of our friends and neighbours knowing that would have destroyed him.'

Anthony glared at the headstone.

'It's so selfish. He prevented your happiness for his own sake.' He turned back to Amy and put his hands to her cheeks, gently turned her head up to face him. 'Tell me that you would have accepted my proposal if we had met as planned that day.'

She covered his hands with hers, lacing their fingers together. Her heart swelled at the urgency in his voice. 'Of course I would. With you beside me, holding my hand and keeping my heart, I could have braved all father's objections.'

He made a small noise in the back of his throat and wrapped his arms around her. 'We've spent enough time here thinking of your father.'

She let him escort her out of the church yard, arm around her. At the gate, she turned and looked back.

'Money and vanity on the part of my father. I can't forgive him for robbing me of the chance to be with you.'

'He didn't steal it for ever. He only delayed it,' Anthony said.

At the start of the path to Windcross, he stopped walking and gave her a serious look.

'I thought you had stopped caring for me back then, but you hadn't. Could you find it in you to care for me again? I know I'm not the wealthy man you thought I was. I'm sorry I don't have a coach and horses.'

'I never cared about that,' Amy said. 'If anything, it's a relief that I am not too poor for a man as rich as I thought you were. I've never cared about money when it comes to you. You really wouldn't have minded that I had no dowry to speak of?'

'I would have married you barefoot and in rags. I never cared about your money.'

Amy looked away. 'Your wife was wealthy. I heard of your marriage and the advantages she brought with her for your career.'

'That was not why I married her. She was kind to me at a time I was feeling vulnerable and wounded,' Anthony explained. 'It was easy to let myself love her as I could not have you. I don't regret my marriage to Henrietta.'

He spoke a little more of Henrietta and Amy found she could listen without jealousy or resentment.

Anthony sighed. 'If only the world could be split into two, where in one life you and I married, and in the other life I married Henrietta and we had Rose and Oliver.'

They had walked as Anthony talked and now they reached the fork in the path. Anthony stopped and held her hands.

'Amy, I want to marry you. Say you will have me now. We can marry as soon as I can arrange it.'

Her heart soared, but beneath the elation was a slight worry. She hesitated only briefly, but it was enough for Anthony's expression of ardour to crumble.

'Have I misunderstood?' he asked.

'No,' she assured him. She wrapped her arms around his neck and looked deep into his eyes. 'You should have no doubt that my love for you will soon become as strong as it ever was. However, I think we should take time to become reacquainted. We have spent less than a week in each other's company. The children may not like me as a mother. We may discover we are too different.'

'Who can say whether the people we are now is who we would have been if we had not parted? I know my love would have been exactly what it is now.' He wrapped her in his arms.

Amy smiled at him but narrowed her eyes. Anthony in the full swing of love was as dizzying as it always had been. 'Do you mean to say you felt this love for me for fifteen years?'

He bowed his head to hers. 'The feeling diminished, as any fire would die if it wasn't fed or stoked, and I was not unfaithful to Henrietta in thought or deed. But seeing you again, kissing you and holding you, has re-ignited the fire, and it burns as strong as it ever did. We are the same inside. Whatever else has happened in the middle of our lives, we are still Anthony and Amy who fell in love. Nothing can change that.'

He kissed her then drew back and smiled. He pointed up the hillside to the path leading back to Windcross. In the fading light, Amy could make out figures carrying lanterns. The merry strains of 'God Rest Ye Merry Gentlemen' floated across the valley.

Anthony turned to Amy with a wide grin and eyes that gleamed.

'It's Christmas Day and there are carollers and hot wine waiting for us at Windcross. Why are we standing on the hillside getting chilled? Come with me, Amy. Let's go home.'

# *Epilogue*

*One year later*

Weddings did not take place on Christmas Day, so it was on Christmas Eve morning that Amy Munroe became Amy Matthews in a ceremony at Priestclough church.

Unconventionally, the bride and groom walked on foot up the hillside path, enjoying the sharp chill of winter sunshine. As they had hoped, they arrived before the rest of the guests, and sat together in the Garden Room while they waited for the wedding party to arrive.

The newlywed couple had decided to revive Violet Chase's practice of having a bonfire, carols, and mulled wine as their wedding breakfast. Many of the guests chose to make the journey from the church to Windcross in carriages and would arrive slightly later. Remembering the effect the weather had had on his destiny, Anthony had sent Mr Carey and three hired men out the day before to ensure the road would be clear.

An entire pig was being roasted in the yard and the kitchen was full of bustle. Amy leaned back in the sofa and rested against Anthony's chest. He poured her a glass of champagne.

'It feels at odds not to be supervising,' she said. 'Perhaps I should just look in on Mrs Carey.'

Anthony pulled her back down to his side. 'We have a housekeeper for that now,' he pointed out. 'Today you have to do nothing arduous.'

'I know.'

Amy craned her head and kissed his cheek. He had rid himself of his beard and looked younger. She felt younger herself.

'I am saving all my strength for tonight,' she said, running her fingers over his chest.

'Very wise. I intend to work us both until we drop, Mrs Matthews.'

His eyes grew serious for a moment. 'Are you happy, Amy?'

'Yes, very. I believe this last year has been my happiest ever. Even in the times when we were apart and you weren't here with me I knew you would be coming back.'

'And I knew you would be here waiting for me.' He took her in his arms, holding her tightly. 'Happy Christmas, my darling. May it be the first of many we spend together.'

'The second,' Amy corrected.

'Of course.' Anthony smiled at her, his eyes brimming with love and desire. 'Here's to us, Amy, and our wedding day. Fifteen years later than it should be, but let's drink to our future.'

They lifted their glasses and drank, looking into each other's eyes over the rims.

'Happy wedding day, Anthony, my love,' Amy said. 'And Happy Christmas.'

\* \* \* \* \*

*If you enjoyed these stories, you won't want
to miss these other Historical collections*

Snowbound Surrender *by Christine Merrill,
Louise Allen and Laura Martin*
Tudor Christmas Tidings *by Blythe Gifford,
Jenni Fletcher and Amanda McCabe*
Christmas Cinderellas *by Sophia James,
Virginia Heath and Catherine Tinley*
A Victorian Family Christmas *by Carla Kelly,
Carol Arens and Eva Shepherd*
Regency Christmas Liaisons *by Christine Merrill,
Sophia James and Marguerite Kaye*